W9-BUM-873

THE
MYTHIC
KODA
ROSE

THE MYTHIC KODA ROSE

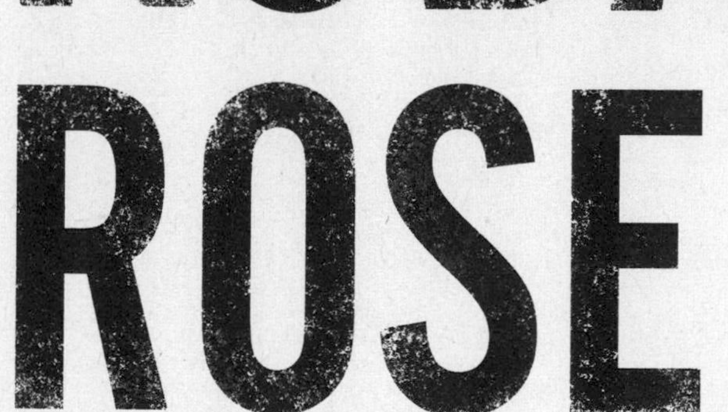

JENNIFER NISSLEY

SIMON & SCHUSTER BFYR

NEW YORK LONDON TORONTO SYDNEY NEW DELHI

An imprint of Simon & Schuster Children's Publishing Division
1230 Avenue of the Americas, New York, New York 10020

Interior designed by Tom Daly
The text of this book was set in Adobe Caslon Pro.
Manufactured in the United States of America
First Edition
2 4 6 8 10 9 7 5 3 1
Library of Congress Cataloging-in-Publication Data
Names: Nissley, Jennifer, author.
Title: The mythic Koda Rose / by Jennifer Nissley.
Description: First edition. | New York : Simon & Schuster BFYR, [2021] |
Summary: Leaving her best friend (and secret love) Lindsay, seventeen-year-old Koda Rose moves with her mother to New York City, where Koda grows close to the ex-girlfriend of her late father, a famous rock musician who neglected his daughter.
Identifiers: LCCN 2020037385 (print) | LCCN 2020037386 (eBook) |
ISBN 9781534466760 (hardcover) | ISBN 9781534466784 (eBook)
Subjects: CYAC: Best friends—Fiction. | Friendship—Fiction. | Moving, Household—Fiction. | Lesbians—Fiction. | New York (N.Y.)—Fiction.
Classification: LCC PZ7.1.N584 My 2021 (print) | LCC PZ7.1.N584 (ebook) |
DDC [Fic]—dc23
LC record available at https://lccn.loc.gov/2020037385
LC ebook record available at https://lccn.loc.gov/2020037386

For Kellie

THE
MYTHIC
KODA
ROSE

CHAPTER 1

MY FATHER'S MOST FAMOUS SONG GOES, *You're not drowning if your eyes are closed.*

That's not how I see it. But as Makeup Lady dabs shadow onto my lids, I hold my breath for as long as I can handle, until the burning in my lungs blots out the chaos around me, and the only sounds are ocean ones. Roar of walkie-talkie static. Photographer's assistants squawking like gulls.

Makeup Lady switches to my other eye and says relax. Relax, sweetie—no need to be nervous.

"Not when you have such striking eyes."

"Thanks." I shiver.

"They're your father's."

My eyes flash open, and I see everything at once: gawkers and Makeup Lady's too-red mouth and the whitewashed set behind her. Last of all, I see myself, in the mirror. I blink and my eyelashes rustle. Not mine—I felt her press them on.

Tragic purple bruises my lids. I've never had this much makeup inflicted on me in my life, but beneath it, my eyes are as uninspiring as ever. Watery blue. I glance from Makeup Lady to the mirror, unconvinced.

"Most people think I look like my mom." My mouth is black, practically necrotic. I squish my lips together. Wearing lipstick makes me immediately want to chew it off.

"Oh." She laughs. "No. You resemble Mack."

A jolt goes through me.

Mack.

Like she knew him.

"He was very talented," she says quietly.

I nod.

She disappears.

A girl with a gravity-defying blond ponytail hustles in to replace her, clipboard clasped to her chest. "Koda?" she chirps. "We're ready for you, hon."

Great. Fantastic. *Lovely*, as Mom would say.

Ponytail leads me onto set. Even the stool they want me to sit on is white. Photographer stands several feet away, viciously adjusting the settings on his camera. He's dressed completely in black. Long and skinny, like a knife, and something about the gleam of his bald head beneath the lights suggests he must be famous, probably the best photographer *ROCK* has to offer.

"Um. Excuse me?" I wait. Photographer thrusts his camera at an assistant, who immediately passes him another, identical one. "Hi, um, do you want me to . . . do I sit?" Our lawyer,

Mr. Todd, strides by, blah-blahing into his phone. I practically lunge for him. "Is that Mom?" I ask, but he doesn't hear me either. Okay. I eye the stool.

Mom promised that makeup, the photo shoot, this whole ordeal, would be easy.

She'd know if I should sit.

Ponytail whispers to Photographer, and his head jerks up. "There she is!" he exclaims. I've been here since noon—three whole hours—and it's like he's just noticed me. "Happy birthday, darling!"

Definitely famous. And French. All those swallowed vowels. "Thanks." My birthday isn't for months. April 1. Ha ha. But we're doing the photo shoot in December because *ROCK*'s editor-in-chief deemed it would be so. Probably this has to do with running a monthly publication—interviews must be conducted, articles written, pics shot and Photoshopped a gazillion weeks in advance, especially when the feature story is as momentous as this one. It's not every day a dead rock god's only kid turns eighteen.

An impatient flap from Photographer—*sit*—and I ease onto the stool, feeling faint. The shirt Wardrobe buttoned me into is only soft on the outside. Inside, it's a web of frayed stitches, scratchy tight. The pants too. Leather. Hair tickles my nose, but it took Stylist so long to set the curls that I'm afraid to move. Clearly he expected me to show up with something he could work with, instead of the same sad haircut I've had since I was four.

Sweat pools in my butt crack. The pants are that hot. I grind my palms into my thighs as Photographer snaps what must be test shots, aiming his camera at my face, the wall, my face. "Hmm." He grimaces. Seemingly in pain, if not blinded. Like the set, I am astonishingly white. Did nobody think this through?

Okay, okay. Right. Mom and I talked about this, and we agreed that inspiration is all about summoning the right mental images. Looking the part. As Photographer advances, hunched behind his camera, I pull my shoulders back. Take a deep breath that is the opposite of drowning.

The set has gone completely silent. Just him and my swim pose and the steady ping of his camera's touch display. Finally, he lifts the camera to his eye. "You are having a big New York birthday?" he asks.

My chest sizzles. Heartburn. Amazing it waited this long. "Maybe. I mean . . ." It's like talking to the dentist when his hand's halfway in your mouth. Am I even supposed to answer? I give it my best. Slowly. Letting my lungs expand. "I want to, but my friends aren't exactly down with leaving LA in the middle of—"

"Don't tense," he scolds. "Give us a pout, eh?"

My nose prickles. Oh no. No. I can't cry. Not now. I'll ruin the makeup. Everybody will be so mad. Quickly, I glance away, tilting my face to rock the tears back. Mom's trick, but it doesn't work. God, if only she could've come. If only she could've been here, instead of whatever it is she's doing at the office.

"Go on," says Photographer. "Show us what made your father famous."

How? My father's face was 90 percent dimple. I don't have dimples. Just fat lips—Mom swears they're not, but they are—and too much forehead and, worst of all, these ugly, blocky cheeks. I am the lowest possible form of my father. A bootleg copy. My lip quivers.

Click!

"There!" Photographer murmurs. "A little bird could perch on that lip."

Was that a compliment? Can't tell. Too stunned by the flash. The camera clicks. *Click click click!*

He retreats to study his efforts on a laptop. I stare at the floor.

Photographer comes stalking back. "What is your favorite memory of your father?"

"Um."

Somebody reaches to fluff my hair.

Does he not . . . can he seriously not know? "I—I . . . I don't have any. He died when I was a month old."

He snorts, like this is entirely beside the point. "Yes, but you have *seen* things? *Read* things? Your father was absolutely unknown when I photographed him, and yet his magnetism was undeniable. *ROCK*'s best-selling cover to date. I need you to channel those images, Koda Rose. Become him. Embody the *essence* that was Mack Grady. So." He taps his camera. "Smile. You can do this? You know your father's smile?"

Everybody knows my father's smile. See above: dimples. And maybe I don't know the exact pictures Photographer's referring to, but if he showed me an example . . .

Somehow, I doubt that's an option. I look up again, avoiding Photographer's glinting stare.

"Go on," he coaxes.

I smooth on what feels like a smile—a Mack smile—and I guess I do it right, because my mouth is so stiff it sticks that way until Photographer announces, "Okay, we are done smiling, Koda Rose. Let's look serious. No, *serious*—how is it possible to have those eyes and not know how to use them?" *Click!* "The key is to not be pretty." *Click! Click!* "Plenty of girls are pretty. It is not so hard to do, and fans' expectations for this feature are astronomical. You must—"

In photos my father is pretty. Not much older than me.

"—look worthy."

"Worthy?" What? My back tightens, this urge to defend myself—*well, I am his kid, whether you think I deserve to be or not.* But my mouth only flops.

Three days since we moved from LA, and nobody has ever spoken to me like this.

Photographer yanks the camera from his eye, motioning frantically for intervention. Ponytail. She lights a cigarette and drops it between my fingers.

"Oh," I say. "I don't—did my mom agree to this?"

Exasperated, Photographer explains that I don't have to smoke it. I'm just supposed to let the smoke snake around me because my father smoked, it'll be like this echo thing, utterly brilliant—he stops. Ponytail manipulates my fingers, showing me how to hold the cigarette without getting ash all over myself. Then she steps back, and somebody goes, *"Shh!"* Through my eyelashes I watch as two mouths, many mouths, drop open.

Slowly, Photographer says, "Move your head."

I move it. This cigarette reeks.

"No! Less!"

I move it less.

"That's it," he mutters. "That's it!" Spasms. "There he is. I knew you had him in you!" *Click!* "Yes!" *Click!* "Brilliant brilliant brilliant. A little more, darling—" I let the cigarette dangle, like the Mack in pictures I have seen, and—"There! Yes! Beau-ti-ful! Extraor-dinary! Blue eyes, and auburn hair, you fucking ex-qui-site china doll . . ."

By the time it's over, I kind of wish I did smoke, and that Mom could've let me in on a few more tips. Also maybe that I could look the tiniest bit more like my father, so I wouldn't have to turn my head to remind people I'm his.

CHAPTER 2

I BLOW THROUGH AN ENTIRE ROLL OF TUMS waiting for Mom to get out of her meeting. Photographer's fault. After wrap he buried me in questions about my father, like what I admire most about him, how very nice it might be if he were, of course, alive? My mouth hurt so much from smiling I couldn't answer. Somebody suggested I might be allergic to the lipstick. Poison Ivy, the color was called. Hilarious.

"Want to throw that away?"

I jump. The Magazine's receptionist clacks away on a computer, her face lit ghostly blue by the screen.

"Your wrapper," she explains.

The Tums wrapper. I shredded it. "Um . . . okay. Thanks."

She holds a small wire trash can out like some kind of sacred offering. I take three creaking steps toward her—The Magazine might be to fashion what Kleenex is to tissues, but its New York offices are depressingly ancient—then hover there, scraping Tums confetti off my palm. "Sorry," I mumble. For her part, Receptionist doesn't seem to mind having me all up in her space. My vision's still strobing from the flash, but as she scoots the trash can back under her desk, I risk further examination. She's older than me, but not by much. Scraggly dark hair, a ring through her eyebrow. She catches me looking and smiles.

I creak back to my chair and hook my feet around its spindly legs. Receptionist resumes typing. A steady clackity-clack.

"Thanks," I say again.

I never know what to do when cute girls smile at me.

To distract myself, I study the deserted reception area for the thousandth time since our driver dropped me off. It's not only ancient but soulless, the creamy white walls and chrome-accented furniture giving me serious competition for "Least Rock 'n' Roll." The oblong coffee table is way too nice to put my feet on, slathered in months-old magazines—back issues, and sister publications put out by the same company. I sift them around, hoping for something science-y, but they're what you'd expect. *Modern Luxury. Philanthropy Today.* I'm about to give up, check my phone again, when a ragged *R* poking out from the pile stops me. My pulse leaps.

Last month's *ROCK.* Not generally my thing. But—after checking to make sure Mom's not coming—I pull the magazine quickly into my lap. On the cover, a girl with an Afro strums her guitar, exponentially cooler than me. Thumbing past her, through pages splattered with more names and faces I've never heard of, it's hard not to imagine Receptionist tucking my issue here after April. My own face unrecognizable, Photoshopped smooth.

I set the magazine down, my gaze creeping toward the door.

4:24, my phone says.

Mom's meeting was supposed to end forty-two minutes ago.

I slip my phone back into my pocket and switch chairs to be closer to the window. Inexplicably, it's cracked open, and city sounds drift up with the chilly air. Blaring sirens and horns that I'm positive, after three days in New York, I will never get used to. At home it's different. Our new apartment, I mean—not Beverly Hills home. The apartment's so high up you can't hear anything except your own breathing, and blood slithering around your veins with the skyscraper's swaying. Mom claims that's just my imagination, but countless Google searches I've conducted in her absence this week proved otherwise. Tall buildings shift to accommodate high winds. It's weird how she doesn't feel it.

Not that this matters now. We live on the Upper East Side, but The Magazine's offices are way across the city, and there are only six floors, not eighty-five, between the street and me. 4:31, and the sky's already ashy, Eleventh Avenue strung with headlights like even shitty, smelly New York cares it's practically Christmas. My phone buzzes with a text from Mom: Almost done! XOXO! Thank God. OK! I reply. Please hurry! <33333 I could tell our driver—John? James? The Magazine's provided so many over the years I don't bother learning names anymore—judged me for wanting to come here after the photo shoot. But where was I supposed to go? Home? Alone? I guess I could've showered.

I drop my nose to my shoulder. Sniff test. Mom has a *thing* about cigarettes.

"Sure you don't want a drink?" Receptionist asks.

My head jerks up. She saw that? She saw me smelling myself?

"We have coffee," she adds hopefully. "A wide selection of teas."

"No thanks." Neither is on my list of heartburn-proof foods. I cool my forehead against the glass, eyes trained on the door. I don't know what Mom is doing in there. I don't particularly care. I can't even pick her voice out from the vague mumblings that occasionally rise, then subside again, little jolts of hope. No. Doors stay shut for a reason. They open when Mom says.

Meanwhile, Receptionist keeps typing, sneaking me glances I pretend not to notice. "Well," she goes on, like I've disappointed her somehow, "I saw you reading *ROCK* just now. You probably get this all the time, but—you're going to be on the cover next year, right? In the spring? And I want to tell you we're so freaking excited. Like, thank you."

I smile and fold my hands, fighting the urge to say, *You're welcome.* Everybody knows that dumb magazine jumpstarted my father's entire career. Combine that with the even dumber photos of me that got posted just before we moved, and we didn't—Mom says—have much of a choice.

But—"We?" I say.

She blinks. "Quixote fans."

Oh yeah. Them. I turn back to the window. Stare at my face etched on the dark glass. Really, it's only a reflection. Electrons. Light waves. I can see Receptionist, too, now blatantly staring at me, as wide-eyed and slobbery as Makeup Lady and Photographer were hours ago. Weird. If she's gawking at me, a nobody, she'd never survive LA. There, celebrities are like those black gnats you find bouncing around after a drought. They get caught in windshields, your teeth, but only tourists freak out about them.

Receptionist gets up, exiting through a door to the left of her desk that I guess must lead to a bathroom. I sit with my hands on my knees, pretending I can't hear her peeing while I practice the look Mom's early admirers dubbed *devastatingly casual.* The effort pulls my eyes to the window again. Tentatively, I trace a finger along my forehead.

You must—

My jaw.

—look worthy.

Idiot. The whole point of the *ROCK* feature is to prove I'm nothing like my father. Setting it up was stressful enough, but Mom will flip anew if my pictures bear even the slightest resemblance to him—she'll demand we shoot the whole thing over. And Mom could do that. She wasn't reassigned to this resuscitation task force at The Magazine's struggling New York offices for nothing. She was famous too once. She has power. And if Photographer really was so amazing, wouldn't he have reconciled himself to this basic fact?

Still, since Mom seems like she might be a while, I take my phone out and google *Mack Grady ROCK*. Might as well find the pics Photographer kept screaming about.

Images pop up of a glossy cover dated October 2001. I recognize it immediately. Anybody would. The caption, WHY QUIXOTE WILL REVOLUTIONIZE ROCK 'N' ROLL, floats above my father and his bandmates, filthy and too cool with their torn velvet shirts and dripping hair. My father is in the middle, obviously, arms flung out and limp like Jesus, one draped around the bassist, Ted, and another around the tomboyish little guitarist. His ex, Sadie. Drummer Vinnie looms behind everybody. Typical.

I flip through several variations of this picture, wondering what it is I'm supposed to feel. The article reveals nothing. Only the same phrases I've always associated with my father: *voice of a generation . . . a brilliant man with a gorgeous mind . . .* and then, on the twentieth-anniversary reprint: *left us most unfortunately*. Like he caught the wrong bus or something.

Receptionist reappears, wiping her hands on a paper towel, and I instinctively lower my phone to my lap. Once she's distracted, I unlock it again. Zoom in on my father's tangled black hair. The dimple. Makeup Lady was wrong. His eyes were nothing like mine. Layers of gray.

On impulse I scoot closer to the window. They brushed my hair out after wrap, but it's still sticky, chemical-smelling.

I pull it back over my shoulders, watching my eyes the entire time. It's weird, staring into yourself like this. Almost like I expect something big to happen. For my father to swim up to me.

Out in the hall, an elevator dings. Stilettos strike hardwood. "No no, that's so kind, but it's right here, isn't it? I'm sure I remember . . ."

I tear myself from the window just in time to hug Mom in front of Receptionist and the magazines and the poor elevator attendant who barely escapes getting trampled. "Koda!" Even Mom seems surprised by my greeting. She cups my cheeks, laughing, and I hug her again. Can't help it. A three-hour meeting, and her hands still feel like the cool side of the pillow.

"I thought your meeting was here!" I say, muffled by the swells of her giant white coat. It's fake. I'd never let her buy real seal.

"Oh no, honey, the designer we're showcasing has a studio downtown, so we thought it'd be best to—it wouldn't have been a problem if it weren't for the traffic! We got stuck coming back. Gridlocked! I swear, if it wasn't thirty degrees out, I'd think we were still in LA." Taking my face back in her hands, she pries me from her shoulder, gives me one of her searching looks. *Are you okay? Today went fine?* And even though it's enough to make me break down right here, I hold still—*fine*—letting my eyes flicker back whatever they need for her to believe it. Somebody clears their throat. Receptionist. I turn to see her standing stiffly in the doorway.

"May I have your coat, Mariah? Everybody's waiting."

Mom bites her lip. Besides the red hair, and vaguely Midwestern accent, punctuality is her most distinguishing feature. "Oh," she says, "oh, I'm so sorry, I didn't realize we still have to—don't worry about the coat. Should I go right in?" She steps forward. Receptionist doesn't budge. My mind's fritzing—still have to *what*?—but I turn to Mom anyway, so we can share that dumb look we share when people are too much.

My mom confuses people. Not on purpose—she's just so beautiful, so *obviously* a former model, that orienting her existence with your own temporarily sucks up all your bandwidth. The definition of stunning. It doesn't matter that her normally pristine skin has that pink, peeled look from scrubbing off her makeup in the car. Face on, hair down or not, she always looks the way she used to, the same Mariah Black who once sprawled across magazines and taxi tops. Receptionist is powerless.

Except Mom won't meet my eye. And the smile she switches on for Receptionist isn't her wispy model smile, but apologetic. Pleading. "I'm so sorry," she repeats.

A pause, like Receptionist is debating this. Then she slides from the doorway. "Follow me."

As we creak after her, I whisper, "What was that?" but Mom gives me a look so sharp I grab her fluffy faux sleeve. "Mom . . ."

And I remember how relentlessly attentive Receptionist was toward me as I sat captive in this ugly room. The poke of her curiosity while I flicked through magazines, watched traffic, compared to how she threw down Mom's name. Not *Welcome back, Mariah!* or *Ms. Black*, the ferociously capable editor who will bring The Magazine back from the brink of irrelevance, but *Mariah*. Some girl who got knocked up and destroyed the band.

The door I've been watching this whole time squeaks open, revealing a conference table. Alien, expectant faces. "Forgive me," Mom breathes, sweeping into the room. My palm registers a goodbye squeeze just firm enough for me to realize I won't be swept in with her.

"But," I stumble. "But I want—"

The door shuts in my face.

I'm not crying, but Receptionist brings me a cup of water anyway. I sip slowly, sitting as far as possible from the window.

Clacking away, Receptionist says, "Nobody's allowed in brainstorming sessions but the editors. It's like, a confidentiality thing."

I glare down into the cup.

It's not fair. I've needed Mom all day. She didn't say anything about brainstorming while she was getting ready this morning. In fact, she said, *It's one meeting, Koda. One meeting and done.* Why did I believe her?

The paper cup is getting soggy in my fist, the rim beginning to sag. Receptionist watches me run it across my sore lips.

Then she turns away and starts typing, practically shouting over the clacks of the keys. "What's your favorite song of your dad's, KR? I mean, if you don't mind me asking."

It takes a sec—very few people call me KR, and they're all assholes—but I refocus on her, accidentally sinking deeper into the couch. It's long and crimson, like Makeup Lady's mouth.

"Um." I avert my eyes from Receptionist's, their feverish glimmer. "To be honest, Quixote isn't . . . they're not really my thing?"

Abruptly, her clacking stops, and I default to staring at my fingernails. A move so foolproof that even teachers usually get the hint to call on somebody else.

Except there is nobody else to call on. Swallowing the lump in my throat, I add, "It's just . . . the screaming? I like 'Drown.'" This is true, but doesn't seem to satisfy her. For a while, neither of us says anything. The only sound a muffled *shhhh* that I don't immediately recognize as coming from the radiator.

It's not like I haven't tried to comprehend my father's music. I've streamed their albums, stalked message boards. Educated myself on the two categories of Quixote songs so I'd know how to react whenever somebody brought them up, not that anybody who knows me ever bothers. First, the raw stuff. "Headbangers," fans call them, though there aren't many. "Drown," Quixote's biggest hit, would fit into this category, but it's mellower, and given my father's interview aversion, it's the closest fans can get to understanding what they've dubbed *Mack's condition*. Depression, I guess. Darkness folding like water over your head. Except the lyrics are incomprehensible, and as for the other category? Who knows. Fans call them "scrapbook songs." Lyrics you might find pasted into diaries, carved like initials in a tree. And they are gentle. Tender even, but as hard as I've tried to lose myself in the murky chords and howling harmonies, guilt stops me every time. As far as Mom knows, I've only ever heard Quixote on the radio. When she couldn't switch stations fast enough.

Then there's the other feeling I get listening to their music. This feeling like—like my father's called from someplace with zero cell service, and there's shouting and static chaos, a message I can't make out, even though it's for me. And that feeling? It's deeper than guilt. Deeper than anything. I don't like it.

Eventually, Receptionist gives up on me, and I find myself staring at the *ROCK* cover on my phone again. It is pretty iconic. My father's black hair, the spark in his flinty eyes. Like I don't have more important crap to worry about than him. Unpacking. Altitude sickness. School—I start Monday. But I can't get my father off the screen, the photo shoot out of my head. Could they Photoshop a dimple onto me?

When Receptionist skulks over to collect my cup, I pretend I'm texting.

Mom finishes brainstorming within the hour, coat tossed over her shoulder in a stab at nonchalance. While she lingers at Receptionist's desk, patiently reciting the details of tomorrow's schedule that we both know Receptionist should've confirmed earlier, I give one coat sleeve an experimental hoist. Its weight surprises me every time.

I forget about my own coat until we're almost on the elevator. "Oops," I say as Receptionist emerges from the waiting room with it. "Thank you." Mom's mouth pulses. Even her non-smiles are smiles, but mine's the real deal: a peace offering. Receptionist's eyebrow ring is so cool.

She thrusts the coat at me. "Everybody likes 'Drown.'"

Driver takes so long bringing our car around, my toes practically shatter in my boots. He starts to get out, but Mom waves him off, jerks the door open. I slide into the car's stuffy backseat.

Mom climbs in next to me and doesn't say a word. Not even to Driver, so he can turn the heat down. She stares straight ahead, folded into herself.

Once we're moving, she says, "That was unbelievable."

I don't answer. My forehead is pressed to the window, attention locked on the shops we creep past. Café, designer optician, Thai restaurant, another café. The night swarms with New Yorkers hefting shopping bags, wreathed in their own breath. As we inch toward the intersection where street meets avenue, a dog cocks its leg to pee on a bicycle. Pigeons peck at a pile of barf.

". . . shouldn't have uttered a word to you," Mom's saying. "I don't care if she was being friendly, making conversation. That's not her job. Back home, nobody would have . . ."

Pizza place. Organic health food store. A cat boutique with kitty mannequins draped in crystal-encrusted collars.

GENUINE SWAROVSKI, brags the handwritten sign.

Of course everybody likes "Drown." There's clapping. Isn't that the point?

Mom yanked me onto the elevator like she was afraid I might start belting facts. Really wowing Receptionist with my Quixote IQ. Which is—what? Two albums. I do know that. I know that when Quixote's debut, *Sheer Folly*, dropped in '97, something in my father did too. The second came out two years later, his voice on half the tracks and that Sadie chick's scraping through the others. They had to release it unfinished.

I know that Mom and I were halfway across the country, in North Dakota, when my father died by suicide. Mom said she heard the news on TV.

Gentle pressure on my knee. "Honey."

I turn to see Mom gnawing the cuticles of her free hand, shadows under her eyes from the city's lights. "You promise the photo shoot went okay? Nobody bothered you, or said anything out of line like that?"

This is my chance to confess everything. Makeup Lady, the cigarette, Photographer harassing me to *act like him. Smile like him.* Fifteen minutes ago, that was all I wanted. Now the truth jams in my throat.

Mom's been negotiating this feature deal for weeks. Eight, to be precise, ever since those pics the paparazzi—*pazzos*, she calls them—snapped of my friends and me swigging smoothies out of unmarked cups hit the gossip sites. IN DADDY'S FOOT-

STEPS, one caption read. Like I'm this big party girl. Anyway, I didn't really care about the photos. A new tide of celebrity meltdowns and birth announcements was all it took to wash them away, but Mom saw them differently for some reason. Mom panicked. Absolutely freaked, like I've never seen. She said if we didn't take control of my so-called *narrative* now, prove to the world that I am not Mack Grady, I'll be screwed. Paparazzi chum for the rest of my life.

So I'm not mad at Mom for setting this up. Not exactly. I just wish she'd prepared me for the fact that people—randos, absolute strangers—might actually care about me here. Like maybe the feeding frenzy has already started.

Then again, the band was based in New York from the beginning. I guess I was just supposed to know.

I'm sure today was a fluke. A random exception to my otherwise lifelong anonymity, fed by excitement surrounding a *ROCK* feature that won't be out for months. Scientifically speaking, Receptionist and the others would be labeled *anomalies*—a deviation from the rule. In reality, they're New Yorkers with nothing better to do.

Mom's hand is still on my knee. I squeeze and she squeezes back, the shadows gone now that we're moving faster. "The photo shoot went fine," I say. "Promise." She smooths sticky hair back from my face.

Definitely anomalous. No use thinking of today as otherwise when there's dinner to choke down, and a locker to find on Monday, enduring this new job assignment that's gobbled up all of Mom's attention. Tomorrow will be easier. Tomorrow, Mom's got the day off, a whole blissful twenty-four hours to pretend everything's the way it should be. The way it's always been. Me in LA, and my father here. Five hours, three time zones, and over two thousand miles away.

CHAPTER 3

MY NEW SCHOOL IS HIDEOUS. ONE LOOK at its gothic brow has my stomach doing backflips. Kids slam doors to Jags and Mercedes, rushing past me up the marble steps, but I'm frozen. Shivering beneath my backpack and layers of eiderdown.

Can't fake sick. Driver's already pulling away from the curb, and now that Mom's working late again, we've reverted to old rules. No fever? No vomit? You're going. I won't see her until tonight—she was gone when my alarm went off at six—which means I have nothing to hold on to as I drag myself up the steps, a Latin-emblazoned banner flapping above the entryway. No final forehead peck to reassure me that everything's going to be okay. Only Mom memories. Mom residue. The same words she shipped me off with every morning in seventh grade, when I officially transitioned from homeschooling to an alien universe, with lockers and class periods and kids my age. *Try, honey. You'll feel better when you get there.*

The Latin on the banner translates to: *Truth calls the . . . wisest is . . . love* . . . there. Trying.

And I don't feel better.

The interior matches the exterior, more curlicues and clammy marble. A spiral staircase twines upward, the wing before me a tunnel of doorways and trophy cabinets. Everywhere I look, there's another kid, another face that means nothing to me. I take a tentative step forward. There's a smell of eraser crumbs. Antiseptic.

When trying fails, there are alternatives. *Picture your happy place*—Mom's top trick for when The Magazine's demands overwhelm her. My happiest place used to be our old pool, practicing flip turns with Lindsay without water shooting up our noses, but after the way we left things—the way I left things—she's the last person I want to think about. So I reach deeper. Grope around inside for something, *anything*, familiar.

Behind me, the hall churns with whispers. Stares crawl up my neck.

Okay. This must not be the type of school that gets many midyear transfers. They probably think I'm some delinquent. Head down, I struggle upstream, but the marble floor, soaked in fluorescent light, makes me dizzy. I have no idea where I'm going. Two boys shove past me, and I shift my backpack to my other shoulder, mumbling, "That's okay," before realizing they haven't stopped to say sorry—only to gawk. A girl traveling with her pack tips heart-shaped sunglasses up for a better look at me. Rude, but this is hardly my first time playing new kid. I smile to show I'm friendly.

She shrieks and grabs her friend's arm. They shriek together. I smack into a cabinet of wrestling trophies.

And so begins my second first day of senior year.

They want to know if "Rose" is a middle name and what California's like, if it's just sexy surfer bods engulfed in wildfires like you see on the news. They ask how many instruments I play and how I did on the SAT and what my preferred brand of pick is, whether I think *Rocinante*, Quixote's follow-up, is as brilliant as *Sheer Folly* or overrated like (*my friend, my cousin, Ms. Gonzalez the chemistry teacher*) claims. They crowd around me to show off their pigeon necklaces. The band's symbol—long story. They clutch my coat sleeves and beg for selfies, even though there's apparently a strict no-phones-during-class policy and four kids get sent to the office just for asking. They invite me to eat lunch—*you're in first wave too, Koda Rose!*—pronouncing my name like it belongs to something rare and wonderful, a fat-lipped fish species with one extant member. They chant, "Sit with us!" "No, us!" "Us!" Ms. Gonzalez takes one look at me and intervenes. "There's a seat right there, Koda Rose." Back row. A tall girl's haven. Except the desk I lower myself into is so far away that the whiteboard is a blur. One of the girls from the hall shoves a notebook in my face and whispers, "Copy off me." I take a pencil from my bag and the lead snaps immediately. Nobody else is wearing a coat.

When the bell rings, I shoot for the door. First period down. But second period? Third? Reruns. In the cafeteria—located on the school's fifth and highest floor, a deafening cavern that smells like wet meat—kids bombard me with questions while I dissect my turkey and cheese.

"Can you sing for us?" somebody asks. The girl with heart-shaped sunglasses, only she's not wearing them now, her blond hair fizzing from a braid that reminds me of Lindsay's.

"Yeah," says her friend. "Is your voice as good as your dad's? *Better?*"

Another kid whacks her and explains how that isn't possible. She whacks him back. I peel what remains of my sandwich from its biodegradable baggie.

When I started school in Beverly Hills, kids were curious about me at first. There was the occasional awkward question, or pity stare during the suicide unit in health class, but even those stopped eventually. They had to. I mean—okay, Quixote was pretty cool, revolutionary, if you believe the articles, but who's *that* into the music their parents listened to? I pick a flax seed off my bun, add it to the pile on my napkin, and when I risk looking back up, I realize the tussling has stopped and the table's ringed with expectant faces. My chest starts to burn.

"So?" the girl says.

Lie, and they'll demand proof. Tell the truth, and they might turn on me like Receptionist did. Just as I'm scanning for an exit, Mom's whisper floats into my head.

Try, honey. She's right.

These are my new classmates. Potential friends. I could really use a Latin buddy.

"Actually," I begin. Thirty kids lean in. Thirty! At least. Something moves inside me—this unidentifiable flicker that could be my father onstage, the lights and screaming fans. For the first time, surrounded by all these strangers, I want to know how that felt to him. I want to know if his breath shortened and throat spasmed, all slicked up in that pukey way. Maybe he hated his newfound fame as much as I do. Maybe.

I exhale. "Actually, I . . . don't sing. At all."

It blows their eyes wide open.

"Wait." Sunglasses Girl laughs. "Are you serious?"

I say I am. Only the other girl, the one who asked the question, steps closer. Suspicion narrows her eyes. "What about guitar? Sadie taught Mack how to play. Did she teach you?"

At the mention of Sadie, everybody shuts up. This reverent hush that whips across the surrounding tables. More faces turn—I lose count of how many.

"No. I . . ." My mouth feels like when I got my wisdom teeth out, full of bloody cotton. "I've never met Sadie. And I've never taken music lessons, or anything, either. I want to be a scientist. Well—a marine biologist, technically." Nobody reacts. A good sign? I rush on. Words pile up, spill into my lap. "At-at my old school, we had senior projects? Anybody could do an independent study on anything they wanted, as long as they had a teacher sign on as their advisor. Mine was going to be about the endangered fin whales that've been spotted recently off Newport Beach."

The girl repeats, "Fin whales?"

"Current numbers, future estimates, I had a proposal all typed up, was going to use the data as part of my application for UC Santa Barbara's marine biology program—it's the best. Not just in California. The entire country. But then my mom's job transferred her out here, so." Assuming that's enough of an introduction, I force my head up. Next question.

Sunglasses Girl turns to her friend. "Of course Koda doesn't know Sadie. *Mack* never even went and met her when she was a baby."

Now everybody's gone quiet, the cafeteria a sea of blinking eyes. Her friend looks at me. She's a redhead too. "Is that true?" she demands.

I nod. This one's easy. "I guess he was just too busy, or whatever." Sandwich annihilated, I gather the scraps, then shove them into the baggie—Sunglasses Girl and her friend can sit with me if they want—but the hush around me has chilled. One by one, the faces slide away.

A boy in the back mutters, "Weak."

CHAPTER 4

DOORMAN SEAN ASKS HOW SCHOOL WENT while we wait for the elevator. I pull my hair over my mouth when I answer, even though Mom says that's rude. "Good."

He smiles.

The Magazine found us our apartment, too. In the lobby, a fully bedecked Christmas tree twinkles beside the world's puniest menorah. Floor numbers tick off overhead as the elevator makes its slow plunge downward. 32, 31, 30 . . . In Beverly Hills, we had a front door. Our own keys. Here Doorman Sean grants access to our floor, and rides the elevator with me, all the way up to the top. It opens onto the so-called great room, which has the most dizzying views of the skyline. Then he touches his hat—"You have a good evening, Miss Grady"—and the doors slurp shut. Instead of heading for the room that will never feel like mine, I slump at the breakfast bar, watching the city glitter. Eighty-five floors, and our building still isn't the tallest, not by miles. Another reminder of how one-level California was.

The school nurse wouldn't let me hide in her office. Not for third period. Not even until the end of lunch. She tapped the COMPLAINT box on the clipboard, which I'd left blank while signing in. *I see no reason you can't go to class,* she said. Like my stomach didn't really hurt. Like I was just expected to write, *I want my mom.*

The late pass she scribbled for me was Pepto pink. I waited until she turned away to crush it in my fist.

The rest of school wasn't any better. I returned to lunch, bracing for round two of the question barrage, only to discover my table empty. Sunglasses Girl and her friend were nearby, picking at sushi, and I felt like going up to them and explaining, *My best friend, Lindsay, and I used to play her dad's old* Guitar Hero *game all the time.* Just to see if that counted.

Fourth period was Latin. Like, one-sixteenth of what the teacher put on the board made sense. In AP bio, somebody made a whale noise.

My nose prickles and I sit straighter, wiping it hard on my sleeve. If I texted Lindsay right now—if I weren't a pathetic coward—she'd answer, Forget them. Those kids are just jealous bc their parents all do boring shit lol. Tomorrow, she'd make rounds of the cafeteria with me: *Your dad—banker or lawyer?* A ruthless, informal poll. But that's Lindsay, who is confident, and blond, and everything else I'm not. I nibble my sweatshirt cuff.

The last time I saw her was the night before we moved. We went to the beach, but it was too chilly to swim, even in our one-pieces, so we found a bench and talked for hours. Lindsay kept saying how much she was going to miss me, that without me school would be shit and home would be shit, her dad making her dance with him all weekend, blasting his old-ass bachata records. *Don't get me wrong, I love bachata. I love dancing.* She elbowed my ribs, grinning. *I love teasing you for not knowing how to dance.* I should've elbowed her back, rolled my eyes, anything. We both knew she could barely keep up with her dad either. But all I could think about was our toes touching, snuggled up under the sand.

Now I slide off my stool, leaving my phone facedown on the counter. Something must be seriously wrong with me. I can't stay away from windows. The city's glare whites me out. Undeterred, I roll my shoulders back, throw my arms out like my father's in that one picture, only it doesn't look right—either because I truly am this uncool, or just need some bandmates to back me up. Adjusting angles, I touch my fingertips to my lips like there's a cigarette between them. If I showed up in different clothes tomorrow? Except I don't own nearly enough black. "Fuck you," I practice saying, my voice sharp and clear. "I bet half you idiots never met your dads either. I bet plenty of them are dead too." But saying something over and over can't make it true. *I'm* the dad-less anomaly here. The outlier.

Usually Mom texts when she leaves the office, but when my phone pings at 7:23, it's only a gossip alert.

KR GRADY PREFERS WHALES TO MUSIC,
DAD'S LEGACY, SOURCES CLAIM

I wonder if he hated school too.

When Mom comes in, I don't look up from the box I'm repacking. My new room is repulsive, so pink it gives me a toothache—I only picked it because it connects to hers.

"Koda? What are you doing?"

"Nothing." I pop the last of my whale posters from its frame while she perches on my bed, legs knotted tight to avoid flashing me. Today's skirt is suede. A sensible nude.

Carefully, she says, "I've already called the principal."

"Yeah, I heard. You didn't have to yell." I mean, the effort's appreciated, but shrieking voicemails won't stop the school she so painstakingly picked out for me from crawling with Quixote-obsessed freaks. Before today, she almost had me convinced that this school would be a good place for me. Somewhere to finish high school in *safety and solitude.*

Emphasis on solitude, apparently.

Mom runs a hand through her hair. "In the long term, I think this might actually be a positive thing for us? Corroboration for the future. I admit I'm a little surprised by the intensity of your classmates' interest, but . . . it seems that . . . I suppose we . . . honestly, I don't know what I'm trying to say, Koda. It's been an eventful day. Let's work on choosing friends in New York wisely."

The whale posters are taller than I am, divided by toothed species and baleen. I grab the toothed—my favorites—and start rolling, my hair so infuriatingly long I have to stop every couple seconds to swipe it back. "Sure," I mutter. "Will do." She hasn't been home long enough to slip out of her work persona. That takes time. And chamomile. Still, it's hard not to feel let down when she turns that ruthless practicality on me. The most humiliating day of my life reduced to bullet points. Does she not realize I've got the solution right here? I sit back, giving her space to see the drastic lengths I will go to in order to prevent total degradation. I'm rolling up my *whale posters*, Mom. Whale posters.

She yawns, fingertips pressed to her eyelids. "I think I'll go take a bath, okay?"

As the door shuts, I bite off a strip of tape and slap it on the rolled-up poster. A few days from now, she'll wander into my room and comment on it looking bare. *Didn't we pack things to put on the walls?* And then I'll tell her. In the meantime, I need to practice, so that when I confront those kids tomorrow, my excuses won't sound made up. "I was just kidding yesterday," I say, mouth slack, letting it frame the words. "I really don't want to be a marine biologist. I want to be a . . . a . . ." The tape pulls free, unfurling seventy-three toothed cetaceans across my carpet. The bottom inset is a close-up: more teeth. Porpoises' are spade-shaped. Dolphins', conical. Most people don't realize.

• • •

Turns out *taking a bath* means *calling my lawyer.* On speakerphone, not that I hear everything through the door. Occasionally, voices rise—Mom's first, then Mr. Todd's, trying to calm her down. I stick tape to my fingertips, then rip it off piece by piece, like the esthetician with Mom's waxing strips. When I can't take eavesdropping anymore, I stand slowly, stick fresh tape to every finger.

I enter Mom's bedroom just as the call ends, and it's obvious despite her casual tapping on her phone that I've startled her. Her mouth opens. Closes. "I thought you were in bed. It's almost midnight."

"Nope. Still redecorating." I wiggle my tape fingers, playing dumb.

Mom sets her phone on the nightstand. The master suite is the biggest room in our new apartment, white carpet as blinding as my room is intestinal. The mossiness tickles my toes as I help Mom with the temperamental curtain controls. Only when we manage to hit the magical combination of buttons do the curtains peel back slowly, like thick mechanical eyelids. She sets the remote down, adjusting her pale blue nightgown. "So it's that button, Koda. The red one. We'll have to put a note on it."

"I'll remember."

We smile at each other, kind of thinly. I don't move as she takes my face in her hands and kisses me good night.

Once it's clear I'm not going anywhere, she gestures at our view. The whole apartment is wrapped in windows, and at night the city sparkles around us in 360. "Isn't this lovely?"

"Lovely," I echo, plucking off the tape. Mom's efforts at selling me on New York are getting old. Can't she just admit that our veranda back home was superior? I miss it almost as much as I miss staircases. Our pool. Central Park is kind of neat, though. Its own constellation. I connect the dots of lamplight, steadying myself, so what I want to say won't fall out all at once. *I hate it here,* I imagine confessing. *I don't care anymore about The Magazine, all the money they're paying you, and what this means for your career. I want to go home.* But how can I say that when it's been the two of us, rooting for each other, holding each other up, since . . . practically forever? Like, before I was born. I mean, if you want to get technical, I had no choice but to stick by her at first, busy gestating and all, but that's just it. I was a fantastic copilot, Mom says. Rarely kicked or complained. It sealed something between us. I've always known that.

I've stayed silent too long. Now Mom's working herself up again, chafing at my shoulder. "I'm so sorry, Koda. As first days go, this wasn't ideal, but you'll be old news to those kids before you know it. You're going to make so many friends."

I can't help myself. "They don't want to be my friends."

"Honey—"

"Those kids"—where to start—"they don't like me." My hands burrow into my sweatshirt cuffs. "I'm not *worthy*, Mom."

Instantly, my face is back in her hands. "Why would you say that?"

No. I touch her wrists. Don't be mad, Mom. Logically, I

get that this sort of scrutiny is about to start happening more and more. It's inevitable. A consequence, Mom has explained, of growing up, exposing myself to a world, *a public*, rife with expectations. Preconceived notions not necessarily of who I am, but what I should be. *Take hold of your narrative, Koda, before it takes hold of you.* Coming from her, that makes sense, but in practice . . .

In practice, it fully sucks.

I am just so awkward. Fundamentally, egregiously wrong. I always assumed he didn't meet me because he was touring, doing music things, when I was born. But he was brilliant, right? Enough to make it happen, if he wanted?

Enough to sense from across a country, a continent, that I was no good.

The thought explodes across my brain, white-hot. I can't answer Mom's question. I *can't.* She wasn't there when Photographer said that to me. Even if she had been. Even if she'd seen the sneers on those kids' faces, heard the things they said, she would've brushed them off. *When people give you feedback, Koda, it's because they want to help you improve. It'd be silly to take it personally.* But I'm not being silly. This *is* personal.

Mom lowers her hands, oblivious, and starts hunting for bobby pins on her dresser. "Ignore them," she urges. "Mr. Todd will take care of the gossip leaks. Moving forward, I . . ." She nibbles a pin open, hesitant. "I mean what I said about choosing your friends wisely. I know you know this, but not everybody can be your Lindsay."

Yeah.

Well.

Not even Lindsay could be my Lindsay.

I stare out at the city while Mom folds her hair into a chignon. A signature bedtime look. All it takes is seven bobby pins.

"Did you have dinner?" she asks. "I mixed tuna with yogurt earlier. It's low-fat."

I shrug. Like she ever lets us go full-fat. "I'm not hungry."

Mom flops back onto her California king. "It's so late, honey. You have to eat something."

My stomachache says otherwise. Besides, I'm already wriggling next to her, frustration shelved. I can't spoil our ritual. The only time that's truly ours, now that she's in overdrive. When she announced The Magazine was changing her role, I acted happy. Rigged my mouth into a big smile, because I knew how important it was to her that she be given this opportunity. Truth is, Mom's worked most of my life. I should know what to expect, and it's not like I'm going to sit here and cry about some missed swim meet or science fair. That's how fantastic a copilot I am.

But sometimes I wish The Magazine really would go under. I picture the two of us back in Los Angeles, no more money or meetings or midnight brainstorms pulverizing her nerves. We could move into a smaller house, far up in the hills, and hang out just like this. Foreheads touching. Legs hinged off the side of the bed. She put on my favorite lotion tonight. A random favorite, since the scent doesn't remind me of anything in particular. Just the sheen on her arms when she's finished rubbing it in. I take a big whiff.

Mom covers my eyes, laughing, and when her hand slides away, I move my cheek onto her comforter, to see her better. Her mention of Lindsay has me thinking. "We're three hours ahead of LA, right?" I ask. Like I haven't been obsessively counting back since our plane hit the tarmac. *I am eating lunch, but Lindsay is just now getting up. The sunset's stinging my eyes, but Lindsay . . .* Mom studies me, squinting a little in the track lighting.

"You know you'll never adjust if you keep thinking of it like that."

"I know," I tell her, but that's exactly my problem. I don't want to adjust.

Not everybody can be your Lindsay. Mom doesn't know how right she is. She doesn't know—because I never told her, because I deluded myself into believing it wasn't happening, even as the changes unfolded right in front of me—that Lindsay is different now. It started over the summer. One day we're at the beach, embarking on the same tide-pool expeditions we'd gone on since seventh grade, and the next she's all about Peter.

I'm still not sure how she met him. At a party, she told me, but we always went to parties together, and once she finally introduced us, I couldn't imagine him hanging out with anybody we knew from school. He's older, for one thing. Not by much, but—enough. And a musician. A guitarist who whams notes so hard you feel them in your molars, the sole reason Lindsay gave up her swim team sweatshirt for smeary eyeliner, and tattered black everything. She says Peter is super sensitive, and totally gets her. The notch in his chin? SoOOoOoOoOoO hot omg!!!!!! I once listened to her describe, step by agonizing step, how he went down on her at a party.

That I was not invited to. That she didn't even tell me about, until then. *What do you mean "What party?" My family's* Dominican, *Koda. I hear about a party, I go.*

Mom sits up, and I swallow hard, breaking the tightness in my throat. "Let's give New York some time," she says, fingering a piece of hair that's come loose from her chignon. "I lived here for a while when I was your age, remember? Downtown. I hated it here at first. I was living off nothing, with six or seven other girls, all models, crammed in a single room. It was so hard, but I got used to it. You can get used to practically anything, if you put your mind to it. By the end I'd absolutely fallen in love with the city."

"That's Stockholm Syndrome," I say. Then, anticipating a *Be serious, Koda* frown: "You know, when you accidentally start to identify with whatever's holding you hostage? Otherwise, the other models would've cannibalized you or something. You don't need to love New York, Mom. I don't either. The air hurts my face."

Sighing, she palms my cheek. "Be patient. That's all I ask."

Patient? I can be that. I guess. As long as she's right, and the kids at school will lose interest eventually. While she goes on and on, saying the things she often says about how lucky she is to have such a good kid, my attention wanders to our reflections. Her shimmery blue nightgown and miraculous legs. I've secretly always suspected I got mine from my father. They look so pitiful compared to hers. Spindly mozzarella.

CHAPTER 5

NURSE SIGHS WHEN I WALK INTO HER office. *Happy Tuesday,* I almost say. My second day at this school, and she already can't contain her joy at seeing me. "Miss Grady, you can't come waltzing in here whenever you please. First period starts in ten minutes."

"I need the bathroom," I say.

She swivels away from her desk. Nurse uses a wheelchair. And I can tell, based on how her *t*'s come out *d*-shaped, that she's probably from around the same area as Mom. Not North Dakota, but close. Wyoming? Montana?

"And the regular bathrooms won't do because . . ."

Insufficient privacy: an insufficient excuse. Fortunately, I'm familiar enough with school nurses as a species to know they never, ever argue with diarrhea—all it takes is one anguished grab of my abdomen, and voilà: a personal escort. She unlocks the bathroom with a key around her wrist.

"Wash your hands," she says, and I swear I will, shutting the door quickly behind me.

The bathroom smells like it looks. Gray tiles. Greasy pink soap suspended in the dispenser by the sink. I let my backpack slither from my shoulders, then sit on top of it, hugging myself. On the other side of the wall, kids laugh. Sneakers squeak. Nothing too scary. If I got up now, I could wash my hands and make it to my locker with time to spare. What vibes shall I beam down the school's hallowed halls today? *Please ignore Koda Rose Grady. Do not approach or make any sudden movements.* Sounds menacing to me.

But as I get up, my gaze flicks to the mirror. I remember Sunglasses Girl. The cafeteria.

And what little resolve I woke up with shatters. What if I'm never accepted here? What if, no matter what I do, I'll never be allowed to do my own thing, be my own person, without hundreds of greedy eyes dissecting my every move? I'll be doomed to star in their gossip. Not *Miss Grady*. Not even *Koda Rose*. This wad of communal gum that's passed from mouth to mouth.

The bell rings. A hot nail through my skull.

Nurse knocks on the door. "Koda Rose?"

"What?" I croak. "I'm still going."

"Well, you need to hurry up. I can't keep writing you late passes."

"Okay." But I don't stand up, or flush the toilet, to convince her I'm not faking. I cram my hair in my mouth and sob.

• • •

My photographs leak the next day. I shouldn't be surprised. I mean, it's been almost a week since I sat on Photographer's stool and pouted for him. One week for—Clipboard Girl? Makeup Lady?—to fire the proofs off to every last scoop-starved gossip blog out there. For that, a week feels pretty standard.

Mom sees it differently.

The bellowing starts as I'm getting dressed, rooting for the head hole of my JV swim sweatshirt. Lately I've worn it every day. It's cozy, a dark navy even Mom would deem flattering, the back covered in names: my old school's, and my own name, and Lindsay's, and all the other friends I made on the team. Inside it, I feel protected. Untouchable. Say somebody tries to speak to me in the halls, gives me one of *those* looks? No problem. I wrap my arms around my waist and scurry away. A hermit crab. The world's gangliest.

The adjectives Mom's chosen for this particular indiscretion are ones she hasn't resorted to for a while—not since she fired a journalist back in LA for making up quotes. *Ludicrous! Unconscionable!* Finally, I find the hole and push through, gasping. My hair crackles around me. I get zapped twice just wadding it into a bun.

In the car on the way to school I hug my backpack, debating what would happen if I surrender completely to impulse and barf all over myself. We pass a corner where kids have already gathered, Sunglasses Girl included, and their necks torque to follow the car. Any hope that they haven't seen my photos evaporates. As we approach the drop-off point, the kids congeal into a seething, pointing mass. Sunglasses Girl elbows to the front. She dyed her hair. Pink, but like certain sea anemones are pink. To remind people they're poisonous.

Pro: barf, and Driver might U-turn to dump me back home.

"All righty, Miss Grady," he says. "You have a nice day now."

Reaching for the door handle, I take a shaky breath. My mouth floods on cue.

Con: I really need this sweatshirt.

Mom's on a conference call when Driver drops me off after school. Surprise. I've barely stepped into her office before she's waving her hands, hustling me back out into The Magazine's chrome-accented hall. Picture frames, this time. My reflection stares back at me from cover after meticulously preserved, glass-encased cover—every issue from 1961 until now. Interns must draw straws to figure out who'll get stuck polishing them each morning.

". . . repulsive . . . to insert herself into . . ."

Startled, I spin around. I accidentally left the door cracked.

"Yes, but why would—you have to call her right this instant. Call that woman and tell her she can antagonize me whenever, however she wants, as long as she stays away from my daughter!"

My heart starts to thump. Not a work call.

Something with our lawyer.

Something about me.

I push the door a little wider.

". . . good question." Mom sighs. "I haven't had a working number for her since 2011. That's Sadie for you."

Wait. Like . . . Sadie? Guitarist Sadie? What would my father's ex, that ragged girl from the *ROCK* cover, have to say about me?

Mr. Todd crackles over the speaker. "This is what Sadie does, Mariah. She makes noise. She makes noise about something totally inconsequential and then vanishes for another decade, so I still suggest that we—"

Mom detonates. "But why torment us? Why now? Because I had the audacity to move to New York? Because commenting on Koda's pictures in a video clip is that little has-been's only means of reminding people she still exists? Half the world thinks she choked to death on her own vomit fifteen fucking years ago."

Holy crap. Mr. Todd doesn't answer, but I can feel his eyebrow rising, feel him thinking the same as me, which is, *Holy crap*. I mean, Mom sends flowers with cease and desist letters to bloggers who make stuff up about her, and now *she's* going to badmouth somebody she hardly knows? That swear alone was headline-worthy. My hand jerks to the doorknob, but something stops me from barging in. A silence that stretches years.

Softly, Mom says, "I didn't watch the clip, no. I assume she's the same."

At school this morning, as I struggled out of the car, Sunglasses Girl shoved her phone in my face. The photo on the screen was of me. Or a girl who used to be me, awkwardness radically transformed by eyeliner and tentacles of smoke. Sadie made a video commenting on . . . that?

I creep to the side of Mom's desk, deliberately out of sight. My hand trembles as I touch her shoulder. "Mom? What's wrong?"

Her face is coming apart like a wet tissue. In a single motion she kills the call, pushes her ultra-sleek desk phone away. "Everything's fine, honey. And you? How was school?"

"Enlightening," I manage.

Her eyes narrow—but it's the truth. We're halfway home, bundled into the backseat, before I work out that Mom doesn't realize what I overheard. "It's nothing, honey, really," she says when I ask what's wrong for the thousandth time. "I just wish . . ." She watches traffic, rigidly nibbling a fingertip. "What was that photographer thinking, giving you a cigarette?"

Normally, I don't mind her nostrils flaring when she lies to me. Tonight, I'm torn between calling her out and admitting, *The kids at school like the cigarette pictures, though.* Sunglasses Girl shoving her phone at me was just the beginning. For the rest of our drive up Fifth Avenue, I imagine Mom liking those pictures too, frowning the appraising frown she brings to film screenings, spring previews.

At school I forded throngs just to lock myself in a bathroom stall. It was too much attention. Too much *Hey, Koda Rose!* and sleeve-grabbing. My first day all over again. Except instead of bolting to the nurse's office, I huddled on a toilet with my feet tucked up so nobody would recognize my sneakers. I chewed my hair and listened to what girls said about me as they applied mascara, washed hands. *Well, I think the resemblance is totally obvious. Why doesn't she come to school looking like that? Doesn't she realize people might actually start to like her?* In a way, it was worse than my first day, because at least then I had nothing to offer them. No definitive proof besides my last name that would legitimize me and satisfy their hunger. Now there is, apparently, something. And I still ran away.

I decide not to tell Mom any of this when I confront her later. She's at the kitchen breakfast bar, legs so endless that her feet are pressed flat against the marble. Taking all this in, I let myself think what I wish were happening actually is: Mom's cooking. Not cooking like she does now, mixing low-fat yogurt with whatever's sufficiently spreadable to last us through the week, but *cooking*. The way she used to. The way she still could be, if she'd allowed The Magazine's offer to be just that: an opportunity. Anyway, I'm good at pretending. So good that as I approach, arms crossed—count on Mom to notice when I'm not wearing a bra—I never quite stop hoping. Even as I reach her elbow, and see she's got her notebook spread before her. A pen between her teeth. Listing. Even then, I rise on tiptoe, checking for clues about what she's making. *Dmge contrl,* she's scribbled. *Call w/ Todd 8:30.* A recipe for getting us through the week.

"Koda!" Mom slaps her arms over the notebook. "Don't creep up on me like that!"

The kitchen is a chrome wasteland. No wonder The Magazine wanted us to live here. Tonight, it seems darker than usual, even with the city's lights. I can hardly see Mom's face as I slide onto the stool next to her, muttering, "Sorry."

She laughs limply. "You're too good at it. It's terrifying."

Terrifyingly sneaky? Or terrifyingly adept at terrifying her? I pull the notebook out from under her arms. *?????* it says. Then, *SADIE*. Ferociously underlined. Mom stares at me, staring at the page. A feeling—the same I felt hearing her utter Sadie's name at the office—begins to rise. I can't name it. But it crashes into me like waves.

"Can we talk?" I ask.

"Talk?" She gnaws a fingertip. "About what?"

Good question. There is so much I want to ask. So much I need to know. Understanding why she trashed Quixote's guitarist should be the least urgent. "You didn't really know my father's ex, did you?"

The gnawing stops. "Were you eavesdropping earlier?"

"No. But . . ." I falter, confused. "You didn't know her well, right? You've never said anything about her. How come you didn't tell me that you knew her?"

"Why would I? That was a lifetime ago."

"You mean his lifetime?" I'm not sure why this distinction matters suddenly, only that Mom seems thrown by it too, her twisting mouth making me sorry I asked. But: "What's it matter if she has something to say about me? Do you really hate her that much?" Because maybe I don't follow Quixote stuff as closely as I should, but I'm positive Mom wouldn't have stayed with my father even if he hadn't gotten back together with Sadie, or lived. Probably he would've been awarded holidays. Thanksgiving. Every other Christmas. I'd fly out to New York for occasional long weekends, and we'd do touristy stuff. Times Square, and Central Park carriage rides, ice skating at Rockefeller Center. Midtown's greatest hits.

At least, that's what I've worked out. The thing about my father—or my mother's thing about my father, which is more or less the same—is that she won't talk about him. I've sort of made my peace with that. Or been forced to. I've always told myself her reluctance makes sense. My father hurt her. Before tonight, I never considered that she was deliberately *hiding* details from me. Info that barely concerns him, but this strange third person. A woman I know only from her smirk on a magazine. Who commented on my pictures . . .

Mom smooths her palms across the counter's shiny finish, avoiding my eye. "I don't hate her, Koda. That would be childish."

"What did Sadie say about me, then?" I demand.

Her face hardens—an expression I've rarely seen outside of YouTube, video after grainy video of pazzos hounding her when my father was still alive. *No comment.* "She's just being an instigator, Koda. This is what Sadie does, so—let me handle it, all right? Frankly, I don't see why any of this matters."

Realistically, it doesn't. I don't care about Sadie. Not really.

Except. "The kids at school like her a lot." I wait a beat, then go for it. "Would I like her?"

Mom works quietly on a cuticle. "I'm sorry you had to hear me getting heated with Mr. Todd. There's just so much going on right now with work, and this trouble with school, and now the leaks, and . . . if I had known coming to New York would be such hell, I would've thought twice about . . ." She stops herself, probably not wanting to get my hopes up about moving back home. Or else just coming to terms with how to answer my question. "Sadie is . . . of course people still like her, she was very famous. Twenty years ago, but . . ." The logic starts meandering. One of those answers. "But you should trust me when I say she's . . . well . . ."

Whatever Sadie said about me could've been really nice, or it could've been really mean. I try to envision it either way. I try to envision what it'd be like to hear from somebody who knew my father and might know me because of him. Somebody whose authority on this issue means she would never join the ravenous mobs at school, or—the other extreme—treat me like I am fatherless. Like I sprang from Mom's forehead, a god in some weird old story.

"Sadie can be very . . ."

Wise. That's what Sadie must be. Incredibly, unendingly wise.

Mom shakes her head, looking exhausted. "Unreliable. Sloppy."

"Sloppy?" That's a new one.

Mom pushes my hair back. "Let's forget about her. Unlike Sadie, I don't revel in the past." She smiles. "Not when there's so much to look forward to in the future." The hopeful twinge in her voice makes me want to believe this. My curiosity withers. And then comes the guilt.

Mom's right. The past is over. Unreachable by definition, but I did okay enough on the SAT that I'll have my pick of marine bio programs in California, even applied early decision to one. That's what I should be obsessing over, instead of this mess. Saving whales. Not letting myself be eclipsed by a Mack-shaped sun.

"Okay," I relent. "Sadie forgotten. Done."

Mom strokes my cheek, her hand uncharacteristically sweaty.

CHAPTER 6

ONCE I START GOOGLING, I CAN'T STOP. That's all I'm doing, though. Googling. Not skipping English to hide out in the bathroom. Definitely not disobeying Mom. One simple, harmless google, to see what she thinks I can't handle and move on. I don't want to upset her. Just for the clammy feeling in my gut to go away. I find the reaction article to my photos that Sadie supposedly commented on—a handful of sentences devoted to establishing me as nearly legal rock spawn. The first paragraph alludes to previous exploits, aka the smoothie photos, followed by speculation about why, with this feature in the pipeline, I would be so upfront about my scientific ambitions. *Start a band, Koda Rose!!!!* one commenter demands. *Take over the world! We have all been waiting for you!!!!* Others concur. I scroll past them, my cheeks blazing, to the very end of the stream. A link posted by somebody calling themselves *RIPMACK*. The comment reads: *Check out* *this video lol Sadie P is wild. It's actually re that news story about KR and the whales but hopefully a statement on the photos is forthcoming?? Regardless, is this her first public statement EVER about our Koda?!??* So Sadie didn't comment on my photos. I lower my phone into my lap, disappointed. Maybe there's no point watching after all.

The bell rings to signal first-wave lunch, forcing my attention back onto the screen: *first public statement EVER*. Either I face Sadie's opinion of me, or the cafeteria's.

The video hardly qualifies as such, one of those pazzo-ambush, iPhone-in-your-face deals that most celebrities probably breeze right past. Still, you'd think these people would have better equipment. When the clip finally loads, it's a pixelated mess. Like the phone it got recorded on was recently dropped in a toilet. But as fuzzy as the background is—some kind of storefront, bricks and a smooth sweep of glass—I recognize her immediately. Even with the bandanna. The sunglasses that eclipse half her face.

"Sadie," the pazzo pants. "Sadie, have you seen the news about Koda?"

Her brow puckers, like, *Who?* My chest seizes. Does she seriously not—but as he hurries to clarify, "Koda Rose? Mack's daughter?" the pixels shift. Sadie smirks.

She knows exactly who I am.

"Yeah." She nods repeatedly. "Oh yeah. Big fan. Though I've always been more partial to her experimental stuff."

A pause. The pazzo seems stumped. Sadie keeps walking,

and as he hustles to catch up, she flips him off over her shoulder. I giggle. I can't help it. *This* is what Mom was so mad about? The screen goes black. I'm about to hit replay when I spot the geotag: Fazes Café, Astoria, Queens.

Queens.

That's part of the city. A fringey part, but still, I had no idea she lived so close. I zip to her Wikipedia page. It's true. *Born: Troy, New York.* Same as my father. *Lives: Queens, New York City.* And she's only five feet tall. Five feet and three-quarters in Doc Martens. The *P* stands for Pasquale.

My stumbling fingers open another tab. I google *Sadie Quixote*, but it's the same things you always read about her and Mack Grady being high school sweethearts, running away to the city to start their band. When they got discovered, they were eighteen and homeless. Scrawny nobodies with guitars strapped to their backs. I keep tapping. Pictures flood my phone like the u ok??? texts from Lindsay I can't bring myself to answer. Old pictures, because they have my father in them. His face is a singing face and Sadie has a guitar on her knee, hair everywhere, the background a haze of smoke and lights. And then there are the interviews I'm too impatient to reread. An eight-second clip of Sadie shouting she'd crowd-surf more if people quit grabbing her junk. Apparently, she gave a spectacularly incoherent press conference the day my father died. I don't watch that.

But I keep going back to the ambush video throughout the day. I don't know why. It's not even interesting. Just my father's ex, walking out of an ordinary café, on an ordinary street. Bandanna and sunglasses and some kind of leather jacket. The skinniest skinny jeans. It's just that . . . in a way, I was right. Sadie doesn't seem to care about me the way other people do here. My *experimental stuff.* What does that mean? I scour the video for clues. Zooming in as far as my phone will zoom, scrutinizing every ragged edge of this woman who everybody agrees knew my father better than he did, and when I get sick of that, I return to the caption. Queens. *Queens, Queens, Queens* . . . until my sweaty palms pulse the words.

CHAPTER 7

DRIVER MATERIALIZES AT EXACTLY 3:15, much appreciated on this frosty afternoon. I set my backpack where Mom usually sits and stuff my penguin beanie over my hair. Wait for his eyes to appear in the mirror.

"Have a nice day, Miss Grady? It'll take about—oh, thirty minutes to get to your mother's office."

Heart pounding, I look out at colorless Fifth Avenue, the sidewalk choked with kids waiting for rides. Some cross the street, into Central Park, which isn't nearly as impressive at ground level as it seems from eighty-five floors up. A mass of fog and dead trees.

Queens. The pounding fills my throat, my eyes, getting louder and louder the longer we idle. *Queens, Queens, Queens . . .*

The car noses forward. Another couple feet and we'll join the clog, Mom-bound. I'll totally lose my nerve.

"Hold on," I say.

He stomps the brake.

My day sucked, I want to shout when his eyes skitter back into the mirror. But as my mouth opens, I think better of it. Too off-script. Instead, I take a breath. My voice wobbles only a little when I recite the address off my phone.

A silent crawl through traffic on Fifth. More gray, tangled streets, so packed with traffic that we make it to the bridge right as the sun flames out. While we cross, the entire island of Manhattan becomes visible along the horizon, skyscrapers like the dips and peaks of a heart monitor. Honestly, it would be breathtaking, if anything in New York deserved that label. Staring at the sunset, the restless gray river, I take deep breaths, one after the other. Willing my chest to loosen.

Crossing the bridge is like getting squeezed through the guts of a giant slug. Driver maneuvers from lane to narrow lane with a stoicism that suggests he's about to murder me. The outer boroughs must offer some prime options when it comes to dumping bodies, but as we near the end of the bridge, an exit pops up for ASTORIA BLVD. We take it.

I switch to the middle seat to make my view more panoramic. No skyscrapers here. Just three- and four-story buildings made of yellowish brick, interspersed with more modern-looking glass facades. Some truly monstrous scaffolding looms ahead. I lean over the console to investigate.

"Subway," Driver explains. As we pass beneath it, a train rumbling by sends a whole new round of earthquakes through me.

"I thought the subway was underground," I say, blinking up at the sunroof.

"Some lines. Others are elevated."

We turn off the noisy boulevard, up a short hill. The sunset turns caustic. Without my sunglasses, I feel more than see tiny front yards, all Christmas'ed out with lights and glowing plastic Marys. "Oh," I say.

It's gotten dark, and I've counted five more Marys by the time we pull up to the curb. We've been on this street for a while, and it looks more like Manhattan than any bit of Astoria I've glimpsed so far. Shops and too many people. Only the brick buildings and tacky decorations haven't changed. I peer through murky street light until I find a sign that says FAZES CAFÉ, the letters wrapped around a fat white moon.

"This it?" Driver sounds doubtful. I never actually explained why I made him bring me out here. I'm not sure I know myself. While the car idles, my eyes jerk to the sidewalk just beyond the doorway. The same place—it must be—where Sadie stood in the video.

Anyway, my motivations are none of Driver's business. "Yeah." I reach hesitantly for my backpack.

Fine. I'll be fine. Chances are she's not even here. "Yeah," I repeat, stifling a burp. "Call you when I'm done, okay?" The locks release. *Chirp.*

The café door says PUSH, not PULL. Embarrassing, but I get there. Warm air flushes into my face like dough rising.

Two things.

First, Astoria gives way too many shits about Christmas.

Second, Sadie isn't here.

I know automatically. It's not a big café. Besides the counter with its row of barstools, there aren't many places to sit, only a sofa, and mismatched armchairs in upchuck florals. Any remaining room has been hijacked by that station all cafés have, where you add sugar and cream, and an art installation. Scrap-metal reindeer, their antlers looped in white lights. Music thumps. Anonymous EDM with fractured vocals, beats that drop. Two girls sit on the sofa, leaning over the same laptop. I try not to stare at them, their knees almost touching, as I move stiltedly toward the counter. A print of my father broods by the espresso maker, but in a weird way I was expecting that and don't make eye contact. That's the first rule of encountering Mack Grady in the wild.

The guy at the register has plugs I could shove a fist through. He slides me a Poland Spring from the cooler and asks if I want anything else.

Yeah, I would say, if I was any good at this. *You know this woman? Mack's ex?* I'd play him the video, saved hours earlier on my phone. But it'd be stupid to just give myself up like that—he obviously doesn't recognize me. He pricks an eyebrow, waiting.

"Um . . ." Only one latte flavor on the chalkboard menu. Called *latte*. I point, and he proceeds to take steaming the milk very seriously.

The girls are still giggling when I perch on a scruffy orange armchair, juggling my bottled water and latte. No harm waiting. I have plenty of time, hours and hours, until Mom leaves her office. What else am I going to do until she gets home? Homework? I carefully pry off the lid and blow, my breath sending shivers through the heart drawn in the foam.

I'm a little relieved Sadie isn't here.

Like, what if she was? I didn't practice introductions, don't have a clue what I would say to her. *Hi, Sadie*—real name? Approximation?—*you don't know me, but my father*—cheated on you with my mom—*was in your band, and* . . . frankly, I'm still kind of obsessed with how she flipped off that pazzo. Would my father have done that?

I sip the latte. Swallow. I'm not facing his picture, but Mack's presence, that sublime smile, makes the foam clot in my throat. There's this interview he gave back when *Sheer Folly* debuted at number one, special because there's a transcript *and* a voice recording—one of only a handful where he isn't singing. Most of the interview's about music stuff, recording, totally boring, but there's this part toward the end where the interviewer asks how Mack feels about their upcoming tour, and he sort of laughs and says, *Well, I'd be lying if I said I wasn't freaking out.* And that's always stuck with me. It's just so honest, a giant *fuck off* to anybody who'd judge him for being scared. And then he got over that fear. He must have, right? He toured the world. He sang for thousands of screaming people, night after night.

Anyway—the voice recording is a start, but not enough. I want to know what his eyes did, his hands and shoulders and mouth, when he said it. I want to know where you get that kind of courage.

So if Sadie walked in right now, I guess we could start there.

"Oh my God, no! Give me the computer." The girls on the couch wrestle for control of the laptop. "Charlotte, I swear . . ."

What does Sadie think about when she sees my father's picture? That interview? Something else? Walking past him seems too cold, even for an ex. She could smile. Press her fingertips to his lips like Lindsay does with Peter.

"Stop!"

My phone's in my pocket. I fish it out, on a mission.

"You stop!"

Sadie's real name is Sarah. Or was until ninth grade, when she made my father give her a new one. Mack and Sarah sounded dumb. Recent photos of her are pretty elusive, but in the blurry shot I find from 2010, she doesn't have a dimple either. Just big, dark eyes. A stampede of brown curls. I close Wikipedia but hold on to my phone, turning the syllables over in my head. *Sa-die. Sar-ah.* For a birth name, it's not so rough. Definitely not as bad as Mackenzie. Or Marianne Blackwell, the person I never think of as Mom, even when we used to visit her hometown and her parents—my grandparents—refused to call her anything but. Maybe when Sadie sees my father, she doesn't think about him, or touch him at all. Maybe she pulls a Mom and stares straight through him. Exactly like she might do to me.

Time to get out of here. I zip my phone into my backpack. Down the latte, pitch the ambiguously recyclable cup, and when I get back to my chair, the computer's on the floor and the girls are kissing.

Kissing kissing.

Making out.

My face flames. It's a truly brazen display of PDA. I don't know where to put my eyes, or hands, so I settle for lowering myself back onto the chair, the Poland Spring bottle throttled between my knees. The girls keep kissing. I can hear this even though I'm not looking at them anymore, hear the slide of their tongues and murmurs of their jackets brushing together and the wide-open surprise of Register Guy, who is so clearly trying not to stare. The girls part, and the one called Charlotte laughs, which guts me. A thousand little hooks. "Wow," she says. "Megan."

Eyes stinging, I study my jeans, sawing a thumbnail along the grain of denim. There's less than ten feet between us. I could say something. I picture myself getting up and tapping Megan's shoulder, disgust and annoyance and spit on her face when she finally looks at me. *Excuse me*, I'd say. They'd think I was a total homophobe. *Sorry—how do you get a girl to say your name like that?*

I push out of the chair. The water bottle clonks to the floor, but they don't notice. Of course they don't. They're Charlotte and Megan. They're kissing. And I'm wearing a penguin beanie.

On the sidewalk, I nearly lose it. One dry bark of a sob, but I get control of myself quickly because I'm seventeen, not seven, and someday I'll be way older, seeing ages my father never saw. Twenty-two. That would've been a big one for him, I bet, even though I can't really fathom being that old. I can't fathom turning eighteen, but it's going to happen, as unstoppably as the feature. *KR GRADY* blared across *ROCK* magazine, still unwhispered.

CHAPTER 8

IT'S MASOCHISTIC. I KNOW THAT. BUT WHEN Driver picks me up the following afternoon, I make him take me to Astoria again. A week. That's all I'll give myself. One week, and if Sadie doesn't show . . . I'll stop. Forget a conversation. I think I just need to see her. Without a sighting, empirical evidence, you can't prove anything is real. Not that Sadie is small and wild and once shared a stage with my father. Not that she knows my name.

Until then, I have lattes for company. This ache in my ribs.

If I'm acting as off as I feel, Mom doesn't notice. I'm in bed before she gets home. This morning, she wakes me up slipping into my room. I just don't let her know it. My face stays slack, my lids don't flutter, when she kisses me goodbye. A distracted peck right between the eyes.

Maybe I don't seem that gloomy. It's kind of nice having somewhere to go that isn't Mom's office or home. Fazes is way cooler than our apartment—twisted-metal reindeer aside—and EDM only plays when Register Guy, with the plugs, works. Otherwise, it's classical. White noise with piano. Notebook balanced on my knee, eye pinned to the door, I attempt calc equations, conjugate Latin verbs. Turns out "Fazes" is the perfect name for this place. I bob along on its tides. Deliveries arrive. After-school crowds disperse. Megan comes in without Charlotte and buys a muffin. Lemon poppyseed.

By Friday—three days without a Sadie sighting—my rib aches only add to the ambience. I read more about her. Articles from when my father was alive. Mack and Sadie crashed black-tie parties. They stuck their tongues out for pictures and trashed hotel rooms. We're talking thousands of dollars' worth of damage, still unpaid. Sadie smeared her lipstick on purpose. My father tried stuffing himself into her clothes.

Hunting for tales of her current exploits proves futile—her social media presence is nonexistent. No Twitter, Snapchat, Insta . . . I'd be impressed if it wasn't so irritating. Blog posts refer to her as *reclusive*, *a hermit*, but if she's not online, then how am I supposed to figure out where she is, when she'll be here? It's like she's ghosted the world.

On Saturday, though, I don't know—I just have a feeling she's craving a macchiato or something. I forsake my orange armchair for a beige floral with retro potential, right by the window. Scanning for her on the brightly lit street, I try to practice. I imagine what I would say to her, if a sighting really wasn't enough. *Hi, Sadie.* My pulse thumps in my fingertips.

The roof of my mouth. *Hi, Sadie . . .* A pigeon sitting on a parking meter tilts its head at me, cooing.

Mom's still at the office when I get home. Big surprise. I change into pj's and starfish across her bed. On the ride back to Manhattan, I was inert. A science word that means "numb with cold and disappointment," but now, buried in Mom's pillows, I start grinning. It's fine that Sadie never showed. Really, truly fine. Tomorrow's her last chance, and then Mom has some time off. An entire Sunday afternoon with one of those fancy cards on it. *Reserved—for us.*

Saturday, I'm up early. Mom's first meeting isn't until eight, which means we get to have breakfast together: PB&J smoothies blended with cooked oatmeal. Almost as good as bread. When Driver returns from dropping her off, I've been itching in the lobby for forty minutes.

"Awake already?" he asks as I climb in.

"Sleep is overrated." Scientists who claim teenagers need extra should hit me up.

The drive seems different today, even though we take the same streets, cross the same bridge. The river is calmer, the sky almost offensively blue and bright until I realize what's happening: I've never seen Astoria in the daytime. The revelation leaves me tingling. As we make our way down the street Fazes is on—Steinway, I learned it's called, like the pianos—jerking to a stop every ten feet for a light, I put my penguin beanie on, jittering. "Isn't there a shortcut?" I demand. Driver doesn't answer. Actually, he rolls his eyes. I'm positive about this, practically feel them rocking in their sockets at me, Mariah Black's spoiled daughter. Whatever. I rub at the grease smudge my forehead left on the window. Three blocks.

Three blocks and we'll be there.

Except—construction. A chasm clawed into the asphalt just to jam us up. It takes five minutes—literally five, I count—for a worker in an orange hat to guide us around it. Then another stoplight. More construction. Some men driving a beer truck urgently decide to start unloading, right in the middle of the street. I'm going to scream.

And then I see her.

Leather jacket. Black jeans. Waiting at the crosswalk.

"*Stop!*"

Driver pulls over so abruptly he must think I'm about to barf. Maybe I am. The light turns red, and I crane my neck as the herd passes in front of us, this impossible stampede of peacoats and knit hats and scarves until—*there.* It is her. Unmistakably. Same sunglasses, even. I scramble out, street-side, and almost get nailed by a bicycle. "Sorry!" I say to the cyclist. Also Driver, who's bellowing for me to get back in. His insurance must not cover this. "Sorry, um"—crap, I can't lose her—"call you whenever."

"Miss Grady!"

I bolt across the street.

Sadie went right. Right? Yes. Safely on the sidewalk, I hang back, wanting a good ten feet of strangers and concrete between us as she saunters down Steinway, fingertips twitching against her thigh. I hesitate. Photos didn't indicate sauntering. Also her hair's not what I prepared for, a mess of dreadlocks, but besides that, she's tiny and cool, my father's *ex*. My stomach boils. I can't tell if I'm breathing air or glass.

But I follow her.

In movies this looks easy. Pick your target, keep her in your sights. Plus I'm tall. Like, mortifyingly, although suddenly being a girl periscope isn't so bad, considering Sadie treats walking like a game of freaking limbo. She swerves around oblivious couples, skirts children—a man cuts her off, carrying a chair over his head, and instead of stopping to politely seethe like I would've, she squirts right under his armpit. "Excuse me," I mutter, edging past him. "Excuse me!"

Five-foot nothing has its own advantages, apparently.

One block down, I start to get the hang of it. My muscles loosen. As the crowds thin, I creep close enough that I could say something to her, if I really wanted to. *Hi, Sadie.* Her white-girl dreads are fuzzy. The leather jacket sheepskin-lined, worn gray at the collar. We pass a Duane Reade pharmacy. Dueling bodegas offering discount cell phone plans. PAY AS U GO! NO MONTHLY FEES!!!! She ducks into one them and reemerges a few minutes later, smacking a pack of Newports against her palm. A smoker, then. Like my father. Of course. Tucked behind the glass case of a bus stop, I watch her root around for a lighter, cup the flame.

Smoking slows her down. Makes her more contemplative somehow. She wanders through this pop-up stall selling Christmas trees. REAL TREES, the sign insists. GROWN IN NEW JERSEY. Sadie strokes a garland while I sidle up to a nearby wreath display, my view of her netted by my eyelashes but still the best yet. Photos don't count, and the video footage was too grainy to capture her rings and gazillion ear piercings. The delicate curve of her neck. She turns and I duck, burying my nose in a wreath. Act natural. Act. Natural. Even in my panic, I smell Christmas morning. Gingerbread and spicy balsam.

"Watch the smoke, sweetie," grumbles the vendor, and Sadie quirks her mouth at him, like maybe she isn't his sweetie.

Outside Fazes, she stops again, but the place is packed. Worse than packed—the line is practically out the door. Her brow puckers like it did in the video.

She dallies on the curb so long, finishing her cigarette, that I pop a Tums into my mouth. Crunch it to oblivion.

Theoretically, this should be enough. That's it, Sadie spotted, time to get on with my life, the Everest of homework I've got waiting for me. Except thinking of homework only yanks me back to my disastrous first day. Koda Rose Grady lingering beneath the school banner. Stranded in the hallway, classroom, cafeteria, with boiling heartburn and nothing to say. Introducing myself to Sadie—*Sadie freaking Pasquale*—won't go any differently. *Get out of here,* this voice whispers. *Stop embarrassing yourself.* I back up—

Into a man I didn't realize was standing behind me. "Sorry,"

I mutter. No problem, he says. And then he crouches to help a little girl—his daughter, I'm guessing—open her juice box. Strawberry apple.

I watch him push the straw through the plastic wrapper. I watch him hand the juice box back all carefully, so nothing spills, and then I continue watching as they move off down the street. Maybe he'll reach to take her hand as they enter the crosswalk, adjust her teddy bear hat to make sure it's on just right. When she burps, he might tell her, *Now what do you say?*

Then they're gone, and I can't say why I'm imagining this at all. The world is perilously full of dads—I've known that, ignored it, since I was small. I just know that I'm aching. Sadie grinds the cigarette beneath her boot, smoke feathering up.

Stepping over it, I follow her inside.

Fazes stinks, the air woolly with body heat and the stench of scrambled eggs. Huddled in my jacket, I scroll through Instagram, reflexively hitting "like" whenever an LA friend's post appears. Pancakes and sunsets and palm trees draped in Christmas lights. Lindsay's latest is a selfie, her turtleneck pulled up so you see only slitted hazel eyes and bedhead curls. My thumb wavers. Liking is not sufficient. A puny heart can't say, *I want to wake up with this picture.* The caption is in Spanish. Weird. Lindsay rarely posts in Spanish, unless . . . it could be for the sake of her aunts and cousins in the DR? But she has a separate account for them, strictly PG, so why post a picture like this, in a language Peter's too stupid to understand? I copy the text into a translation app: *Why can't I be where you are?* it says. Definitely for Peter. I swipe the window away.

Meanwhile, Sadie snakes to the front of the line.

It's kind of amazing how nobody else seems to notice her. Even if she grew five inches, and ditched the sunglasses, she'd be conspicuous. It's like . . . I'm not sure. Like the same energy that twanged her down Steinway won't let her be. Her fingers alternate between twitching a beat out on her thigh to twitching at her jacket, adjusting pins and zipping zippers. She fidgets with her shirt cuffs. She fidgets with her rings, pulling them off and on. One pings to the floor, and she dives after it, almost brains herself on the counter. Then she notices a display of chocolate-covered espresso beans and fidgets with them. Once or twice her hand jitters to the pocket where she stashed her cigarettes. Her leg jiggles. Everybody else stands patiently.

The EDM makes my head hurt. I burrow deeper into my phone, wincing at every newcomer and gust of cold that comes through the door. *Sorry*, my smile says. *Waiting*. People sidestep. Ignore me.

Finally, it's Sadie's turn. She pushes her sunglasses up and my heart catapults into my throat. The Mack picture. I forgot about it, taped to the espresso maker. Her back is to me. I rush the line—as much as I can rush it without getting decked—for a glimpse of her reaction. Maybe an eyelash flicker. Another quirk of her lips, but I'm too slow. Can't even hear her order over the simmering beat. She shoves her change into her pocket and moves to the pickup area. Seizing my chance, I sneak closer. Elbows help. "Hey," somebody says. I catch more than a few dirty looks. "Sorry," I hiss, only I'm not. At all. They just don't get it.

Sadie's already sidling away. Oblivious to my creeping, she stops at the cream-and-sugar counter and pops the lid off her cup, and now I'm right behind her. Towering. Literally. While she examines sugar options, I contemplate the pale seams of her scalp.

Okay. White-girl dreads are irrefutably trashy, appropriative, messed up, but her hair's the same color it was in those old pictures, dark as mocha. Plus an unexpected spritz of gray. She chomps open a packet of Sugar in the Raw, and without thinking, I whip my hair across my mouth.

Now or never.

Say something.

Anything.

"Um," I try.

No response.

"E-excuse me?" The Tums turned my tongue to cement. I inch slightly left. "Sadie?"

Warily, her eyebrows rise, but she doesn't look at me, engrossed in opening more sugar. I try again, cheeks burning. Obviously, she deals with fans, random idiots, strutting up to her all the time, acting like she owes them. "Hi, Sadie, I, um. I know we haven't met before, but . . ." If only I could've seen the way she looked at my father back there, I'd know what to say. But I press on, mumbling through my hair curtain. "I mean. We haven't met, like, officially, only . . . I'm. I-I'm K—" It won't come out. My own name, and it sticks. "I'm—"

She glances up.

The cup plunges from her hand. Coffee splatters as she staggers backward.

"Shit! Oh God, did I bump you?" I'm a disaster. The actual worst. I fling her soggy cup into the trash. "I'm sorry, I'll get you a new one. I just . . . here, let me . . ." The napkins are 100 percent post-consumer, unabsorbant crap, but I've got nearly the whole mess sponged up before she pries her hands from her face. If other customers don't hate me yet, they definitely do now. Sadie too. She stares up at me, eyes big and black as vinyl LPs.

"I'm so sorry," I say miserably. Without my hair covering my mouth, I feel skinned. Exposed. "What did you order? I could get you another." I look at the line. It's endless. "Maybe, maybe somebody will let me cut—"

A man barks at us for blocking the creamer, and Sadie snaps to, grabbing my coat cuff. I flinch, even though as grabs go, it's gentle. Well. Gentle enough. She tows me toward the door, doing her twisting, ducking thing. I stumble to keep up. Wind blasts us when we hit the sidewalk, whipping tears into my eyes. I want to ask where we're going, if she can slow down, I don't know these streets, but she doesn't seem in the mood for explaining and I've already said so many wrong things. At last she veers onto a side street. Releases me. I touch the indentations her fingers left in the wool.

"Sadie?" I pant.

Pivoting from me, she squats low, arm hooked around a piece of that green sidewalk scaffolding that's as endemic to New York as pigeons and seconds-long walk signals. It seems to belong to . . . a pizza place? All I smell is pepperoni. "Sadie, are you . . . ?" Her shoulders buck, and—oh God—I jerk back. Is she going to throw up? "Please don't!" I smack my hands over my ears. "Just, just breathe, okay? Through your nose first. Deep breaths." I walk her through my method. "In five, out five through your mouth, until the feeling goes away." My eyes are shut, so I can't tell if she's listening, but I really, really hope she pulls it together because I'm no hero in the bodily fluids department. Ironically.

Another minute or two, wind sawing my cheeks, until it feels safe to peek.

Sadie didn't throw up. She's gripping her mouth, trembling like she's about to, but that's okay. As long as she's making the effort. Her shoulders heave. In five, out five.

"I didn't mean to startle you," I say.

Sometimes talking helps. Any distraction.

"I . . . I wanted to . . . I saw this video of you online? Leaving that café? And I thought—I mean, I've always known who you are, like, conceptually, but . . ." Wait. I still haven't introduced myself. How could I forget? Stretching a bit of hair across my mouth, I say, "Is it okay if I start over?" which is a question for a teacher, not a rock star. Either way, I have massively fucked up this presentation. "I'm—"

"Koda Rose." Sadie says my name in the same voice as her singing one, thin and sweet but still kind of a surprise. She pulls her hand from her mouth and spits. "You think I wouldn't know that face?"

I blink. Sadie pushes herself up, back to twitching at her pockets. "My face?" Why would . . . but she doesn't go online, right? So she must not bother with gossip blogs. And they only started publishing photos of me recently. "How do you know my face?"

Her lips part. This little fissure.

"Oh." Instinctively, I touch my mouth, but my fingertips are numb. I can't feel him pulsing there, or anywhere.

Sadie lights a cigarette. She doesn't ask if I mind. Backing up, coughing anyway, I hear a crunch—my boot landing in unidentified frozen ooze. "Ugh," I say, but if Sadie registers this, she doesn't comment. Behind the sunglasses she put on, her own face is unreadable. Snapped shut.

"So," I say. "We just moved here. The other week, actually?"

She sucks the cigarette. One pin on her jacket says, I'M HERE TO HELP. Another, FUCK YOU.

"I lived in California before," I go on. She doesn't seem especially interested in this story, but I'm slightly oxygen-deprived and way, way more out of practice talking to people than I realized. Deep breaths. I have to remember. *Deep.* Breathing prevents rambling. Instead, I stammer cities. "Los Angeles. Well, Beverly Hills, technically, but then—"

"I know," she snaps.

"Oh." Right.

She smokes two more cigarettes, one right off the other, while I count her ear piercings. On the left alone she has seven holes, including an industrial, which I've secretly always wanted. Before I can stop myself, I ask, "How long did that take to heal?" Incredibly, she seems to know what I mean. She fidgets with the bar, not quite meeting my eye.

"Never really did."

"Wow," I say, too quickly to suppress my awe.

A blue vein hops in her throat.

Maybe it's the cold making me light-headed, the purplish stink of her smoke, but I'm not sure what else to say. She's a recluse, sure, but even recluses must have lives. More so than me, anyway, and here I am, eating her valuable time up with my flailing. I gaze down at my boots, trying to think of something, anything, that might salvage this. *So I saw this video of you making fun of me but I actually don't mind I actually thought it was funny Sadie how you flipped that pazzo off and I guess I was hoping, I was just hoping you could . . .* A snap picks my head up. Sadie's lighting another cigarette. Her fourth? Her hand trembles.

"Are you sure you're okay?" I ask.

Freckles. That's all I see when she pushes her sunglasses back. She's so pale and sweaty they spark from her cheeks. Still, as she plucks the cigarette from her lips, I decide she still is the girl from those old pictures. Minus this more recent, regrettable hair. Those lines in the corners of her eyes that tighten as she peers up at me. My tongue tingles. An impulse to say, *You can get those filled in, you know*. Mom does.

Thinking of Mom only makes me wobblier. I back up, jumping when my elbows brush cold bricks. Sadie ignores this, too.

"Me? Fine." She seems about to add something but reconsiders. "Fine."

"Oh," I repeat, not sure where to put this information. *Fine*, as in, actually fine? Or fine like me, and liable to spew at any moment? The peering continues. I stand still, trying not to feel too dumb as her giant eyes bounce all over me.

Then she turns away again. Ash from the cigarette drifts between us.

My mouth opens. Words assemble. Not the right ones, probably, but direct enough, so sudden in their clarity that they startle me: *Tell me about my father*. But then Sadie laughs. A throaty chuckle, at a joke apparently too good to share. I look back down so she won't see me darken.

I'm so stupid.

Sadie Pasquale is important. Taught herself guitar and ditched school to tour the world, made two hit records. Why would she bother with me? She was my father's *girlfriend*, the love of his life, and I thought she'd open up, just instantly spill her guts to me about this person I never met? Who never wanted to meet *me*? Maybe I shouldn't be talking to Sadie at all right now. Instead I should track down that kid I saw outside Fazes, with her dad and teddy bear hat and juice box. I know exactly what I'd tell her. *Hey—someday your dad might not be everything that he is to you in this moment. He might leave or be nasty to your mom or hurt your feelings. You might find out he's done some stuff that you won't like. But at least you'll have that juice box. You'll have this one moment, this single, precious speck of proof, that he loved you.*

The tears come so swift and sharp I can't look up in time to hide them. "Sorry. I-I'm sorry, I shouldn't have bothered you. Please don't tell anybody about this. If it gets out, my mom . . ."

Sadie doesn't budge. In fact, she looks kind of stricken, the cigarette smoldering between her fingers. "Your mom?"

Would tell her, *Put that cigarette out, it's bad for your face.* But I'm not Mom. I'm nobody.

And that's why Sadie doesn't call after me when I spin away from her, and run.

CHAPTER 9

I WAKE UP PANTING SUNDAY MORNING, soaked in more ways than one. Charlotte again. Or Megan. My dreams don't exactly differentiate. I squeeze a hand between my legs, get off within seconds.

By the time I scrape myself up and go into Mom's room, it's after seven. She should be asleep, but her bed is empty, the covers mussed. Bundling myself in her comforter, I pad toward the en suite. White carpet gives way to icy marble and tub tiles. "Mom?" My voice sounds wispy. Not quite my own. "Mom? Where are you?" At the vanity, making faces. Serious. Somber. Sultry.

She squawks when I throw my arms around her. Too easy to sneak up on—even with a mirror.

"Koda!" She looks flustered. It's been a while since I caught her checking for cracks. "What did I say about scaring me like that?"

"Good morning to you, too." The joke scrapes out, not that Mom notices. She squashes her cheek briefly against mine, then scoots over, making room for me on the padded bench. I sit, and the mirror shows me a puffy down chrysalis. Two new zits. Mom wipes a thumb across her eyebrows.

"There's nothing there, Mom." The vanity lights even my pimply morning face to perfection.

"I was just—"

"No. You'd have to be like, Nana Blackwell's age to get an eyebrow wrinkle."

That makes her laugh. "Nana isn't so old, you know." But she drums her fingertips against her lips, thoughtful. My eyes wander.

One thing I wonder about Sadie, even though I shouldn't wonder about her anymore: Does she have any Mack pictures I haven't seen? On her nightstand maybe, or the walls? Because Mom's vanity would be a good spot for one. She could put it next to our favorite of us, taken when I was still little enough to kiss her on the lips. Other photos stuck around the mirror are pretty random—she's either supremely pregnant or riding a sleek palomino horse. Buster, his name was. From her rodeo queen days. I make myself point to him.

"Remember that trip we took to Zap, and you let me ride Buster all by myself?"

She smiles a little. "That was so long ago."

"You taught me how to make him go backward." My arms feel seaweedy, but I push them from the comforter, fists loose, like I'm holding reins. Mom turns them so my thumbs are on top. "I knew that," I say.

Mom quit dragging me to North Dakota when I was five, for lots of reasons, I guess. Mostly the custody battle, which Mom never mentions but basically involved my grandparents deciding LA was a bad place for me. Too much smog, not enough Jesus. Anyway, we haven't been to Zap since that. I still think about it sometimes, though. Not Nana or Grandpa Blackwell—I have only sketchy memories of them—but the sky at the ranch, and the grass stretching beneath it for miles and miles, like it's a race to see which can go on the longest. Maybe Mom's thinking about that too. She covers my hand.

"Honey."

I really screwed up yesterday.

"Koda, look at me. You're acting funny. You've been acting funny for days. Did something happen? Why are you wearing this?" She tugs the comforter, releasing a cloud of lotion scent, her warm, sleepy smell. I clutch it tighter. "Koda, please. Tell me." She frowns. My jaw thumps with what I can't say.

If Mom had been honest. If she'd told me she hated Sadie because she was impossible to read and kind of rude, I wouldn't have looked her up in the first place. But she didn't. So now we're here, and where there should be excitement at having Mariah Black all to myself, there's disappointment and guilt and the same parts on shuffle: twitchy fingers, cigarettes. My own name lodged in my throat.

You think I wouldn't know that face?

"What can I do, Koda?" Mom rubs my shoulder. "You still haven't made up with Lindsay? Is that it?"

"No." I fidget. How did she know we're still not speaking? "That's not it, Mom, I . . ." Helpless, I scan the vanity. Her makeup is arranged by function. More brushes and bottles, powders and serums, than I'll ever know what to do with. A tube of fine-line eraser catches my eye. The shiny pink reminds me of something we might eat on her cheat days, full-fat and creamy. Mom watches me roll it between my palms. I guess it wouldn't hurt to tell the truth about Lindsay. To go back to a time when she was my only problem. "It's just"—where to begin?—"I feel like . . . I don't know. Ever since she started dating Peter, she's been—"

"Friends get boyfriends, Koda. That's part of life."

My eyes boil. Frustration tears. I try again. "I know that, Mom. I'm not stupid—"

"What did she think of your pictures?"

My . . . ? It takes a second to realize what she means. *The* pictures. From the leak. "You said we're reshooting them," I remind her.

"Oh, absolutely. The velvet, that cigarette, it's all wrong." Mom says this all so succinctly. The matter settled, brushed quickly aside. "But the photos are still of *you*. So what did Lindsay think?"

"I don't know." Incredibly, I haven't devoted a single byte of brain space to worrying about whether Lindsay saw them. Of course she did. Maybe she even texted me about them, texts that I instantaneously swiped away. "I—I'm sure she likes them. But that's not the point. It wouldn't change anything."

"Why not?"

"Because . . ." More pressure behind my eyes. "If she liked my pictures, thought I looked beautiful or hot or whatever, it's because we're *friends.* Because she's trying to be supportive. It's not proof that she wants to date me." A subtle shift in Mom's expression; she's searching for a way to refute this. But I know there's not. I know because that night on the beach, my last night in LA, Lindsay touched her forehead to mine and whispered, *You are going to meet so. many. girls. in New York.*

Mom starts rearranging vanity photos. The kissing one. Buster. Mom and some model friends when they were my age—all bangs and lipstick and cheekbones. Standing, she slides the kiss picture across the counter. "You *are* beautiful, honey. It's Lindsay's loss that she can't see it. Once you start making friends at school"—a knowing glance in my direction, like she's so sure this is exactly what I have been doing with all my spare time, making friends—"you could meet a new girl, somebody you'll like even better. Lindsay will be so jealous." She smooches the top of my head.

I don't point out that finding your own kid beautiful is a biological imperative—it doesn't make me any less of a platypus. Once she leaves, I stick the photo back to the mirror. My phone buzzes. I forgot I slipped it into my pajama shorts.

KODA ROSE!!!!!

hmu? Pls???

haven't heard from u in forever

I almost check to make sure my microphone isn't on. How did Lindsay know I was talking about her?

Hey! sorry

busy with hw and stuff

u sure?

I feel like ur avoiding me

Avoiding her? That night, I had a plan, every word lined up about how I'd had feelings for Lindsay—not just feelings, but a massive, pulsing, electric crush—since before I knew what that meant, since ninth freaking grade. But then she said that thing about other girls, and I froze. She was going to reject me. I'd never been more sure of anything, except for when I told her I was gay. I couldn't survive rejection. Not now, not ever, but especially not right then. Lindsay was so incredible, the waves so loud. Their roars filled my ears.

Eventually, she brought Peter up. He was being a dick again.

Now I scrutinize the picture of Mom and me, trying to measure that little girl against this new half-molted Koda who can't be honest with her mom or best friend, either. When my phone starts ringing—Lindsay, demanding to FaceTime—I abandon it on my dresser.

I'd tell Mom all of this if I thought she could help me. But Mom, as supportive as she is, doesn't give the greatest girl advice. *Friends get boyfriends, Koda. That's part of life.* Sometimes I worry I will never tell Lindsay how I feel. What if this isn't the sort of thing you need a mom for? What if that one person is the father you don't know, and my one opportunity to do just that—to not only *know* him, but step into his carefree world—I have completely, irrevocably blown? It's just so hopeless. Like that night with Lindsay, salt and sand and her hair stinging my lips. A thousand ways to drown, and not one involving the ocean.

CHAPTER 10

LINDSAY TEXTS AGAIN THE NEXT MORNING.

She and Peter broke up.

She calls me sobbing. I have to huddle in a locker room shower for privacy, but basically, they went to a party over the weekend, and Peter disappeared for like an hour. She just found out he was in a bedroom upstairs, making out with another girl.

"God," I tell her once the sobs dry up. "I'm so sorry."

"He's an asshole, Koda. I hate him." She sniffles. It's just after eight a.m. in California, which means she should be at school. Or is at school? I'm afraid to ask. She swore to me, after she got busted, that it'd be the last time she ditched. "I should've listened to you when you said he was bad news."

I don't remember saying that. Thinking it, obviously, but . . . sometimes my face does get a little ahead of me. I clear my throat, try to sound consoling. "You can move on from this. Find somebody better."

She breaks down all over again. "But I want Peter . . ." Afterward she apologizes for not asking what's new with me. "I keep forgetting to tell you," she says, her voice still rubbery from crying, "but I saw your magazine photos." She giggles. "Was the lipstick your idea?"

She means the black stuff. Poison Ivy. I close my eyes and remember Makeup Lady, coming at me with a bullet-shaped tube. The tug and itch.

"Yeah," I lie.

"Whoa, really? It looks amazing! So . . . daring. I don't think I've ever seen that side of you. I love it."

I mumble thank you, and she says she has to go. I stay in the stall a while longer, glowing atomic red.

When Mom texts saying we should do something fun tonight, I assume she means dinner. Not hitting up health food stores in a trendy downtown corner of the city I immediately hate, searching for a cereal that resembles rabbit turds.

"My God." Mom pushes her hair back, then continues sifting through boxes, crouched low to avoid mooning the entire breakfast aisle. "I don't see the seven-grain anywhere. Do you?"

This store is the same as the five others we've ransacked on our quest. Skinny aisles with skyscraper shelves, the lighting faintly post-apocalyptic. I pull a lock of hair forward, hunting for split ends. "No."

Sifting resumes. I close my eyes. In my head, Lindsay giggles and says, *I don't think I've ever seen that side of you!* Almost worse than no comment at all. Worse than hearing her tell me I'd find a girl in New York, which, except for that time she put her head on my shoulder after swim practice and joked, *Why can't* you *be a boy?* ranks as my most demoralizing Lindsay interaction to date. And now she's broken up with Peter. And loves me in black lipstick, the side it apparently brings out in me that I didn't know existed. A color I never would have chosen myself.

"Aha!" Mom hauls herself up by my belt loop, dumping the cereal box into the caddy we grabbed at the entrance. "Got it. Now—quinoa. Go." Bullet points again. I follow her to the next aisle, wheeling the caddy carefully behind me.

The grain aisle has a cat. Two cats, spooning on a bag of rice. Mom freezes. Her hand jerks to her throat.

"I've got this," I say.

Her eyebrows flutter with gratitude. Like she'll go into full anaphylaxis right here. "Make sure you get the—"

"I will."

She whips out her planner, which is basically a cross-section of her brain, red ink and stickies hemorrhaging all over the place. "Get black. We need it for protein bars—"

"Mom, I know. It's freaking quinoa." I just want to pet the cats.

A hard look emphasizes the importance of my mission. Then she clacks away.

I sink immediately to my knees. "Hi there." The cats don't acknowledge me, a purring bundle, but when I scratch one on her bony noggin, she leans in for more. Calico. That's how I know she's female. "You're very"—I struggle for an adjective that isn't *cute* or *pretty*—"patchy." The purring intensifies. Drool slips from her mouth and onto the bag. I keep scratching, not thinking about Lindsay, or Peter, or my father. Blank. That's how I'm going to be from now on. The burst of a flashbulb. A page where nobody's written a word.

Soon the calico starts wiping her drool on me. Knees aching, I grab the quinoa, then search for Mom, who, predictably, is nowhere. Not with dairy substitutes, or hydroponic herbs, or individually packaged servings of nuts. Annoyed, I head up front and stake myself by the checkout line. Old habit. Eventually, she'll come clacking up with a mystery fruit, some toxin-purging wonder she'd been wanting to try. Until then, it's me and the checkout boy, the half-hearted look he slides me before returning to his phone. If I had the guts, I'd snap, *Well, I don't like guys anyway, so.* Tabloids leer. I avoid the shouty headlines and decontaminate, picking cat fur off my coat. Knowing Lindsay, she'll be back with Peter by tonight. So it's not my fault for letting this chance slip away. The fact that right now, 3:25, California time, Lindsay is probably waiting for Peter to pick her up in his Audi, toeing pebbles off the sidewalk in front of our school. If I was there, maybe I would say something—the words I couldn't form at the beach fizzing on my tongue already. But I'm not there. She told me, *I want Peter!* You can't be blamed for accepting an inevitability.

The blankness is working. It looks good on me, better than the lipstick. I study my reflection to be sure, staring at myself in the store's dusty plate-glass windows. Mom doesn't know that Lindsay and Peter broke up yet. I don't think I'll tell her. She'll want me to do something nice for her. Flowers. Or worse, a grand gesture, like my life is a movie, and Lindsay just needs convincing. Part of me worries she's right. Another part, the teensiest sliver, still wonders what my father would say.

I shake my head, canceling the thought entirely. I've got to stop with him. Have to stop gazing at myself like this. Street light's pretty anemic here, but enough filters down for me to catch faces floating by. Most are neutral. A couple of scowls. Some smiles. Everybody looks cold. And then—

Something inside me recognizes her before my eyes do. I can't say how, only this time, there's no second-guessing. She's one-of-a-kind. Her own species. Blood rushes to my head. This electric hum.

"Koda?" Mom appears, lugging the caddy. "Almost done. Did you get the—what's wrong? Where are you going?"

I don't know. But I call, "Back in a sec! Don't worry!" with quinoa rattling, flung behind me. Outside there are as many people in my way as bags of garbage. I can barely see around my own breath, but I hurry, and now I'm right behind her, at the sweaty mouth of the subway. Her dreads sway as she starts down the steps.

"Sadie?"

She stiffens. Turns.

No sunglasses tonight. Too dark, which might be why, when she realizes what's happening—that I'm happening, again—her eyes don't seem so LP huge. They flicker. A spasm of disbelief.

"Are you stalking me?" she demands.

A giggle squirts past my lips.

The subway steps seem narrow. Sadie eases back onto the sidewalk to let people pass, and because she doesn't tell me not to, I edge with her beneath the neon glow of a sushi restaurant. The OPEN sign flashes: pink, red, orange, back to pink, and I flinch, unsure what to do next. *No,* I should say. *I'm not stalking you.* I want to take back that giggle. But I can't.

And maybe I am stalking her, a little.

"I was at the health food place," I say quickly. It's a funny night, raw and wet. Our breath pillows in front of us. "I saw you out the window. What are you doing here?"

Her eyes widen. Shit. Was that rude? I didn't mean to be rude. This is just beyond weird. Sadie scratches her head, clearly thinking the same. "My label's got offices here in the East Village," she says.

"Label. You mean . . . record label?"

She blinks, like, *What else?* and wiggles her fingers at me. "I use their piano?"

Somewhere down the block, a store blasts music. Staticky Christmas carols. Sadie turns red. Orange. Pink. I look away, hiding my disappointment.

Suspicion confirmed: Sadie Pasquale has no time for my problems. She's a musician. A rock star, no matter what Mom says about her days in the spotlight being over. And being blank means not caring. Not needing anybody anymore. Except . . .

Do-overs don't happen for me very often. Some days, I doubt one with Lindsay ever will. But I've known Sadie five seconds, and I'm positive she and my father would never say anything, to anyone, that they didn't mean. I don't think I totally grasped that at first. Now, neon flickering, this ache in my chest, I understand exactly what I'm chasing. Exactly what a second chance means.

Watching me, Sadie parts her lips. An almost smile. The humming surges back.

"Could my father play piano too?" I venture.

She smirks. A stupid question. I know he was a genius. Still, I figure it's best to start small.

"Of course he couldn't," she says.

Two men in suits exit the sushi restaurant, pushing us apart, but when we step back together, our gazes tangle. This time, neither of us looks away.

"Really?"

She ignores me. "This your hobby? Accosting people?"

Frankly, my real hobbies are more embarrassing—if the past week has taught me anything, it's that I can't tell her about fin whales, or the six generations of mutant flies I bred in the lab at my old school. Even swimming seems terminally pathetic compared to her accomplishments. So I shrug. "It's a coincidence. Well—the first time, on Saturday, that was on purpose."

She tilts her head, and a dread brushes her cheek. "What purpose?"

My teeth settle deeper into my lip. Something's different about her tonight. Her hands aren't jittering. She hasn't reached for a cigarette once, even though I can see the outline of the pack in her pocket. Head tilted, she gives me this look. Curious? Mocking?

Another couple enters the restaurant, forcing us back apart, and with a jolt I remember Mom. Sticking around to explain myself would mean making her wait. Possibly raising all kinds of suspicions, which is the last thing I need. Even so, I can't seem to pull myself away. Back to normal size, Sadie's eyes kind of remind me of the chocolate chips Mom tosses into her quinoa bars. Semi-sweet.

My father couldn't play piano.

How else was he like me?

"Can I have your number?" I blurt.

Her mouth bends.

"I can't. Explain. I mean, there's just so much happening, but if you . . . maybe if I had a way of getting in touch that wasn't, you know, an ambush?"

A thousand thoughts I can't decipher spill over her face. Please.

"Frosty the Snowman" starts playing.

Sadie, please. If she says no, I'll die. The lights twitch.

Red.

Orange.

Pink.

Sadie plunges a hand into her pocket and twists my palm up with the other. She chomps off a cap—her pen red, like a teacher's—and I don't realize what role my hand plays in this equation until she starts writing. Couldn't we have texted each other our numbers?

I hold my breath, trying not to squirm as the ballpoint scrapes across my lifeline.

She says, "Have your people call my people. We'll do lunch."

"Lunch?" I hesitate. Like her need to demonstrate how pianos work wasn't testament enough to my eternal unworthiness. "I could do that . . . but . . . a late one? I have school."

Sadie laughs. Not the gritty chuckle from before, but huge, head thrown back. I pull my hand away.

It's confusing. She is, but totally isn't, the same person I met last weekend. We say goodbye—I say goodbye, spluttering—and she turns to go into the subway. "Bye," I repeat, thinking she didn't hear, and she flings a hand up. Rings flash in the yellowish light.

Mom's just finishing at the checkout when I burst in gasping, spitting hair from my lips. "Sorry!" Plastic SHOP LOCAL bags wait at the end of the conveyor. I grab two, but of course she won't let me off that easily. Her eyebrows prick, demanding an explanation. "It was nobody. A girl from school. She lives around here. In the East Village." That's what Sadie called it, right? As Mom reaches for the remaining bags, I smile, tucking my hand against my hip.

In the car, I sit up front, head swimming from Sadie, and Driver's crappy cologne. I got her number. Sadie Pasquale's actual *number.* Heat roaring, Mom instructing, "Eighty-Ninth and Second, please," I risk a peek. Ones and sevens stagger across my palm.

I snap a secret pic, in case I sweat them off.

CHAPTER 11

WE DO GO OUT TO DINNER. THIS LITTLE Peruvian place that Mom insists on. It's so dim I read the menu twice before finding empanadas, but Mom seems unperturbed by the murkiness, a creature perfectly adapted to life by candlelight. She orders chili chicken but spends most of the meal nudging it around her plate.

She got a phone call from her boss the moment we arrived, but I bolted to scrub my hands and missed most of the details. When I crept back to our table, sucking my stomach in to avoid knocking everything over, she had the phone braced against her ear, saying, "Yes, yes, of course. Tomorrow, we'll—of course." Now she makes an effort to seem unbothered, lifting her chardonnay as she says, "So tell me about this friend, honey."

Beneath the table, two sets of knees jostle for primacy. I steer mine surreptitiously away, nibbling an empanada and wishing I hadn't said anything to Mom back at the health food store. Or that I could at least be a better liar.

"What's her name?" Mom prompts.

The napkin is paper. I tear a tiny piece off in my lap. "Um."

Her smile widens. No escape.

"Sarah," I relent. Technically not a lie. "Her name is Sarah."

Mom's cheeks crease with her grin. If both parents have dimples, the odds of their kids getting them are 50 percent. "Sarah," she repeats. "That's great. It's—it's really wonderful, Koda. I'm so glad that . . ." She rubs a finger up and down the stem of her glass. "I'm glad one of us is starting to fit in."

I shove my mouth full of beef.

The restaurant is tiny. Intimate, I guess, with half a dozen small square tables arranged beyond the bar. To our right, a woman eats rice alone, absorbed in a magazine that isn't The Magazine. On the left, an awkward date, the boy telling the girl she has incredible hair, incredible eyes. I'm not sure how long anyone's been here, if they recognize me or not. We'll find out when the blogs update. The notion zaps my appetite. Fork lowered, I drift. Our waters get refilled. Flames wiggle. Then I realize I'm being a downer, and that's probably not what Mom had in mind when she suggested dinner. So I raise my water glass and whisper, "Mom, your tonsils are *incredible.*" She laughs so big you can almost see them.

Once the waiter's walking off with Mom's Amex, she shifts closer, the red curtain of her hair tumbling down between us. "So does this mean things are finally looking up at school?"

I nod. My smile's starting to itch, but Mom matches it, rubbing my back with her cool, dry hand.

"I'm so relieved." Her hand glides on, and I don't tell her stop. It feels good, even though she's making the burpy pressure in my chest even worse. My father couldn't play piano. *Of course he couldn't.* Why did Sadie say it like that? What would she have done if I'd confessed I couldn't play either—couldn't play any instrument, for that matter? Maybe she'd be surprised, or disappointed, or confused. Maybe she wouldn't care at all.

But I'm going to find out, because her number is in my phone now. I added it in the bathroom before scrubbing the red off my palm.

Mom leans her head on her hand, watching me. "This new friend, Sarah," she says. "What's she like?"

I consider ignoring this, but Mom seems genuinely interested, her face open, smooth as the tablecloth. Swallowing, I say, "Weird."

Mom laughs. "Sometimes weird is good."

No. Weird is weird.

But I've learned tonight that certain lies don't count, if they're true.

"I mean," I explain, "not weird like me. Weird as in, she's her own person. She doesn't care what people think of her."

She frowns. "You're your own person."

"I'm not," I say, shaking my head. More like an outline of a person. With Sadie's help, that could change.

Back in the car, Driver says we have to get a move on. "That place closes at eight, Ms. Black."

"Place?" I turn to Mom. "What place?" I thought we were going home.

Her smile returns, only something's off—there's this sadness behind it that wasn't there before. *What's wrong?* I ask with my eyes. Does she . . . no, that's impossible. She can't know the truth about Sadie. How could she? But as soon as it appears, the sadness evaporates, and Mom is her usual self again, squeezing my face between her hands.

"You're so red, honey! But trust me, this is a good surprise."

A pet. That's the surprise. Another Frisky, the African dwarf frog I had when I was too young to understand that word had other connotations. We're in the fish store almost half an hour because the clerk is stoned and has bad aim.

"That one." I keep pointing. "*That* one."

Eventually, I grab the scooper and get the frog myself, plop him gently into a plastic bag that I cradle in my lap the whole way home. Mom leans for a closer look, her long thigh pressed against mine. "Do you know what you want to name her?"

"She's a he," I inform her. "The tank was all males. You can tell because"—I hold the bag up carefully—"he has these white glands on his back legs for mating." Mom winces, then resumes tapping on her phone.

Whales. Glands. Frog sex.

This is why I have no friends.

But the truth is, Frisky was an exceptional pet. Didn't demand anything except the pellets I dropped, twice daily, into her aquarium. Freeze-dried worms. Every couple months she shed her skin and ate it. "Thank you," I whisper to Mom, and we wriggle so she can get an arm around my shoulders. Seat belts be damned.

At home, we fill the aquarium with gravel, and set a pitcher of water on my desk to reach room temp. "You're really happy?" Mom asks, and I tell her of course. I mean, the new guy does remind me of Frisky, but that's to be expected. They're the same species. When I say this, she nibbles a cuticle, eyes moving about my room. "The pink is a bit much. Do frogs see color?"

"I don't think so. Actually"—I dip my fingers in the pitcher—"did you know their pupils can't dilate? They adjust to different light by shifting the lenses around inside their eyes." Mom nods slowly, in acknowledgment of this fact.

She says, "The last tenants must have had a baby."

The frog pops his head above water, and I tilt the bag slightly, to watch his sides contract. He's a guilt present, for the feature, the leaks, moving—I know that. But he's still pretty cool. Once we've nudged the plastic plants into position and the filter's going, Mom kisses the top of my head, murmuring, "Good night." Her lips linger longer than usual.

It's safe to put the frog in now, but once Mom leaves, I sit at the desk with the baggie in my lap, hands cupped around it. Frisky lived her whole life on my desk back home, her filter bubbling conversationally while I studied or played *The Sims,* but this frog doesn't know me that well yet. He lies motionless, assessing me with his beady frog eyes. "I'm going to call you Spot," I say. That's why I wanted him, because his back had the most freckles, but he doesn't seem to like this name. We examine each other. Nothing between us but water, this thin plastic membrane.

Another moment or two, for observation's sake, and then I set the baggie on my desk. Get out my phone.

In the restaurant bathroom, I was frantic, didn't know what to put for Sadie's entry other than *S*. Now I type, *Sarah*. Enter. New text. The cursor blinks.

I'm being stupid. Obviously, Sadie wouldn't have given me her number if she didn't want to hear from me. Even so, I stumble and stall like texting her is this high-stakes Latin recitation, 40 percent of my grade. *Hi Sadie.* Reliable start. *It's Koda Rose*—delete. *Koda. Thank you for*—not almost barfing at the sight of me again—*giving me your number.* Wait—I can't believe I just thought of this—what if it's not her number at all? What if it's random, because she wanted to get rid of me, and once I hit send, this perfectly crafted text will zing off to nowhere? Devastated, I put my phone down. Snatch it back up. A test: *Hi Sadie. Thanks for your number. I realized you didn't have mine! So here it is.* Send.

Painless, really.

I run and put my hair up and brush my teeth, throw pj's on. When I come back, drying my mouth on a washcloth, my phone's on my desk. Where I left it. Waiting. Spot crouches in his baggie. I undo the twisty, then lower the whole thing gently into the aquarium, plastic billowing, so he can come out on his own time. Tomorrow, I'll have Driver bring me back to the pet store, to replace these musty plastic plants with real ones. Amazon swords and java moss. I bet there's enough light for them to thrive.

9:45, my phone says. No new messages.

I move it to my nightstand, climbing gingerly into bed so my pj's won't wad up in my crotch. I survey the city, my chin resting on the satiny trim of the blanket. This place sucks. Always will. But tonight, it's not so bad. The darkness everything I don't know about my father, and the lights everything I could.

My phone hums.

It's a text: Message Undeliverable. Or so I figure. But then I unlock the screen and read: k :)

Sadie's number.

It's real.

Cool, I write back, hitting send right as my frog kicks free from the bag—one solid, decisive stroke that propels him to the surface. My favorite fact about African dwarves? He's fully aquatic but has lungs. Breathes air. Neither of us is equipped for life on land.

I think I'll call him Vinnie, after the drummer. They have the same chin.

CHAPTER 12

THE NARROW THREE-STORY BUILDING IS one of endless narrow three-story buildings we pass after turning off Steinway. Yellow brick exterior, cement stoop. My hair's still damp, shampoo scent suffocating, but I was so nervous getting ready after Mom left that I could barely dress myself, let alone operate a blow dryer. So here I am. A lavender typhoon.

The car idling behind me sounds like gnashing teeth. Driver grips the steering wheel, anxious about blocking both a fire hydrant and a driveway. He can't leave yet, though. Not until I give him the signal.

I press the doorbell labeled PASQUALE. Apartment 3F. Buzzing rattles through the icy dark.

Technically, Sadie did not specify that this was a good time.

This past week, everything happened kind of quickly. Well—everything and nothing, because when it comes to texting, Sadie's even more baffling than in real life. We're talking one-word responses. Hours creeping by without a reply. When I finally gathered the courage to ask when we could meet up, she didn't answer until the next day. Yesterday, while I was supposed to be reading for English. And that text was only another pile of numbers, not immediately recognizable as an address. Stop by.

So, yeah. Sadie didn't say Saturday at seven a.m. But she didn't *not* say it either.

Glass panels line the door, too bleary to peer through. On the stoop, a pot-bellied planter overflows with leaf muck. Stomach rocking, I resist the temptation to check my phone. You can only refresh Insta so often without feeling pathetic, and the pictures I'm expecting I don't want to see anyway—Lindsay with Peter, all, *We're back together!* Incredibly, it hasn't happened yet. She's probably still at his place in Mission Hills. Probably spent the night, which is why she hasn't posted. Phone silenced, I square my jaw. 3F, Sadie's text said.

This time, I keep my finger on the buzzer.

Come on.

She must be home.

Come on—

The intercom crackles. "What!"

I jump, fumbling for the—talk button? Straightforward enough. "Hi, it's me. Koda?" My name comes out cringing. Embarrassed, I clear my throat. "Koda Rose."

For too long there's nothing, only blood roaring in my ears.

Then—I'm not sure, but it sounds like a door opens somewhere inside. And then another door, and then footsteps. Though that could just be my own heart.

She appears suddenly. A shadow-Sadie, blown to smithereens by the glass's fractal pattern. The door opens. This tentative creak. At the last second, I whip my penguin beanie off and stuff it in my pocket.

She wears a blanket over her shoulders. Dorky black glasses that make her look simultaneously nine and ninety. Darting in the hazy porch light, her eyes are huge and startled, like a nocturnal animal's. I should apologize. Explain myself. But all that comes out is a shaky "good morning."

Sadie says, "You're lucky I don't sleep."

"Oh. Um"—her freckles are on mute, voice thicker than I remember—"your text said 'stop by'? My mom got called into the office early." To be safe, I told her I might check out the New York Aquarium today. They have sea lions. She seemed so pleased, she obviously forgot how much I despise aquariums. All that pointing and chattering, people tapping the glass like the signs tell you not to. I'd only go to the one in Santa Monica when Lindsay wanted.

Honestly, now I wish I was communing with sea lions. They're at least predictable. Averting my eyes from Sadie, I say, "Is this not a good time?"

She doesn't say no, but she doesn't step aside or ask if I want to come in either. Actually, I get the sense she's keeping the door between us for a reason, which is kind of insulting when you think about it. Wasn't she the one who invited me? Hand balled in the pocket with my beanie, I add, "That's medically impossible, you know. Everybody sleeps." Even me. Even last night, as I lay terrified of exactly this.

Anyway, this comes out sharp. Sadie softens a little, resting her cheek against the jamb. "You're a funny kid," she says, which is frankly even more insulting—the kid part—so I don't answer. Her eyes inch across my face.

It's just surreal, how my father loved her.

She pushes the door wider. "Kindly remove your shoes."

This is a joke. I think. The door opens into a vestibule, which opens into what should be a lobby, but is basically a stairwell encased in swirly faux marble, no shoes in sight. Her blanket is black and white, a zigzag pattern—I try not to stomp on it as I follow her up the creaky steps. It's a long climb. The hallway smells like pencil shavings, and I want to say something but don't know what, because Sadie's silent and I'm sure that behind every door we pass, people are sleeping. My stomping footsteps echo loudly enough. We round a landing. Trudge up another flight, down another hallway. The door at the end has been left ajar. Brass gleams above the peephole: *3F*.

Sadie says, "That creep in the Mercedes?"

"Oh." Shit. "Sorry, that's—it's just our driver. Hold on." So much for the signal. I grope for my phone, hammer out: Everything's fine don't worry see you in 30!!!! If Sadie and I even make it that long. Her forehead wadded at the mention of Driver, and now she takes her hand off the doorknob, like she's made a tragic miscalculation and my entry's no longer guaranteed. Shoving my phone back into my coat, I stammer, "He doesn't know I'm visiting you, trust me. He's—everything between us is strictly confidential." Thinking it over, I add, "You're right, though. He is kind of a creep."

Oddly, this seems to reassure her. The door creaks. "Men, am I right?"

A wall of stale smoke hits me before all the other stuff, vague outlines of a couch and some other furniture I can't make out in the dark. "You live here alone?" I wheeze, like it's not obvious enough I'm breathing out my mouth. Do smokers not realize how gross they are? After this, I'll need three freaking showers to thwart Mom's nose.

Behind me, the door shuts. I hear the latch clatter and then Sadie's voice, far away for how close we're standing. "I do." She hits the lights.

And I can't help it. I start looking for him. The square room is divided between some kind of living area—black couch, coffee table, bookshelves—and, off to the right, a tiny kitchen swamped in dishes and takeout containers, the fridge the color of an old desktop computer. My father is not on the fridge. He's not on any of the walls, which are plain white, blank except for a swath of exposed brick I think Mom would really like. On the shelves, books lean haphazardly, like at some point they all tumbled off and were flung back in a hurry. Stepping closer—my father was very literary—I spot a battered blond guitar resting against the bricks. Sadie says something, and I whip around, disappointment ricocheting through me. Shouldn't the guitar be electric? "What?" I ask.

"I said, 'Maid's on vacation.'"

That explains the chaos. When I ask how many times she comes a week, Sadie just looks at me.

"Oh." She was kidding. Again. "Sorry. I—I thought—"

Sadie chuckles. "Shockingly enough, us regular folk make do on our own." She tosses the blanket onto the couch, revealing a loose gray T-shirt, the front stuffed into her joggers, effortlessly cool. Papers cover the living room. Nothing official-looking, but notebook pages with the tufts teachers yell at you for not removing. Most are stacked on the coffee table, hidden beneath ashtrays and half-empty glasses and plates and bowls, or piled on the couch in drifts. I secretly lift one as Sadie tips forward, bundling her dreads on top of her head. TERRIBLE IDEAS FOR TERRIBLE SONGS, the paper says.

There is nothing remotely *regular* about Sadie Pasquale.

"Want my advice?" she asks. I cram the page back where I found it. "Ditch the driver. You won't be a proper New Yorker until you experience the subway's subterranean wonders first-hand. You going to keep your coat on?"

"No." Her apartment is stifling. I peel my coat off, and even though I'm fine holding it, Sadie gestures for me to chuck it on the couch too. "Thanks. What wonders?" Beyond the guitar and bookshelves is a short hallway. One door, open, displays a toilet. The other's closed. Her bedroom, probably. Sadie continues wrestling with her hair.

"I mean it's a rite of passage. The other night, for instance, after our little rendezvous? Got stuck on the 4 train. Watched the man across from me eat a jar of Vaseline for forty minutes. Almost wet my pants." She straightens, grinning, flushed from bending over. Her earrings are visible again and I try to think of what to say next. Some clever way of edging the conversation where I need it—but she almost peed herself *because* of the Vaseline eater? Or there was no correlation?

At last, I land on, "Ew."

It's clearly not the reaction she was expecting. Sadie twists a tiny silver ring on her pinkie. Slips it off, then back on a few times before saying, "You like coffee, right? I made some earlier. Probably still good."

My chest is on fire—I nod strictly because it might help her to trust me. Coffee people are like that. As she moves into the kitchen, I check my phone. Eight minutes down already.

Banging things around inside the fridge, Sadie says, "You'll have to excuse me if I've seemed standoffish. I'd blame it on needing to pee, but that would only account for the one time. Mostly I don't like people up in my business. The World Wide Web has surely informed you."

"It's okay." Still, Sadie knowing I googled her overwhelms me with shame. Like I've been caught trespassing, rooting through drawers without permission. Cautiously, I ask, "Why do you? Stay out of the spotlight, that is." It doesn't compute with her guitar-shredding, hotel-trashing image. She could hire a new publicist?

Sadie sniffs a carton of milk, then puts it back. "Fame's like booze, you know? Got my fill in my youth, moved on to bigger and brighter." She says this kind of sarcastically, knuckling her glasses up the bridge of her nose, and I think of her laugh lines, those threads of gray hair. My next question feels inevitable—even if it is super forward.

"How old are you? Forty?"

She cringes. "Thirty-eight."

Right. Duh. She's my father's age. They met in ninth grade—who doesn't know this? Sadie gets two mugs down from a cabinet, and when she holds them out, I point to the smaller one, feeling like a colossal fraud.

The coffee is black acid. One whiff and I know it'll make me sick, but I grip the mug with both hands, terrified of spilling, while she clears a spot for us on the couch. Everything except my coat—which she drapes courteously over the armrest—gets pitched to the scraggly, mud-colored rug. "Just had a birthday, in fact." Sadie sniffs, reaching for a bag of cough drops. "November thirtieth. And you're what—seventeen? I remember the day you were born. Motherfucking April Fool's to me, all the way from North Dakota." She slaps a cushion. "Sit."

I sit.

The leather squeaks. An old couch, cracked like my itchy December skin. *I know where you were born*, I want to say, to redeem myself. *Upstate, like my father. I know you dropped out of high school together.* But that would also mean admitting her Wikipedia page is seared into my amygdala.

She takes the opposite cushion, skinny legs tucked underneath her. "Now." She touches the industrial. "I've got questions for you. First and foremost . . ." She sets her mug down, starts fiddling with her rings. Can she literally not stay still? "It's not that you managed to track me down. People still do. All the time. But you said you had a purpose? A *reason*? Doubt it's as simple as an autograph, but here's hoping."

Did I say that? I must've, but the problem is where to start. What if I make her hate me more? "Well, it's . . ." Instinctively, I pull a strand of damp hair forward, hiding my mouth. "I'm doing a feature with *ROCK* magazine in the spring"—Sadie makes a face—"I mean, it's coming out in the spring, but we already took the photos. They leaked recently, and if I thought my new school was awful before, now it's . . . the kids there are obsessed with the band. *Obsessed* obsessed. They have these necklaces. With pigeons on them, and—"

"Diehards," she interrupts, unfazed. "Diehard fans."

"Right. Diehards. And it's like . . . they have all these expectations. About me? And who I'm supposed to be, just because this famous guy was my father, but the problem is . . . the problem . . ." Maybe something hidden in this mess will help. A piece of him that I could point to and say, *Start here*, but how can I manage that when I've been told my whole life I can't have this one thing, and now he's here, invisible as ever, but *alive*? It's paralyzing. The clutter alone makes my mind feel like a book with the pages all out of order. My gaze ransacks dishes on the coffee table. Her crappy old guitar.

She perks up. "You play?"

"No," I whisper. Like in the cafeteria, when my classmates realized how unworthy I was. Like Sadie must realize now. Clonking my mug down, I say, "I'm useless." Sadie cocks her head. She doesn't get it. I'm screwing this all up, and if I don't pull my shit together, she'll never invite me back. Every word the press will ever wield against me, every smear, will be true. "I came here because"—we're back where we were, me stunned and stammering on the street—"well"—*KR GRADY: A TOTAL COWARD*—"because I don't know my father at all, not really, not like everybody thinks I should, like *I* want to. Like, just that little thing you told me the other day, about him not knowing how to play piano, completely blew my mind, so I thought since you knew him so well, that you could tell me some more about him, and . . . if I just knew him. If I could know who he was, what he might've thought of me, then maybe I could . . . this makes sense, right? Please, please, be honest. Tell me it makes—" My stomach finishes the thought for me. A massive belch.

"Sorry," I say quickly.

Sadie's smile isn't quite a smile. The corners of her mouth turned up.

"I'm sorry," I babble. "Excuse me, oh my God, that was disgusting." There are fish so cunning they change colors to escape danger. All I can do is burrow against the armrest and pray I'll be devoured.

After a moment, the couch squeaks. A raw voice says next to me, "Get your hair out of your face."

Obediently, I paw it back, trying not to flinch as the dreaded skinned feeling overtakes me. Sadie's close. Too close. I see every freckle, smell the honey cough drop clicking around her mouth. I can't stop staring. My inadequacies are on full display. Yet she squints at me like she's making out a far-off constellation.

"I didn't," she says slowly, "*know* your father. We were in love. Got it? And I don't mean like I was going to marry this man, pump out a litter, and live happily ever after, blahty blah blah. We're talking big-time love. Like every breath I breathed, every word I wrote or spoke, only wanted to be his name. Ever felt that?"

Every word she . . . how does that make sense? But then I think of Lindsay. Our toes in the sand. And I know. I know. "Yes," I say.

Sadie sits back. Satisfied? It feels like I've passed some kind of test. She doesn't need to know Lindsay's reunion with Peter is imminent. That Lindsay and I will never run away together, or start a band. Sadie jiggles her leg. I look out the window, at the clouds doing their sorbet thing.

Finally, Sadie says, "Your fucking father had a nervous stomach. Puked every gig."

Struggling upright sends my hair tumbling. "Seriously?"

"So what's the deal?" She leans closer. "Do I make you nervous?"

My stomach lurches. Clearly, this is a trick question. My hair is in my face again, but before I can swipe it back, Sadie intervenes, pushing a lock behind my ear just firmly enough to say, *I don't have to be this gentle.* It makes my decision for me. "You do. Except," I hurry to add, "I think it's the kind of nervousness I could eventually learn to handle? You're just . . . really up in my space right now. But I could . . . I'll get used to that. I promise. And"—I hesitate; surely this will not help—"I'm sorry. About being born April first. Believe me, if I could go back and do it differently, I would."

Sadie's eyes sparkle. They truly are enormous for somebody so small. "At least it sucked for you, too."

The sea lions' underwater viewing area is closed for renovations, but I don't mind, my butt already numb from the cold stone of the outdoor amphitheater. Sea lions snore on a platform. Three females, and a gigantic male who was honking his head off when I arrived. Gray sky seethes over their rocky enclosure, and the air tastes like it smells, like dead mackerel. But for once it doesn't burn going down. Thanks, I text Sadie. That antacid really did the trick! I add a smiley, then a thumbs-up and an octopus. For visual interest.

My thumb veers toward Instagram, but I back out and make my way down to the sea lions, stepping over Pepsi cans and McChicken wrappers. Brooklyn is so far from the city it almost isn't the city at all, despite Driver's repeated assurances that we're not *too* far from the apartment. Distance is like that here. Two hours since I left Sadie, and the couch, her face in mine, might as well have happened on another planet. The urge to tell Lindsay gnaws at me. Guess who I met?! But she gets her secrets. No reason I can't have one too.

Reading exhibit placards helps regain my bearings. The print is small, bleached from decades of New York grime. According to a laminated index card, the big male is on loan from Santa Monica, and named Leo. Original. If the partition wasn't so unnecessarily thick, I'd climb down there to ask what he misses most about California.

My phone rings as I turn to leave. Mom. I answer right away. "Hello?"

"Koda! Honey. Hi." Mom always sounds vaguely out of breath on the phone. "I thought I'd—we're between meetings. What are you up to?"

"What do you mean what am I up to? I'm at the aquarium, like I said."

"Oh." She pauses. "I'm sorry, I guess I . . . you made it sound like you weren't going for sure."

My hair isn't damp anymore. I rake it over my shoulder, summoning patience. "No, I'm here. They have sea lions. And guess what? One's from Santa Monica. His name is Leo."

Santa Anas. That's what I miss most. People say winds that fierce and dry mess with your head, but I never noticed. In fact, without them, Christmas doesn't really feel like Christmas. Realizing a family's joined me, I move to the edge of the enclosure. Once they're distracted by placards, the male's honking, I crush my nose to my coat cuff. Inhale Sadie's char.

"That's lovely," Mom says.

A pull in her voice. She's not really listening. I tell her I have to go.

"Okay," she says doubtfully. "Are you sure everything—no, you know what, never mind. I'm just happy you're enjoying yourself. Call if you need anything. Have fun. Love you."

"Love you too," I say into my cuff.

When I hit end call, a text from Sadie appears. ur welcome. My fingers hover over the keys.

After she pressed the antacid into my palm, I told her about the doctors Mom dragged me to growing up. Assholes who made me drink liquid fireworks and threaded cameras down my throat. Sadie smirked. She said that sounded about right to her. *Nervousness, Koda? Anxiety? This all-consuming panic you've come to understand as life? That's him too. One hundred percent genetic.* The way she set that word down, *him*, made me grin. I plugged my nose and chewed.

Glancing at the family—a mom and dad, two rowdy offspring—I type, Is it ok if I come over again? Then I shove my phone away, confused by the heat beating through me.

Knowing Sadie, it'll be another week before she answers.

A honk from Leo cracks the family up. I smile—his vocalizations are pretty spectacular—and as I head back indoors, the kids rush past me. My phone buzzes. If u got nothing better 2 do.

I stop in the doorway. The mom and dad assume I'm holding the door for them and thank me. I thank them back, like an idiot. My eyes snag with the dad's. Only for a second. But they do.

"Come on, Steve," the mom says. I almost laugh.

Whose dad is called *Steve*?

CHAPTER 13

MONDAY, SADIE REQUESTS THAT I MEET her at the Thirtieth Avenue subway stop—part of the elevated line Driver clued me in on during our first trip to Astoria. He drops me off beneath the trestles, where I shiver for an eternity in the subarctic dark, getting jostled by pedestrians as trains shriek overhead. My gloves drip from wiping my nose. Snot icicles. A truly New York phenomenon.

Sadie, on the other hand, doesn't seem to notice weather. When she finally appears, barging through a pack of commuters down the rickety metal steps, her hands are bare, bomber flapping unzipped. Beneath that she wears a checkerboard flannel. Also flapping. A guitar case bangs against her calf, plastered in stickers. She thumps the case between us, and I squint to make them out. Smiley faces and pot leaves, mostly.

"These goddamn songwriting meetings," she mutters, fumbling for a lighter. "Lucky you haven't gone the music route yet, but if you do, take my advice. Music is a business. These corporate fucks need oxygen to grow, *my* oxygen, and before you realize it—boom. You're sucked in. Somebody's little hit maker."

A music meeting, then. I brush my hair from my lips, marveling at how easy she makes it seem that I could ever do something like that. How possible. "That's what you do now?" I ask. "Write songs?"

The commuters Sadie rammed past walk around us, radiating judgment. She slides me an uncertain smile. "I'll let you know if we hear one, but you've got to promise not to hold it against me. Em—that's my songwriting partner? Emmy Chapeau?—and I have been writing some real basic shit lately. No judgment, though. Whatever sells." She flicks her lighter, and it looks like the spark is coming from her fingertips. "You wait long?"

"Oh." I scramble to answer. How does she talk so fast? "Nope. Just got here."

"Ah. Got me all worried for nothing, then."

Incredibly, her base layer is barely a layer at all—a thin black tank top. As she puffs on the cigarette, I tuck my hands in my pockets, to hide my snotty gloves.

We head uphill. Toward her apartment, I assume. Not that Sadie clarifies. Like all New Yorkers, she has this innate sense, an understanding with the city that informs her when it's safe to cross seconds before the lights do. I hustle after her, pretending I have it too. Thirtieth Avenue is a slice of Astoria I haven't seen, as busy as Steinway but with trendier restaurants. Streetlights amplify colors, smudge edges. We pass dry cleaners and eyebrow-threading salons, makeshift stalls selling fabrics and fresh fruit. The screen of a LinkNYC kiosk informs us that the suspended blue whale sculpture at the Museum of Natural History weighs over 21,000 pounds. Excitedly, I turn to Sadie—but the intensity of her smoking, the distant look in her eye, makes me reconsider. Surely her day's been exhausting enough, and when it comes to revealing details about myself, I want to choose carefully. No way I'm replicating any more of my classmates' disapproval. Their curled lips. I pull my hair over my shoulder and take my gloves off, fashion an impromptu braid.

At Thirtieth and Steinway, the intersection with the two shouty bodegas I can't believe I actually recognize, Sadie thumps her guitar down again. So far she hasn't asked any of the questions adults are programmed to ask after five p.m. on weekdays, like how school went and if my stomach hurts, although I guess she already knows the answer to that. Not that I'm complaining. It's kind of refreshing to know there's one person out there who expects me to say stuff other than, *I'm fine*. What that might be, though, I have no clue. Hoping to make conversation, I point to the case. "Do you . . ." *want me to carry that*, is where I was going, but the walk sign flashes and she hefts the case up like it's nothing. As we hurry across, she glances at me, eyebrows rising—*do I what?*

"Smoke?" I improvise quickly. "Like, a ton of pot?" She

looks alarmed, so I add, "You have three different stickers that say, 'It's always 4/20.'" I don't add that I only know what this means because of Lindsay. All the stupid pot memes she continues to post even though she still, from what I can see, hasn't gotten back with Peter.

Sadie laughs. A squawk-laugh, startling me. "Last I counted, there were a couple more on the other side. Not saying I haven't been known to partake, but . . ." She flicks the cigarette away. "Stickers aren't mine."

"Oh," I say.

It takes two keys to get into her apartment. One for the front door and another for her own. She hits the lights, same as before, and then proceeds to do a series of things I never imagined my father doing, let alone his ex—like shed her jacket with a sigh and flip through the mail she got from a metal box with her name on it downstairs. While she fumbles around in the bathroom, I lay my coat over the couch again.

"You want anything?" she calls over the toilet's roaring. "Help yourself."

Mom's rule: nobody who says *help yourself* actually means it, but I figure I might as well assess the snack situation since my stomach's doing all right. In the kitchen, I nudge a step stool aside to investigate the cabinets. Fingers crossed for sugar.

Frankly? Not much to get excited about. Peanut butter, granola bars, and a folded-up bag of Lay's. Salt & Vinegar. Gross. I scope out a granola bar's sugar content. 16 percent. Disappointing.

Sadie's taking forever in the bathroom. I close the cabinets, then edge silently into the hall. A stitch of light shines beneath the door. Feeling awkward, I hang back, but the hallway's stubbiness leaves few options. What appears to be a framed poster on the wall is actually a map, with street names I puzzle over way too long before realizing they're in Italian. Duh. I back up, and my elbow brushes a door shut firmly behind me. Her bedroom.

If she does decide to ask how school went, I'll tell her, *Terrible.* I'll tell her about Lindsay's latest video, which I was stupid enough to watch before a calc test, how my AP bio teacher caught me hyperventilating on the fringes of the cafeteria and invited me to have lunch with her instead. A tempting offer. Not that I for one second considered accepting it. Everybody knows teacher pity is the worst pity. I went to the nurse's to lie down.

My braid hangs over my shoulder. I stick the tip in my mouth. One last good nibble before Sadie concludes what must be a ridiculously complicated freshening-up routine, and makes me stop. There's the sound of a drawer opening and shutting, then water. She coughs.

I beat it back to the living room just in time for her to find me by the bookshelves. Her eyes twitch at me, too big again. Oh God. Does she think I was browsing for dirty stuff? "I can stay a little longer," I tell her casually, thumbing the wet end of my braid.

She goes into the kitchen. "Yeah?"

"Until . . ." The guitar case is by the door. Positive Sadie isn't looking, I crouch down, caress the hard black shell. "Like, seven thirty? My mom will be home around ten." The stickers look even more busted in the dim lighting of her apartment, each in their own state of flaky, faded decay. Besides the pot stuff, there are slogans: JUST DO IT, and a Chihuahua barking, ¡YO QUIERO TACO BELL! which, I don't know, seems racist. The most perplexing says, MELTS IN YOUR MOUTH, NOT IN YOUR HANDS, except somebody crossed out NOT and scribbled AND. The corner pokes up. I smooth it, realizing too late that Sadie's standing over me.

Quietly, she asks, "You really don't play?" I shake my head, and she chomps at the rim of the plastic cup she's holding. "You smoke pot?"

I laugh despite myself. "Never."

"Drink?"

"No. Well . . . actually, there were pictures. Paparazzi shots from a few months ago where it looks like I'm drinking, but it's really just a smoothie my friend Lindsay made." Sadie shifts her weight to the other foot, probably wondering why I'm cringing up at her. Why her ex's only child has to be this musically inept. "Never mind," I say quickly. "Lindsay's my best friend. We just . . . don't talk that much anymore." Maybe I should tell her how pointless pot is. About that one time Lindsay and I were supposed to hang out, just the two of us, until Peter and his stoner friends showed up, and Lindsay inhaled too hard to impress him and puked into a barbecue pit. Maybe I should get her opinion on Lindsay's new video.

But then I notice Sadie peering at me again, like that day on the street. Except now there's a cup in the way. And I swear she's grinning.

"Mack smoked lots," she says.

I can't stop my eyes from widening. The parties, and hotel trashings—it makes sense. But I genuinely never considered the possibility of my father doing drugs. "I thought he just drank. That was the point of the paparazzi pics. They would've said—people would've said if he smoked pot. Online and stuff."

Sadie shrugs. "Different time. No social media—or at least not like there is now. We had more privacy."

So she must be right. But I don't want to talk about this anymore—I want to focus on learning the parts of my father that connect to me. Parts I would recognize. Impulsively, I thump the guitar case. "I want to play. Can you teach me, too?"

I expect a swift *hell no.* Instead she taps the cup pensively against a canine. "Where *did* you come from, Koda Rose?"

"California," I remind her.

She howls.

Sadie ties back her dreads and twists off her rings and says, don't worry about the junk on the couch, chuck it anywhere. I make tidy piles, then un-tidy them, while she explains what I should've intuited all along, that the banged-up case and guitar were my father's. The respectful distance I intend to keep lasts only until she undoes the latches. Then I drop beside her on the rug, plunging my hands into the case's musty red lining.

"Velvet," I whisper. Like they wore on the *ROCK* cover. Like he basically lived in, except this isn't a picture, and there are patches the guitar hasn't rubbed away, so blissfully soft they practically stroke me back. The case reeks. I mean, if it weren't for Sadie's chain-smoking, I'd blame it for the stench in her apartment—but I refuse to let it overpower me. Glancing at Sadie, who nods permission, I let my fingers creep from the velvet to the guitar itself. I don't know where to start. Never really touched one before, unless *Guitar Hero* counts. Trusting Sadie to stop me if I mess up, I press a fingertip to the neck, run it down a string that he—plucked? Twanged?—either way, it's tighter, sharper than you'd think. Somehow, that sparks confidence. I explore the scuffed-up body. Trace every scar that he made.

Probably there are stories behind them. Stories Sadie might tell me. I kind of lost her in my wanderings, but lifting my hands, I spot her cross-legged, watching me from the edge of the rug. Her forehead has that crease. But then she smiles. "Real piece of shit, right?"

She asks this so fondly I can't decide if I'm supposed to agree, whether she'd think I was making fun of her if I confessed this guitar is actually the prettiest thing I've ever seen. Heart pounding, I trace the strings again. The chipped ruby inlay, shaped like a teardrop. I barely hear her murmur that red was their color.

Smiling back, I say, "Well, then he'd like my hair." Only to remember, as her smile vanishes, where my hair comes from. Sadie stands, so I do too. Mom's voice rushes up with the blood to my head. *Unlike Sadie, I don't revel in the past.*

"One lie I enjoy telling myself"—she gestures for me to sit on the cushion I cleared—"is that Mack's responsible for your hair too. Sometimes that helps. Other times it makes shit worse, which is why I'm told it's an 'ineffective coping mechanism.' Got plenty of those. Although you figure a guy named Mackenzie Grady's got some redheaded genes tucked away somewhere." She sniffs. Then—without asking if I'm ready—thrusts the guitar into my lap.

"Um"—I freeze—"I don't know—"

"She won't bite."

"O-okay." I place my hands where I think they should go. One on the neck, while the other supports the guitar's bottom. That time I held a baby kind of went like this. "I thought it—she—would be heavier," I say as Sadie, seated across from me on the coffee table, leans to make corrections. She pushes the guitar so it's perpendicular to my thigh. Grabs the hand that's cradling the bottom and brings it to the strings. "Strumming hand," she explains. Then, curling my fingers around the neck, "Fretting hand." I sit straight, trying not to giggle. Her touch . . . it's so scratchy. She worms her thumb beneath my fretting fingers, and my breath hitches. They arch up. "Like that," she says. "Not—" She squashes the tips flat again. "Got it?"

"I think so." It's already so much to remember.

But this is a test I refuse to fail. When Sadie says, "Let's see that strummer," I hold out the right one. "Everybody's got their own style," she goes on, and another giggle hatches in my belly but I swallow it down, concentrating extra hard on how she molds my fingers. Thumb against index. Middle, ring, and pinkie tilted slightly toward my palm. "Try this. It's how I like it." Returning to the strings, my fingers inadvertently graze hers. The pads are bumpy. Little knots.

"Your calluses," I say.

"Ah—they get you?"

"No, just . . ." That explains the scratchiness. Sadie shifts closer, flannel gaping, and I bend my head quickly over the guitar. Between crunches of a cough drop, she asks how it all feels.

"Good." And for once I'm not just saying that. My head stays bent so she won't see my goofy smile.

Sadie runs through what must be the basics. String names, starting from the top—E, A, D, G, B, E, her palm hovering over my fretting hand the whole while, so I'll keep my fingertips straight. "This," she grumbles, "was your dad's biggest problem. That and losing his—dammit." She reddens. "His picks."

"What? Do I need a pick too?"

"No, it's not that. I . . ." She drums her fingertips on her thigh. Looks away. "After you left the other day, I kept thinking how uncomfortable it was, having to be all, 'your dad' this, 'your dad' that, out of some twisted sort of deference to you, when in reality he never was that. Not to me. To me, he was just Mack. Always will be."

There's this phase I went through when I was little. A pointing thing. It was just easier than explaining, opining, *interacting*, which was what Mom always meant when she knelt down and whispered, *Koda. Use your words.* Sometimes I still think there are too many. Hearing Sadie, I feel millions jostling in my throat. "To be fair, he . . . I don't call him 'Dad' either. There's a difference, right? Between a dad and a father? Like—a dad does things with you, takes care of you, but a father just . . ." I don't really know what I'm saying. "There's distance. That's all I think when I hear that word, when I think about him. Distance. My father didn't visit me when I was little. Not once. Like he just . . . didn't care, or something." Sadie winces. My fingers tremble on the frets. G, B, E, where she placed them. I realize, looking at her pink ears, that I've never seen her blush before.

She scoots forward. "Strum."

"Huh?"

She mops her nose on her flannel—"You know"—and demonstrates, air-guitar style. "Hit it."

The sound that zings out matches the sting in my fingertips exactly. I flinch, and Sadie laughs, freaking *roars*, like she knew all along how much that would hurt me. "Merry Christmas!" She slaps my knee. "That's a D chord, kiddo!"

Kiddo. Like I'm five or something. My fingertips throb. My knee throbs where she whacked it, but I doubt my father would've let a little pain stop him. Teeth gritted, I drag my fingers back down the strings. Notes spark at weird angles—not so much a chord as a guitar falling down the stairs. Sadie laughs harder. I hear myself laugh too.

"I think I'm bleeding."

"Get used to it." Sadie inspects her own hands, frowning.

"You taught him too, right?" But I already know this answer, and Sadie seems to get that. Without meaning to, I shift back to what we were talking about before. "I could learn to call him Dad someday, you know. Even though he's dead. It's not impossible." That day is easier to imagine with her by my side. A day where I wake up thinking of Mack Grady, my father, as *Dad*. Not some unreachable moon.

Her eyes glisten. She turns away, wiping them hard with the flat of her hand. "Maybe not."

The skinned feeling only gets worse around crying people. But I sense Sadie would appreciate me pretending she isn't. As she takes a breath, I press my stinging fingertips to my lips. They smell, taste like metal. "Are you going to make me learn Quixote songs?"

"What?" She busts back up.

"Because I'm sorry, but—"

"Listen, you think I don't know they're shit? We were kids. Younger than you, even, but you can blame Mack for the clapping in 'Drown.' He didn't want a song about depression making him feel any worse." Her smile falters. "Doesn't matter how many hits I'll write, Koda. How many we could've written together. All the world cares about—all they'll remember us for—is what we did at eighteen. That terrifies me. You know?"

I nod. That is extremely terrifying. What if you'll be eighteen in three and a half months, and haven't accomplished anything yet? "I could never do what you two did," I confess. "You were so brave."

Abruptly, Sadie hardens. "I'm not brave."

"Yes you are. You—you and my father dropped out of high school, and sang and played guitar in front of all those people. I can't even find a table at lunch. I . . ." I push my stinging fingertips against the strings, and as Sadie adjusts their positioning, a clock chimes on the wall. Six o'clock. Three o'clock, California time. "There's this girl." The tremor in my voice is pitiful, even for me. "My best friend. I'm gay"—reflexively, I glance up, expecting to see that seismic ripple that means an adult is shocked but trying to hide it. Sadie doesn't so much as quiver. Her stare is so intense I can't tell if it's aimed at or through me. But there's no going back. "You told me about breathing my father's name, remember? And, well, I breathe her. Lindsay."

Sadie sits back. Cold chafes my jeans—I didn't realize our knees had been touching. And I can't tell what she's thinking as I catch her up on everything, practically barfing it all into her lap, from the beach to the Peter breakup to this new video of Lindsay feeding a squirrel on her patio that I can't stop scouring for clues. Cigarette smoke, or a hairy toe poking into the frame, whatever it'd take to prove that they're back together and there's no use trying. Sadie doesn't waver. Not until I finish, and her gaze flits to the rug. It truly is hideous. The color of old blood.

"Koda."

I like how she says my name. Like it's real. The perfect mix of special and ordinary.

"Koda, look at me. I want you to understand something. The person I was back then isn't who I am now. I'm a mess. A goddamn wreck. You couldn't fathom how bad."

I sort of squint, to make her think I really am looking, only, Mom called her messy too. That's reason enough not to believe it. Sadie's leg's jiggling again. I want to reach out and stop it. But instead I say, "Well, if I couldn't fathom the messiness, then there's no point making me understand it, right? That means I don't have to care either way. It's basically breaking even."

Sadie turns away, her jaw flickering. I've touched a nerve. "Fine," she mutters. "If you're going to be so *Mack* about it."

My fingertips have crept back to my mouth. She guides them away, and maybe it's her gentleness—real, this time—or those words, *If you're going to be so Mack about it*, but when she releases my hand, it finds its place on the frets without me looking. Magic. We grin at each other. Sadie says, "Look at you." I wish I could. Wish *he* could. But I just laugh and flip my braid to my other shoulder. I shape my sore strumming fingers thumb to index, index to thumb. The way she likes.

CHAPTER 14

SADIE DOESN'T ANSWER MY TEXTS ON Tuesday. She doesn't answer Wednesday or Thursday, either.

Friday, school gets out early. Mom emerges from the car, heaped in faux seal. "Surprise!" she beams. I'm so startled I almost drop my phone, but mercifully, she doesn't expect a hug in front of the entire student body. In the backseat, her arms lasso me. Mine squeeze cautiously back.

"What are you doing here?" I ask when we part. Mom grins, the back of her hand pressed to my cheek.

"Tomorrow's Christmas Eve, honey—even we're off for the week. I thought we could spend the afternoon together, go shopping, just you and me." Then, seeing my face: "Unless you had other plans?"

"No, I—hold on." Phone tilted away from her, I bring up the message I've been agonizing over since lunch: Hi Sadie, are you mad at me? It's just that—we had such a great time together?

Playing her guitar? And now she's vanished. Ghosting me. I should've known this would happen. Sometimes, Lindsay won't tell me she's mad until the day after we hang out, and all my texts have gone unanswered. I don't see a reason why Sadie, who is equally as spectacular, so wholly herself, should be any different. This is what I get for sucking at guitar. For making her cry. But how to make it up to her? I put my phone away, sinking deeper into the backseat as Mom confers with Driver.

Mom and I have a kind of haphazard relationship with Christmas. Now that I'm older, we don't bake dairy-free cookies, or put up a tree or exchange gifts the way most families do. Why bother, when we already have so much? Basically, the holidays are just an excuse to be together—slurp cocoa in our pj's until her gaggle of fashion industry friends shows up for dinner. This year, Mom hasn't said how we'll celebrate. Probably some Magazine people will come over and they'll drink too much, end up screaming Ace of Base in each other's faces. As for today's shopping trip . . .

Well. Such expeditions are not unprecedented. Actually, as we edge into traffic, and Mom pretends to adjust her immaculately tousled ponytail, I'm surprised by my surprise. Three weeks ago, when our plane touched down, I would've sooner died than skip this tradition—even if Fifth Avenue has replaced Rodeo Drive. The car lurches. Stoplight. Like I'm not already nauseated, staring down at my phone where Mom can't see it.

Bravery isn't hiding from your mother. It's not holding the

backspace, and gobbling your text all up.

Quietly, Mom says, "I'll need your help picking something out for Nana," and I nod, slumped against the window.

Are you mad is a little kid question anyway.

The personal shoppers at Saks practically cream themselves at the sight of Mom in her fluffy coat, but she demurs, perfectly polite: "No no, we're fine! Thank you! Thank you!" The escalator ride is like ascending to a frenzied, fluorescent heaven. A father and daughter cruising past us to the lower levels scream, "Koda! Koda Rose!" The kid's jacket flops open, and on her shirt is my father's face. Slight smile, hair in his eyes, classic Mack. I turn, but Mom's fingers are stapled to my shoulders. The shrieking intensifies. "Koda! Hey! Koda! Over here!"

Diehards.

Even freaking department stores are infested.

Stepping into the throng of last-minute shoppers results in pandemonium—namely, an off-key rendition of "Drown" belted out by a grown man in suspenders. He's trying to be nice. To honor me, I guess, but it's so unexpected and scary that I lunge for Mom's hand. "Hush," she says into my ear. Calm, even though her long leg is tense against mine, our hearts jackrabbiting together while her face remains the pressed-on public one from her modeling days, smiling, benign. I don't have a public face. Never thought I'd need one, and these aren't pazzos anyway, but ravenous, phone-wielding New Yorkers. Hands snatch at us. A flash of checkered flannel, and for a second I think—but she's too tall, her hair all wrong. "Excuse us," Mom says, pulling me against her. "Excuse us." The man bellows on. "YOU'RE NOT DROWNING IF YOUR EYES ARE CLOSED. YOU'RE NOT DROWNING IF"—the next verse is meant to be unintelligible. This wild Mack Grady howl even his most devoted fans can't decipher, and yet here is Suspenders Man, going for it. The crowd cheers. As we push past him, shielding ourselves from photos and the possibility of a spontaneously ejected larynx, Mom kisses my hair. The slightest brush of her lips, and it's pathetic, how much that grounds me. Blinking, I look up. Fluorescent lights sear tears from my eyes.

Soon security gets involved. Through sheer bulk and repeated warnings to "Stay back!", they manage to sculpt a protective bubble around us. Mom and I pretend-shop, wandering from Gucci to Prada to Yves Saint Laurent, until gradually, the covert pic-snapping subsides. Gawkers get bored and drift away, but I can still feel them, pressed against our edges. Hanging back like that, they're not *so* scary. A couple of times I get curious and glance toward them. Catch a gaze, hold it a beat longer than fear wants to let me.

Only when the looks get reciprocated do I back off, grabbing subtly for Mom's sleeve. A calf whose gangly new legs will get me chomped up the second I stray.

At Chanel, we contemplate racks of silk scarves. Mom lifts a pink one, chewing her lip.

"You got her a scarf a couple years ago," I say.

She lowers it. "Did I tell you what my friends said to me? They think"—we approach another scarf display, functional wools—"I shouldn't get Nana anything this year. Or Grandpa."

"That's wild," I say, and Mom nods, satisfied by my outrage.

Her friends say this every year.

With scarves no longer viable, Mom convinces herself that what Nana really needs is a sweater. A clerk rushes to escort us to the appropriate section, not that that's necessary. These places are pretty much vacant. More sparkly linoleum than clothes. Mom holds up her selections, and I nod and shake my head at intervals—yes merino, no ruffles. My timing's gotten better over the years, so much so that Mom might actually suspect I've discovered some long-dormant fashion sense. "I don't know, though," she says, more to herself than me. "I can't picture your grandmother—the turtleneck, that suits her. But the color . . ." is monstrous. Fresh-squeezed bile. I point to the white version, which she considers carefully. "She'd never wear it. Not around the cows . . ."

Honestly, what does Nana Blackwell do with Mom's gifts? Is the room in their creaky farmhouse that was reserved for me now just warehousing a decade's worth of scarves and sweaters and hand creams?

The thought thuds into me. I can't take it anymore. I have to get away. "Koda," Mom warns—I tell her I'll only be a minute.

You ask me, it's not that Nana deserves *nothing*. Just close. A card saying, *Warmest wishes*. Five bucks inside.

The wool scarves are softer than expected. Cashmere. Rubbing tassels between thumb and index finger, I sneak a peek at my phone. No texts. But I knew that. I would've felt it vibrate, and—oh my God, I'm overthinking. That's all this is, and if Lindsay was here—if she knew about Sadie—she'd snatch my phone away, all, *Let's chill the fuck out, shall we?* and wring logic from bad feelings. Like, okay. Sadie's terrible at texting and busy anyway. Meaning, it's possible she's not mad. It's possible that she's just stuck in meetings, working on songs. Still, as I stand here, fondling scarves, I can't shake the sense that something else is up. Even if she didn't mind my questions . . . I could've done a better job not noticing her eyes were misty. Could've gotten the hang of the chord faster, like my father must've. I bet he learned every chord at once. Nailed them all, first shot, but if Sadie invites me over again, I could practice.

Unless her silence means she doesn't want to see me at all anymore. Unless she's concluded that getting to know each other is too much—too painful—to be worth it. Like I'm not hurting too. Four days later, I'm still getting twinges in my fingertips. Yesterday at dinner. This morning when I brushed my teeth. And now, as I slip a red scarf from its ring.

Chocolatey red. Not too flashy or anything. Perfect for chilly hikes up Thirtieth, or getting trapped on trains.

Mom approaches with a giant shopping bag, guilt scribbling all over her. "I got both," she announces. Her eyes brighten when she sees the scarf. "That's exquisite, Koda, really. Do you want it?"

"No," I mumble, wadding the scarf up. Apology gifts

embarrass people. One day, she'll understand.

Even so, as we descend to the jewelry department—Grandpa is way easier—I decide to try something new. I'll browse Saks with my father's eyes, since Sadie thinks I have them. Probably he'd be overwhelmed by the selection. And too broke to shop here, which is fine considering I won't really buy Sadie anything. This is for fun. An experiment. What else am I supposed to do while Mom hunts for old-man watches? Heads turn as we step off the elevator. I swear the linoleum pulls beneath me. The two of us sucked into the inescapable tidal wave of Diehard enthusiasm, but this time, the excitement fades quickly. I wait until Mom's eyes are the only eyes. Then I swallow my nerves. "Can I look around?" I ask. "By myself?"

She frowns. "Koda . . ."

"I won't go far, I promise." I swallow harder, trying to project the confidence that I in no way feel. "I've got shopping to do too, you know."

Miraculously, that seems to convince her, although she couldn't look more pained as she signals for a security guy to follow me. *Stay close,* she mouths. Like I need a reminder.

Jewelry overlaps with Cosmetics. I wander down the central aisle, to be judicious. Tinsel abounds. Almost as disorienting as the techno remix of "Silver Bells" that's been blasting for the past ten minutes. Cosmetics is tricky. Sadie hasn't worn any makeup around me, but thanks to old pictures, I know she used to. Razor-fine blush and tarry eyelashes. Purple lipstick that she'd smear on purpose, right as they took the stage.

Ensnared by a MAC display, I pick up the darkest I can find, a black so deep that the test swatch I dart onto my hand smears like ink. It reminds me of Lindsay. Of sitting on her bed, watching her get ready for Peter's shows. My mouth goes dry from all the spit it takes to scrub off.

In Women's Jewelry, I part seas of anxious men, using Security Guy's might to linger at case after case. This stuff's ridiculous, way too red-carpet, but there are some pieces where I think, if I was Mack Grady . . . dainty gold hoops. A topaz ring, dark as her eyes. I get as far as sliding it onto my own finger before deciding it's not right either. Would my father stoop to getting her *another* ring? Unlikely. He was too original. Perfume's next. I flap test strips under my nose, but it's hopeless. She already smells so good.

The sales girl's eyes flick from me to Security Guy as she approaches the counter, her expression all, *Why her?* Not the first I've noticed while browsing. Lots of people recognize me. Lots still don't. "Can I help you?" she asks, and I pretend to consider this, tucking a lock of hair behind my ear as shyness seizes me. *I need a gift for somebody.* Would he say that? I bet after they both found out about me, my father got down on his knees. Begged Sadie, begged her, to take him back. But I shake my head—"Just looking"—and grab a random test bottle. Oval-shaped, with amber liquid sloshing inside. I bring it to my nose. Sniff.

And smell velvet. A battered guitar in my hands.

A tap on my shoulder, and I whip around, clinking the bottle hard on the counter. Mom giggles. "Sorry to scare you," she says. "I just thought . . ." She shows me something twined around her fingers. A delicate silver bracelet, with a single charm. The letter *L*. I stare. "For Lindsay?" she explains. Then, suddenly doubtful, "That's who you were looking for, right? Is it too much?"

No. No, it's perfect, is the thing. So perfect that the moment Mom held the chain up, I saw it shimmering on Lindsay's wrist. She wouldn't even have to take it off to swim. "It's beautiful," I manage, but she doesn't seem to hear, her attention hijacked by Salesgirl, who talks quickly. Hostage to the nervous awe Mom inspires.

"Your daughter was looking at this one," she says, pointing to the oval bottle, and of course Mom is too nice not to play along. Helpless, I watch her spray a test strip.

Her nostrils quiver. "Wow." She glances at me, the bracelet forgotten completely. "Musky."

I shrug, reading the box that Salesgirl sets on the counter. It says MUSK, so Mom must be right. Deer secretions. Not velvet, or guitar. Briskly, Mom thanks Salesgirl and leads me away. "So?" she says, lifting the bracelet. The *L* spins, sparkling like silver shouldn't. Pool water on Lindsay's lip.

I could never give that to her.

Looking away, I whisper, "Where did you get it?"

She brings me to the case, and the sales girl here is nicer, doesn't judge or question me when I hand the bracelet back and ask to see other *L* designs instead. I study them, doing my best to appreciate their subtleties while Mom looks on. It's excruciating. Forget my father. I have never felt more powerless, more desperately alone, than in this moment. Sadie—the only person in my life who seemed to get me—has already cut her losses. And the only person I have left, the girl who might get me, if I let her, is the same girl I can't stop pushing away. Bracelets sparkle before me, tempting, teasing. Mom's distracted now. Poking at her phone.

If my father *was* here . . . really here. Not just in my imagination . . .

Would he help me choose?

Finally, I just point. Mom and Salesgirl exchange smiles, like we all share the same taste.

"You could've gotten one for Sarah, too," says Mom while Driver loads our packages into the trunk.

I don't answer. Tourists flail at yellow cabs.

Mom smiles, brushing my hair from my lips. "Honey? Don't you think?"

"Stop." I pull my hair back into place. "She's not even my real friend." Her silence this past week confirms it. And now I have a bracelet for Lindsay, a card to pick out and send to California. The same bullshit scribbled inside.

CHAPTER 15

WHEN *SARAH* HUMS ONTO MY PHONE SCREEN that night, I slam my hand over it, dismiss the text by accident. Turns out Sadie isn't avoiding me. Just upstate for the holidays, with minimal service. Back next week. C u then? she asks, and I reply, OK sure! suppressing the drumbeat in my ears. Next week. Sadie Pasquale wants to see me next week.

Christmas goes exactly as predicted. Mom, some designer friends, a bottle of prosecco, and me. Our gift ban doesn't stop me from showering Vinnie with the java moss I promised him, plus Amazon swords and a dwarf anubis, so he can hide under its leaves. New Year's Eve, we go to a party—some ball The Magazine throws at a fancy Midtown hotel. The entire office shows up and gets shitfaced. I fall asleep on a couch in the lobby. When I jolt awake, dry-mouthed and groggy, it's after one a.m. Behind the ballroom's ornately carved doors, a beat simmers. Laughter rings like glass breaking. I sit up, smoothing the shimmery scales of my gown.

The doorman here doesn't ask where I'm going. Only tips his hat and says, "Happy New Year, miss," as he swings the door out into the empty black night. It's cold, but I have Mom's feathery shawl that I borrowed. Combined with my gown and the heels that have been gnawing my toes all night, I look half mermaid, half poached swan.

Also, the night isn't that empty. I guess New York never is. On the narrow sidewalk, groups of friends form drunken whirlpools, laughing and shouting and helping one another into cabs. I should probably avoid them, but with Sadie due back soon, I'm discombobulated, so frantic to see her that nothing can penetrate the static in my head. She and my father could've gotten bagels with cream cheese at this bodega. Sat on this exact bit of sidewalk with their arms around each other, shivering, half-dead. Lately, I've built them into everything, but for some reason tonight the visions seem especially vivid. Maybe I snuck more champagne from Mom's glass than I thought.

When I reach a certain corner, the static stops. That street sign—West Forty-Ninth. I've read about it online somewhere. I'm sure I have.

I find a girl who seems knowledgeable. Standing beneath a dribble of streetlight, vaping and alone. "Um," I say, "what neighborhood is this?" and she sucks the e-cig before answering, "Hell's Kitchen. Why?"

To make this awkward, I could say, *Because my father died*

here. But the girl doesn't wait for a response. She laughs a cloud of cherry vapor, eyeing my sparkles. "What's with the dress? You rich or something?"

"Yeah," I tell her. Though I don't really think of it like that.

I wander farther, rustling in my shawl feathers. For all I know, my father and Sadie could've lived a block from here. The fifth-floor walkup where he died is some kind of shrine now, the ultimate Diehard destination. They leave flowers on the stoop—daffodils, like my father and Sadie stole for each other on their first date—and birdseed for pigeons. Take selfies. But I don't want to visit a shrine. I want to step into their apartment, deeper than any picture could go. Cracked linoleum, I'm thinking, my father and Sadie jumbled together with mismatched everything. A couple of plates and coffee cups. Five minutes of hot water each. In the only photos I've found of their apartment online, they lounge on a balding plaid sofa. Sadie sprawls across my father's lap, pixie feet propped on the armrest. A beard shades my father's cheeks. They both seem dazed. Rumpled. Like they slept in their clothes and might go back to sleeping in them once the photographer leaves. In the next pic Sadie's the same, but my father has his head tipped back to blow a smoke ring. A perfect lavender O.

The risk of cancer, and heart attacks and lung disease, can't stop me from wanting to blow my own smoke rings, just so my father could watch me try. He probably wouldn't have lectured me on the risks anyway. He probably would've been the kind of father who lets his kid make her own choices. I mean—he did drugs. At the very least, I doubt he'd judge me.

The sky's a chemical spill. Purple ribbons, zero stars, which is one thing—besides traffic—that New York has in common with LA. But there's this burst of light in the distance, clear and bluish bright like it's radiating from a TV, and I know, even without knowing anything, that it must be Times Square. This certainty is freakish. Totally instinctual, which means the city must be changing me somehow. Altering my DNA.

I walk until I can't anymore. Until the blocks all run together and I need a navigation app to limp back to the hotel. As Doorman does his thing, my reflection flashes across the glass. Not so much poached swan as too-tall girl in clopping shoes, her cheeks chewed pink from the cold. The party's still raging. At this rate, we'll definitely skip brunch. I clop over to my couch and flop down. So tired that I'm already slipping beneath the waters of a dream when my buzzing phone wakes me. "Oh my God! Happy New Year, baby!" I can barely hear Lindsay over whatever's happening in the background, a jumble of shrieks and bass. "Happy New Year," I manage, but my mouth is Styrofoam. It doesn't sound like I planned.

"Hold on," she says, and there's this sense of movement—the noisiness fizzling out behind her as she goes somewhere more private. "Okay. Sorry. I'm at this party and . . . it won't be midnight for a while here, but I wanted to be the first to tell you Happy New Year. Was I first?"

I sit up. One heel slips off and I overreact, trying to hush it with my other foot so both go clattering to the marble. Doorman jumps.

"Yeah," I lie, once my ears quit ringing.

Lindsay giggles. "Hooray!"

I can't tell if she's drunk.

"How's the party this year?" I ask. "Fun?"

She goes quiet. "It's okay." Then, in a voice barely above a whisper, "Everybody here is so dumb."

She must mean because it's not one of her boozy concerts. Because it's at a swim teammate's house, girls only, and Peter—even if they were back together—would sooner die than show up at a high school party. I lie with my cheek against the armrest, curled around this fact. "Everybody here is dumb too," I reassure her. "Except one person." This is the closest I've come to mentioning Sadie, and I bite my lip, waiting for Lindsay to demand, *Who?*

"I miss you, Koda."

She says it two more times.

"I miss you, I miss you."

It's January 1. In exactly three months, I turn eighteen. What if I don't come up with the words by then? What if all these feelings will become like the bracelet I still haven't sent her? Shoved to the back of my nightstand, locked inside a pearl-white box. I don't know how to bring up my birthday without giving myself away. *I miss you* doesn't mean *I love you.* Not remotely. You'd have to be seriously pathetic to seize on a hope that small.

"Miss you more," I say.

• • •

The rest of the day proceeds blearily, like it always does after a big night. While Mom recuperates, wobbly from her hangover, I tear apart my closet.

It's all shit, is the problem. Baggy sweatshirts and jeans, the Converse I've slouched around in my entire life, are okay for kids, but with my birthday on the horizon I've got to get serious about making improvements. This isn't your typical resolution, me promising myself, *I'll do better this year,* a brand-new chance that I'll still mess up. Worthiness is the goal. Like I deserve my father's legacy. Deserve Lindsay.

Also, I'm seeing Sadie tomorrow.

And three months, I understand now, doesn't give you much time. Not to record an album, in my father's case. Definitely not to learn everything there is to learn about him, to ask Sadie question after question until I quit feeling so stripped and shy. How do I do that? Channel him. Obviously.

I stand in front of the full-length mirror. Almost naked, but not quite. My undies and bra are plain white cotton. Childish. Old clothes are strewn over the carpet like beach trash. I pick through them again, one eye on the mirror to supervise my stomach folds, the swing of my breasts. Lindsay liked my black lipstick, so whatever I come up with will need to be some echo of that. And then there's all the stuff Sadie's said to me about how much I remind her of my father, my stomach and face and twisty logic. The right clothes would cement that point even more. *Hello, Sadie,* those clothes would say. Not hi. *Hello.*

The lacy black tunic I settle on isn't new. A Mom discard that requires tights. But I turn and turn, my fingers tucked in the drapey sleeves.

Driver doesn't comment on my transformation the following morning, or when I dive into the car after school. My classmates don't notice either—thank God. Hard to tell when you're always greeted with a pile of stares anyway, but keeping my sweatshirt on helped. Now I struggle out of it, zip my coat back up. As we cross the bridge toward Astoria Boulevard, inspiration strikes. I dab my lips with nude gloss, then spend the rest of the ride with my mouth open, guppying it, to avoid licking the stuff off. *Hello, Sadie.* I've been practicing all day. Memorizing each syllable, their edges and curves, like I'm going to sing them. I picture her funny smile. Those big eyes bursting wider with surprise. *Hello . . .*

I know the second Sadie opens the door that she isn't wearing a bra. I process this before her dorky glasses, the torn-up jeans accented with safety pins. Lifting the guitar, she says, "Got to tune her quick."

"Cool," I reply, a beat too late. She must've just gotten home. There's a suitcase and black backpack piled by the door that I have to sidestep to reach the couch. The cushion beside her has been cleared already. I sit down even though she doesn't invite me to, slipping my coat off along the way. It plops to the rug, and I remember—crap. "Hello, Sadie."

Naturally, this comes out nothing like I practiced. A total splatter.

She chuckles and cocks her head at me. "Hello yourself?"

I'm blushing too hard to do anything but watch her with lashes lowered, fists wrapped in my sleeves. Something about her isn't quite like I remember. Not in a bad way, just different. Again. Sawing her nose on her cardigan, she mutters, "This is what happens when you're out of town for a week. Everything goes to shit, poor baby. Listen." She twangs a string. The B string, if I remember correctly. I'd ask, but she zooms on without me. "That's flat. The G's sharp, see?" She twangs the B string and then the other, over and over, until my smile convinces her I hear the difference. There's more, and I try to pay attention, but it's all so distracting. My leggings, for one thing. Turns out I don't have the resolve for tights. And Sadie's freckles. The sunset, her papers smeared with orange light. Her scratchy fingers pluck notes, coax knobs on the guitar's neck, and it's hypnotizing, how one hand always seems to know what the other is doing. Sweat glimmers on her forehead. Her tongue sneaks between her teeth. "Yup," she says. "Sounds awful. A goddamn travesty, but you know Teddy. Actually, you don't know Teddy, but he's got a real bug up his ass, let me tell you. Won't let me bring my girl anywhere near him, not even for Christmas, if you can believe that. He's got this big old farm upstate, suppose you googled. Wife and kids. Alpacas—"

"What?" I say.

"Those cuddly-looking fuckers—"

"No, I know what alpacas are." If she wasn't talking like a fifty-car pileup, I would've caught on sooner that by Teddy she means *Ted.* The bassist. "You guys really keep in touch?"

Sadie bends her head, fiddling intently. "Teddy's my best friend."

"That's awesome." I didn't realize he'd moved back upstate or had a farm. Contrary to Sadie's assumption, I've never really bothered to research him. Like most people, probably. He seems all right in photos. Black, handsome, but a different direction of handsome from my father. This narrow, serious face. "Why doesn't he let you bring your guitar?" I ask, and she laughs. This joyless bark.

"Teddy's that sort of person—thinks he knows what's best for me, better than I do. You got one of those?" A self-conscious flick of her eyes. But I'm stuck on Teddy. The injustice of it all.

"Why would leaving the guitar here be best? You're literally a guitarist."

Sadie doesn't answer. The guitar looks so content on her knee, like a cat curled up.

Once it's tuned, she passes it to me, then shifts onto the coffee table while we get reacquainted. "I've been practicing," I explain. When she seems more startled than impressed, I add, "In my head, I mean. The way your fingers are supposed to go. There are YouTube videos and everything. See?" My fingers slot onto the frets—not magic this time, but hard-earned muscle memory—and Sadie grins, clearly pleased. My cheeks blaze hotter than ever.

Sadie hops up. "Hold on. I've been thinking . . ." She rummages around the clutter, displacing cups and papers. "Got to warn you, picks are a different feel, but I trust you can handle—aha."

The pick is green plastic. Painfully attentive, I watch her show me how to hold it. Between my thumb and the side of my index finger, covering the cartoon turtle. "Exactly," she says. "You know, this is how Mack preferred it too." I return my strumming hand to the strings, not caring for once if she sees my dumb smile. She matches it, her pupils big as moons.

"All right." She cracks her knuckles. "We'll start slow. . . ." It should be easy. Strum using the pick from the thickest string down. Sadie demos the technique a hundred times, but the pick keeps flying from my fingers and I get so frustrated, so freaking angry, that when she moves from the coffee table onto the couch, next to me, I almost push her away.

"I'm trying," I say. "I swear." How could I still suck so bad? She said this was how my father did it. I don't have *time* to fuck this up.

Sadie blows out her cheeks. Even with the windows cracked, her apartment is sweltering. Then she smiles—an authentic Sadie Pasquale half smile—and grabs my elbow, moves it up and down. "Unclench."

I can't.

"Relax, Koda."

She makes me so nervous, but I try to relax. To pretend I'm water.

"There we go." Sadie's still making my arm flop. "Lock up and you can't hold on to the pick. Strumming's all about staying loose, in the wrist especially. Mack used to imagine he was"—she pauses, moves my fingers up the frets about an inch—"flicking a booger off his finger."

I laugh. Like a balloon bursting, though. Not on purpose. "Gross."

"Says you! Everybody's bad when they start out, and he was no virtuoso." Her grin slips, and she rests her elbow on the back of the couch. Softly, she adds, "He tried real hard for me. Sweet how you do too."

I look back down at the strings, do a quick mental check to make sure I actually do know how to hold them: EADGBE. "I know you said he couldn't play piano, but the guitar . . . I . . . I guess I figured he was born good at it."

"Nah," says Sadie. "Started bad, stayed bad, frankly."

"Really?" I press my fingers down, testing the bite of the strings. "So all those people online, and the people who come up to me, telling me he was this musical genius, that he was brilliant . . . they're wrong. He was more like . . . like me? Kind of . . . ordinary."

Sadie rests her chin on her hand, eyes twitching, assessing. For what I can't tell, but I sit extra straight. Part my lips slightly, so she'll catch their shimmer—except as soon as I do, her gaze twitches away. "That's one way of putting it," she tells me.

Like I'm deterred that easily. Already I'm imagining him instead of Sadie sitting down to teach me. Both of us laughing, stumbling over the same chords over and over until eventually, one of us got it right. *Like father like daughter*, they'd say.

Only . . . that would mean missing this. The moment that Sadie and I are sharing, right now. I pick through the chord some more, getting a little better each time, and then we sit together awhile, listening to her neighbors bump around downstairs, a bus idling outside. The silence that's opened between us isn't the regular kind, a blank I'm rushing to fill. This is important silence. Grown-up silence.

Once I'm finished savoring it, I say, "Thanks for not being mad at me."

She frowns. "Mad?"

"For making you cry before."

"Oh." Her ears redden. "That."

"I'm sorry. It wasn't my intention. I just . . . I cry too, you know. All the time. My crush called New Year's Eve. She said she missed me, and it felt significant. The way she said it. But I know that's wishful thinking. So." I shrug. "Anyway. That's what I've cried about lately."

Sadie's chin is still in her hand. "There's one thing he was good at. Bawling his eyes out all the goddamn time."

Breathless, I whisper, "Why? His depression?" I don't feel depressed. Not really. More like, stupid, and cowardly, and wet from Lindsay's voice being in my head all this time. *I miss you.* But I can't tell Sadie that. Can I?

She leans closer. Her breasts brush the loose fabric of her

shirt. "Sometimes," she says, "this being alive business rubbed us raw."

A breeze slithers through the window, rustles my hair. I nod, amazed. "That's it. That's totally it." I mean, if I had the words, those are exactly the ones I'd use. Sadie sits back, and I notice for the first time how much paler she seems than the last time I saw her. Thinner, too, if that's possible.

She rolls the pick between her fingers. "You look different tonight. Wasn't sure if I should say."

"Oh." I blush. Guess we've both kind of changed. "Yeah. I was . . . doing some spring cleaning, I guess. A closet purge? All my clothes suck. But then I found this, and I remembered you and my father wore lots of lace. So."

She smiles, smoothing the collar that hasn't stayed flat all day. "He'd approve."

My stomach butterflies. "Really?"

"Sure. I thought so the second you took off your coat. One look and I said to myself, 'He would've loved that.' Loved me in it. Same difference." She fiddles with an earring, avoiding my eye. "It is nice. Seeing you again. Whole time I was up at Teddy's, I kept wondering . . . maybe I shouldn't. Maybe this is all bad news. I mean, we've gone this long not knowing shit about each other, right? Me in my bubble, you in yours? But the truth is, kiddo, I don't mind having you around. A little cry now and then might be good for me."

I smile. It's just incredible. The seemingly infinite space between this idea you have of a person and the Sadie I'm getting to know, a dawning sense that as much as I need her, she might need me a little too. Incredible, and exciting. Like the feeling tumbling around inside me is a song we're both writing. I want to tell her how glad I am that she's decided I'm worth keeping around. I want to whisper, *Nobody gets me like this.* Not even Lindsay . . . but that could change.

I put my hand out. "Let me try again."

Sadie flips the pick up like a coin. For good luck, she explains, slapping it turtle-down into my palm. "Now blow."

Somehow, I get what she means. She blows on the pick and so do I, like we're starting some kind of fire. Her breath is hot ash. Mine catches at my sticky lips. "Does this really help?" I ask, once the plastic's warm. And Sadie giggles and whisks a finger down my jaw, filling me with shivers. Good shivers.

"Want advice? About this girl?"

"Of course—"

"'Fear's always there.' That's what Mack used to tell me. This was before we were famous, back when I still believed him. 'Fear's there, Sadie, so . . .'" She pushes my hand toward the strings. "'Do it afraid.'"

CHAPTER 16

THE BRACELET HAS JUST ENOUGH CHAIN to twist around each of my fingers once, then back again. I test the *L*'s tip with my thumb. Sharp, but I pretend it isn't. I try to imagine myself here in my room six months from now, or however long it'll take calluses like Sadie's to form, digging this silver *L* into the rind of my thumb and feeling . . .

Confident.

But it'll be summer in six months, my birthday far behind me. *Fear's always there,* Sadie said. Or said my father said. Same thing. He'd probably want me to make a move this very instant. He wouldn't tolerate me standing here, wrapped in a bath towel, dripping all over my carpet, when there's a girl you love out there, noise to be made. I loosen my hold on the bracelet, drizzle the chain onto my desk so the *L* rests on top. With a fingertip, I make minor adjustments. Poke and poke until the silver glints exactly right.

A muffled crash. I scream and almost let go of my towel. "Mom?" It's just after eight. She shouldn't be home for another hour. Acid surging, I step to the closed connector door. "Are you back?" God—what do I do? Did she notice I wasn't home? When she doesn't answer, I creep into her room. It's dark. Like, deep-sea nightmare dark, a faint light emanating from her en suite. "Mom?"

I find her rooting around in the vanity, lip and eyebrow pencils still rolling across the tile. "You scared the crap out of me," I say. Frowning, Mom uncaps a lipstick, reaches for another with the intensity normally reserved for hunting down gluten-free oatmeal. It's dark in here, too, except for the vanity bulbs. They're on full blast. Mom's photos around the mirror, her trays and trays of ransacked cosmetics, glow like offerings on some kind of crazed fashion altar. She stands with her back to me, studying a tube of lipstick. "Mom? Hello?"

She grabs my arm so swiftly I yelp and pull away, but it's no use. I've been swatched. A slash of pearly pink.

"What do you think?" She returns dubiously to the tube. "Too sheer, right?"

I pretend to examine the tuna-fish white of my inner arm. Why . . . ? When I look up, Mom's sitting on the vanity bench, strands of hair springing from her bun. "It's nice," I say at last.

She groans—her head drops to her hands. "Too sheer. Everyone is obsessed with mattes now . . ."

I spot a pencil she missed beneath the bench. It'll take real talent to reach it without dropping my towel. "We're having trouble coming up with colors for the spring issue," she goes on as I strain and stretch. Luckily, I did inherit her freakishly prehensile toes. "We've been beating our heads against the wall for weeks, and I finally thought I had just the color, but it's not right. Nothing is right. It's humiliating. We're expected to be at the forefront of such things, and we can't even predict what colors will trend . . ." She trails off, tapping her tongue against her teeth. Then her eyes snap to mine. "Where were you?"

My skin prickles. "My room."

"You weren't there when I arrived half an hour ago. I was calling for you. Didn't you hear me?"

"I—I was in the shower."

I don't need the mirror to know my face is getting hot. Mom eyes me. Not menacingly. More like, that weird, invasive curiosity that's recently got her asking all sorts of unnecessary questions about my life. When she scoots closer, I swear it's the Peruvian restaurant all over again. Dim lighting. Zero options. Studying and homework excuses are out, with the school quarter ending soon. Must keep expectations minimal.

Cautiously, she says, "You've been taking a lot of showers at night lately." This throws me too—until I realize it's the result of careful guesswork. Most nights she doesn't get home before I'm in bed, but she could've smelled my lavender shampoo clogging the air, seen the damp towels that I'm not exactly diligent about tossing in the hamper.

My foot slips, sending the pencil rolling farther beneath the vanity. "What's wrong with that? I always took night showers before. Because of swimming, remember?"

"Nothing's wrong with it, honey, I just figured . . ." She shrugs. "I don't know. New routines."

"I like my old routines." And not reeking of cigarettes.

But even that, I'm beginning to enjoy. A reminder that Sadie and I have something, no matter how fragile. Mom's nose crinkles like she's smelled what I wish I still could: Sadie's smoke twined around me. I dip my head, keeping these thoughts private as I stretch my leg farther, ignoring the warning that zings up my hamstring.

I could tell her I was with "Sarah." I could tell her we flung ourselves across Starbucks couches and talked for hours, like Lindsay and I used to do. But now, even uttering Sadie's alias feels one step too close to the truth.

"Got it." I pluck the pencil from between my toes and clink it onto the vanity. The color is unexpected. Blue deep as an ache.

Mom says, "You can talk to me, Koda. About anything."

Except I can't. Not when Sadie's given me all I need to know, when the last time we spoke about Lindsay, Mom told me friends having boyfriends was just something I'd need to get over. Joke's on you, Mom. Because my father believed differently. Because I am done, so thoroughly, violently *done*, with this sewn-up world that Mom has tucked around me. Mom's never done anything bold in her life. She organizes drawers. Conference calls.

And Lindsay still doesn't have a boyfriend.

Mom's eyes are the inky blue that means tears are imminent. She regards me so intensely I can't look back, end up running my finger down the photograph of her kissing me on the vanity that she showed me weeks ago. When I figured I'd never see Sadie again. *Do it afraid.* Her words drum in my ears. *Do it afraid.*

That's the real reason Mom didn't want me meeting Sadie. The danger that I would make my own decisions. Think my own thoughts.

"Whatever," I tell her.

I almost cringe. Seventeen years of the Mariah-and-Koda show, and this is the nastiest I've been to her, ever. I brace myself. Expecting tears, a slap, even though she's never hit me, doesn't have the *guts* to hit me. The anticipation's so massive I almost don't notice Mom's preoccupied with the picture too, and that her wondrous face doesn't look right. Bones rearranged, shadows falling where shadows shouldn't be. She stands up. The gauze of her skirt swishes as she crosses to the Jacuzzi.

"I think I'll take a bath, then," she announces, bending to yank on the tap. Water thunders into the tub, blotting out the rest.

"What?"

"Nothing, Koda, I'm just talking to myself. Good night."

That's it? I'm . . . dismissed? Okay. That was easier than I thought.

I'm halfway to my own room when she calls me back.

"Koda."

Water glistens, the tub nearly full. Mom sits on the edge in her work clothes, the swishy skirt and aggressively rosetted blouse that I'm through wishing would look good on me. Her eyes widen, like she's just now, for the first time, really taking me in. I mean the essence of me: beyond my height and stringy hair and barely managed skin.

My fingertips sting. I switch the hand that's holding my towel. Too close to being naked—*all the way* naked—in front of my mother.

"I was just going to say"—she reaches to unlace her boots—"that I know I'm busy. Incredibly busy, and that's not always fair, to you or me. But . . . I'm still your mom."

She pauses.

"Okay, well . . ." I'm backing away. "Good night."

Mom turns back to the water. "Love you."

I say I love her too. My hair separating into tentacles, like it always does half-dry.

When my phone pings the next morning, I'm braless, sweating in front of the mirror. An email, probably. School stuff. I bite open another bobby pin, wishing my heart would stop pounding.

It's after seven. Mom would flip, but I don't care if I'm late. Chemistry sucks. My hair resembles something put together quickly by birds. I tear out every pin, all twenty-two, and fling them onto the counter. Default hair it is. Lank on top, wavy underneath. Baffling. And I can't wear the same thing I wore yesterday, which means I'm officially out of Sadie-and-Mack-approved-clothes. Luckily, I do have a backup. Tugging on my chunky sweater, I try to figure out if this will work, if I can really go to school without anybody noticing my nipples. They don't show, but still.

My phone pings again, and my chest spasms; metallic excitement floods my mouth even though I know it's just another email. Before returning to my bedroom, I take one more look at my boobs. Various looks. Side angles. It does feel good, not having them all smashed together. Why have bras always felt mandatory in public? I can't believe I'm just now trying this out.

In my bedroom, Vinnie hunkers beneath a leaf. I drop him a worm pellet, then untangle my phone from the covers. Not email alerts but texts. From Lindsay. For Vinnie's benefit I try to seem indifferent, cool, as I swipe them open.

Hey Koda. U at school yet?????

I can't sleep

It's about peter

Vinnie's filter bubbles. I lower myself to the edge of my bed.

oh. What's up?

ugh idk it's just that we've been talking more lately and
idk. Idk idk idk what to do

y?

well bc he says he misses me

While I wait for her to say more, I pull up my conversation with Sadie, but there's no way to tell if she read the message I sent after talking to Mom last night, or if she's on her phone right now or wants to text me. I swipe back to Lindsay.

I think he wants to get back together

I stare at the screen.

ok lol
is that what u want??

Idk what I want lol!!
That's why I'm telling u

The bracelet is still on my nightstand. I loop it around my fingers again. And again, watching the chain shimmer. I don't know if Lindsay would even like it. But I've also resolved to be done with that type of thinking.

My fingers are turning purple. I shake the chain free and start typing.

I say u shouldn't

he'll just break your heart again

Yaaa but . . .

He breaks it so good :P

It strikes me as something Sadie would say, and for a second, I almost envy Lindsay. Her willingness to get her heart pulped over and over, just because of who's doing it. Without thinking, I type, So u breathe his name then, only to realize when her reply comes through—huh????—that I'm using a code she can't read.

It's not that I don't want to tell her about Sadie. I want to, absolutely, but how? Every time I try, I lose hold of what to say, end up typing and deleting the same message a thousand times. We barely talked about my father or Quixote in LA. Besides, you can text about guitar lessons, chords, picks . . . but they're not just lessons. Not just picks. And if Lindsay's going to get back with Peter, then she doesn't deserve to know about Sadie anyway. The one person left in the world who is entirely my own. So I decide to drop it. I take every memory of Sadie and press them against the top of my mouth, like candy I'm not done savoring.

nvm lol sry

need caffeine

She ignores this for a while. U there???? I add.

yeah sry just asleep haha it's 4am

LA is 3 hrs behind remember???

Well. Maybe I did forget. But the thought of Lindsay lying awake, thinking of me . . . I remember sharing a bed during sleepovers. Her breathing dreamy slow beside me. All those nights I pressed myself into the mattress and wished . . . what if she moved her head onto my pillow? Touched her lips to my lips? Once she flipped onto her side, and her curls spilled across my pillow. I took one in my teeth.

I can't give up this easily again. I can't miss this one, final chance, to tell Lindsay the truth. But what am I supposed to do? She's so far away, and this isn't the kind of thing you can say with a text. Is it? I take the silver *L* and press it to my lips, tasting the clammy metal.

The solution arrives so suddenly you can hardly call it one at all. A blur across my brain. It's risky. And . . . kind of wild, but I've got to trust Sadie. *Do it afraid.* Nothing short of wild will count.

I have some investigating to do first, some big-time making up with Mom, but there's no question that this is exactly what my father would urge me to do, if he were here. Call me, I text Lindsay. After swimming??

". . ." flickers onto the screen. I hold my breath, waiting.

Ok ☺

My pulse quickens as I head to Mom's en suite.

Her makeup, formerly arranged by color, is still all over the place. It takes a while to find the blue pencil from last night, and even longer to find a lipstick that might match. I take a chance on a Pacific blue, smear it immediately. Cursing, I whip a glance over my shoulder, half expecting Mom to come to my rescue. Spit and Q-tips.

Scrubbing at the sink turns my mouth pink anyway. Figures Mom doesn't own a single stick of black.

On my way out, I slip the blue into my pocket.

Sadie grins when I show her my torn-up fingers. "Part of the process."

"Yeah, but . . ." I move so she can reach the tap, accidentally bump into the fridge. Her kitchen is microscopic. "Isn't there something I can do to speed it up? Or reduce the pain somehow?"

Water splutters over dishes in the sink. "You mean actually enjoy life? What's the fun in that?"

Sighing, I right a magnet. FACE THE MUSIC, it says. "You're pretty dark, you know." Her mouth quirks. Either because I shouldn't have said that, or because she caught how winded I am from taking the stairs two at a time. Embarrassing. I make an effort to breathe calmly as she chugs a glass of water.

"Realistic." She smacks the cup down. "Isn't that what you meant?"

"Yeah, definitely." I follow her back to the living area.

Sadie's on a cleaning binge. Or what she considers cleaning—gathering her papers into haphazard stacks. When I arrived a few moments ago, she was grumbling about her songwriting partner, this big rewrite deadline they both somehow forgot about. She hasn't noticed my jumpiness yet, how I still haven't taken off my coat. Now I do. Just—shrug it off, drape it over the couch. Super casual. Nothing to be self-conscious about here. I force a smile, hook my hair behind my ears.

"Want help?" I ask.

Her eyes lift skeptically from the page she's reading, and you can see all over her how helpless she thinks I am. Which, okay. Maybe I haven't cleaned much up, personally. But anybody can make piles. As I trail her around the room, she loads my arms with loose leaf, quizzing me on stuff. Stupid stuff, like how to light a gas stove and flip pancakes and unclog a drain. "Eggs," she says after my millionth shrug. "Can you cook an egg?" Probably, I tell her.

"If I watched you first."

She thrusts more papers at me, sleeves pushed back to reveal skinny, speckled arms. And biceps. Since when? They're nowhere near as developed as Lindsay's—swimming and guitar likely require different muscles—but still. Cool.

Sadie pricks an eyebrow. Whatever she sees on my face, I fold quickly away.

"Anyway," I say in my defense, "I don't even like eggs."

It's 3:57. 12:57, in California, which means I have precisely . . . four hours before Lindsay calls. Three and a half hours, roughly, to clue Sadie in on my plan, and win her blessing. Not that I doubt she'll support me. I just want to see the pride lighting up her eyes. The recognition.

But it's hard when she's so distracted. When doubt worms in with every second I don't speak up. Groaning, she crouches to grab a page beneath the coffee table. The papers she gave me, I hug close to my chest. Anything to shield her from my bralessness. What was I thinking?

"You really are like Mack, princess." The paper is crumpled to hell, a tight little fist. Sadie picks it open, then blinks a sec. Shoves it into her notebook. "Certifiably helpless—" Music interrupts her. Eight-bit calypso. "Dammit." Sadie stalks off. I crane my neck to watch her rummage around the kitchen counter, pat her jeans. "Where did . . ." The music's reaching its frantic crescendo, and she's resorted to flipping couch cushions, by the time she apparently remembers her bomber jacket, hanging on its peg by the door. She plucks a chunky silver device from the pocket.

"Wait." I crack up. "That's your *phone*?" I've never seen one this ancient in real life. It's hilarious. Like if somebody from a hundred years ago closed their eyes and imagined *The Future*. Sadie squints at the screen.

"Christ," she mutters. "Got to take this, sorry." She disappears down the hall, shutting a door behind her. Click.

"Okay," I say aloud.

Probably Em. Her songwriting partner. I wait by the coffee table, cupping my elbows. Minutes slide by.

The papers I helped collect are piled on the coffee table, the notebook nearby. It's not even special. The black marbled kind you see in drugstores and high school movies. Snooping is wrong, but I want to know what the paper says. Need to know so badly what she deems worth keeping that I slip a hand inside the cover, tug the crumpled page just enough to read: HER MOUTH IS A SLICE OF—

The rest is scribbled out.

Sadie's voice rises, muffled by the door, and it occurs to me that she must be in her bedroom. The one place in her apartment I haven't seen, that I've come to think of not as a whole room but just a door across from the bathroom that stays politely, firmly shut. Other things about Sadie are more interesting anyway. I don't need to see the colors of her bed set, or whatever trinkets she's got cluttering up the shelves, don't need to dig up *every* secret to feel close to her. Tugging the page out from her notebook, I lift it to the light, peering through storm clouds of ballpoint, but the words beneath are impossible to make out. A slice of what, Sadie? Whose mouth?

I tuck the page back inside the front cover and venture after her. Slowly. So the floorboards won't creak. I press my ear to the bedroom door.

"Look." She sounds exasperated. "I appreciate your concern and all, really do, but you're not"—she huffs—"so what if she's here? You going to drive down? Kick her out? Give me a goddamn break, Ted."

My bladder tightens. The same irrepressible urge to pee I used to get playing hide-and-seek.

It's Teddy on the phone. The bassist.

And they're talking about me. I press closer, rising on tiptoe, like that's going to help me hear better. Sadie continues, a whiny edge to her voice that I've never heard. "Support it? Of course you don't. Like I'd really expect *you* to support anything I—bullshit. I'm a big girl." She pauses for a freaking century, and I can't take it anymore. I'm going to pee myself. I dart into the bathroom, which, no surprise, wasn't built for tall girls. Knees folded against the lip of the tub, I pee forever, wrapping my hand in a one-ply mitten.

Should I be scared or elated that Sadie told Teddy about me? Not that I think Teddy would go blabbing to the media. He seems like a private enough person, with his alpacas and kids and stuff. But . . . why wouldn't he want me visiting Sadie? Her voice comes more rapidly now. Their conversation's wrapping up. "Yeah, yeah, well, you know I could quit whenever I wanted. Cold turkey . . ." I flush the toilet and go to wash my hands. As chaotic as her apartment is, Sadie's bathroom never changes. The sink is cracked ceramic. Spattered with toothpaste stains. I pick at one while the water takes its usual eternity to get hot. A toothbrush, its bristles all frazzled, sits in a cloudy drinking glass. I move it back, then open the medicine cabinet.

An antacid. That's all I'm looking for. The magic one she gave me on my first visit, a preemptive strike against the reflux now percolating inside me. Except there are tons of bottles up here, and most are for pills. Curious, I spin one around to read the label. *ALPRAZOLAM*. A word I know but don't. Otherwise, there's only cough syrup, scattered tampons, a stick of undereye concealer. One, two, three bottles of nasal spray, which explains her runny nose. Allergies.

A rap on the door. "Koda?"

I flip the cabinet shut. "One sec!" Sadie's right there when I emerge, fidgeting in the darkened hall. Behind her, more hardwood. A slash of unmade bed.

She left the door ajar.

"You heard all that?" she asks.

"A little," I hedge. "But—"

She slams down the hall, then reappears just as suddenly, a cigarette lit between her fingers. She sucks on it hard, then says, "You seen a bedroom before?"

"Oh." I'm still staring over her shoulder. "Sure." I shrug. "Obviously." But I'd be mortified to show her mine. Sadie, after a brief hesitation, pushes the door tantalizingly wider. Granting . . . permission? I slip inside before she can change her mind. Hands shoved under my armpits, determined not to touch anything else.

Her bedroom is smaller than I imagined, as cluttered and

cramped as the rest of her apartment. A shipwreck of tattered notebooks and flung-off clothes. Jewelry box, overstuffed bookshelf, picture frame placed facedown on her nightstand—my attention snags on all of it. But the open closet beckons most of all. Heart thumping, I inspect the velvet jungle.

"You have the coolest style," I say.

She snorts. "*His* style."

"Even better." I free a hand despite myself, stroke a gauzy black sleeve. Sadie comes up beside me, flicking ash to the floor, and I hate to say so, but: "Don't quit smoking." Smoke twines around her like the girl in my pictures. The girl that with every visit, every zing in my fingertips, I'm one step closer to becoming. Smoke means impressing Lindsay. Night showers. The thrill of giving Mom a reason to wonder. Only, Sadie doesn't know any of this. She tilts her head at me, confused. "Teddy wants you to, right?" I remind her.

Sadie pales. The hand holding the cigarette drifts uneasily toward her hair. "Ted's like a brother to me," she says, looking away. "Overprotective. Especially after . . . everything that's happened. You understand."

I nod, like I do understand. Like I've actually had a brother, or any friend who was a boy. "Why doesn't he want us hanging out, though?"

Smoke whooshes out her nose. "Dramatics. Nothing worth worrying about."

"Okay." Silence edges between us.

Sometimes I suspect she's not as carefree as she seems.

She nods at her clothes. "Haven't worn most of that shit in years. Feels sort of entombed, you know? Just hanging there, gathering dust. I'd say help yourself, only, I doubt much of it would fit."

Obviously. From top to toe, Sadie's the length of like, my femur. But . . . I tug the gauzy shirt off its hanger. It's collared like the tunic I wore yesterday, with velvet trim and, importantly, pockets. Why would she want to get rid of it? "Lindsay would love this," I say, unable to stop myself. "Her boyfriend—*ex*-boyfriend—is a guitarist. His band's terrible. Like, Quixote wannabes, but she'd wear this kind of thing to their shows. Every time she looked more amazing. If I could just . . . well . . . when she visits—" Crap. I smash my lips together. That totally slipped out. You're not supposed to talk about a possibility as if it's a sure thing. That's bad luck, isn't it? Sadie doesn't seem to have heard. Unless this is another one of her tests, a courage check, and that's why she's watching me so closely. Daring me to repeat it.

There's just so many boxes to check until I'm ready. Lindsay's dads and Mom all agreeing to let her fly across the country, stay over, potentially skip school, all for the sake of one measly trip. What if they make us wait until summer? What if—

What if Lindsay says no?

Sadie looks on as I hold the shirt up to myself, biding time. Of all moments to sense the thoughts clanging around my mind, this has got to be it. Sadie's so good at that, no *Tell me what you're thinking, honey.* She just knows.

But she waits too long, and I'm forced to break the silence.

"I-I'm inviting Lindsay to come to New York so I can give her her Christmas present, tell her I love her in person. I'm not sure if she'll want to come, if our parents will even let us, but I'd never have thought of this if it weren't for you—well, you and my father, basically—telling me to do it afraid. So . . . thank you." My cheeks burn. When I finally feel like I can look at her again, it's not pride lighting up her eyes, or recognition.

Something even more intense. Something I can't read.

She wipes sweat off her lip. "Got to be home soon?"

"Not exactly—"

"Good." She pushes past me. "Let's go."

Peter's band is called Ghost Ocean. Sadie screams when I tell her.

"Oh my God." My grin practically splinters my face. "Okay, thank you, isn't that so stupid? Lindsay swears it's some anti-oil drilling thing, which she's been totally obsessed with lately—political statements, I mean—so I've had to go along with it, but all I want to do is tell her how much that name sucks. Stupid's just the beginning. There are so many adjectives." I'd list them, but Sadie's wheezy laughter is killing me. Walking on the street with her—not *close* close, but just enough that our fingers graze accidentally—will go down as the highlight of my week. At first I assumed she had a destination in mind, but now I'm not so sure. Every block gets more and more desolate, like we're not exploring Astoria but leaving it behind. It's awesome. I don't care how sketchy Steinway gets. Blacked-out shops and the stammer of traffic down nearby Astoria Boulevard, shadows greasy in the dim streetlight. Men loiter in the doorway of an abandoned furniture shop, smoking cigarettes and giving Sadie ideas. She lights up but can't stop roaring long enough to take a puff. I blow hair from my lips, giggling too.

Another couple blocks and it's like the laugh is holding her hostage, dissolving into a wet, barking cough. I'm contemplating giving her a thump when she pulls away from me, hawks, and spits. I wait until she wanders back.

"Are you okay?"

We're outside what must've been a lingerie shop, empty except for mannequin legs dangling in the windows. Ignoring me, Sadie jerks her chin at them. "Dismemberment. Now, that really gets me going."

I laugh and squeeze closer, shaking my head when she asks if I'm getting cold. Next block, we find a thrift store with the *Th* burnt out in the sign. "Look." I point. "Rift store."

Sadie whistles. "That's heavy."

Hands in my pockets, I admit, "I've never been thrifting before." Thrifting? Is that the lingo? I might as well admit Mom buys all my clothes. "You and my"—*dad* squirts out of reach—"my father used to go all the time, right?"

"Sure did."

Together we look up at the sign, Sadie's whistle echoing in

my head. Of course she can whistle. Of course. But that's what makes her so exciting.

Even the obvious things surprise me.

Slyly, she catches my eye, and the invisible wires rigging our brains hum back to life. We both grin.

Patchy blue carpet. Odor of mildew. Not so much a thrift *store* as the world's most chaotic prop department. Long and narrow, the lights getting squintier, shelves more crowded, the farther back they go. I linger in the doorway, trying to gauge what exactly I'm at risk of contracting here (bedbugs? Something flesh-eating?), and next I know, Sadie's vanished. I've been marooned.

Okay. I'm okay. Sadie wanted to go in too, which makes this disaster worth both our whiles. And this place is pretty cool. The anti-Saks, no sparkly linoleum or garment racks in sight. Whoever's in charge dumps clothes right on the floor. Memories waft up of personal shoppers kissing Mom's cheeks, offering champagne, and I can't help it—I crack up all over again. Lindsay would freaking love it here. "Sadie," I call. "Where'd you go? I can't see you over all this junk."

No response. Figures. Wincing apologetically at the ancient man behind the counter—for the junk comment—I skirt piles of horrifically outdated blouses and sweaters, a brave explorer traversing never-before-seen mountain chains. Shelves along the wall hold stacks of plastic plates and bowls, mugs that say WORLD'S BEST TEACHER and ASTORIA PARK DAY FUN RUN '87. I draw an uppercase *K* and *L* in the dust around them, smiling to myself. *"Sa-die,"* I sing in the low, leaky voice it probably kills her to hear. "Come on, where are—"

"Over here!"

Thank God. I thread my way to the back wall, where Sadie's on her hands and knees, excavating a mass grave of denim. She's had some luck already—a vest lies by her feet, and a pair of black jeans so long they must be for me. Instinctively, I check the inseam. Thirty-four inches. Promising.

I gather them up, then await further instructions.

"You look like you're on a mission," I say, once it's clear she's staying quiet. We've moved on to a pile of shirts, which she rummages through seemingly by feel. Anything velvet she teases out hand over hand, like a magician. When the heap in my arms starts to teeter, she prods me to a dressing room. No—technically not a room. An alcove with a musty curtain drawn across it. I hesitate—is this . . . legal?—only for adrenaline, my jumping nerves, to push me across the threshold. The clothes I'm holding tumble. I am immediately confronted by myself, proportions warped by the cruelest of mirrors. "Ugh," I say, but then, since Sadie can't see me, I make the storky redhead hold up her fingers. Their rawness gleams. Except for the tip of my right index finger, still furry with dust.

Right. Clothes. Where to start? Jeans are easy. Fit okay too, that kind of stretchy fabric that gives the illusion of skin-tightness while still allowing you to breathe. The fabric's distressed, clawed open at the knees. Shoving my right leg in, I lose my balance, topple against the grimy mirror. "Oops," I say without really meaning to. "I'm okay." Sadie doesn't respond. Did she vanish again? No. I feel her waiting. See the scuffed toes of her Doc Martens beneath the curtain. I clear my throat, summoning more coordination as I pick through the shirts. "These are all cool," I tell her. My voice echoes inexplicably. I stare down into the heap of velvet and flannel.

So cool. So right. How am I supposed to pick? Is there a particular one she wanted to see me in, that Lindsay would especially like? At the bottom of the pile is a blouse similar to the one I admired in Sadie's closet, this lacy, velvety thing, soft as a crushed rose. I grab it. There's buttons. Half have crumbled, but I get them open and wrestle off my sweater. Air knives across me.

I forgot I'm braless.

And the shirt? See-through. I know this before I undo the collar button, before I push my arms through sleeves stiff with cigarette smoke and other girls' sweat. Loose threads jab my belly. But filled by my massive shoulders, the shirt dangles just so, and suddenly the storky redhead in the mirror doesn't look so out of place anymore. Her jeans are torn, hair wild, nipples dark as cherries beneath their black lace veil. This girl looks indomitable. Ready to flip off the world.

"All good?" a voice rasps.

Sadie. Reflexively, I cover my chest. My eyes ricochet to the girl the mirror says is me, her cheeks flushed, but . . . not from embarrassment? I press them, and heat beats against my fingertips. Breath fogs the glass.

"Yeah." My heart pounds so loudly the word barely sneaks out. "One sec." I tug the curtain back.

Sadie doesn't flinch.

Or maybe she does. There's so much warmth and noise churning through me, I can't tell for sure, only sense her drawing nearer until we're practically toe-to-toe. "This'll work?" she murmurs, gazing up into my face. Her tone's steady. Did she . . . not notice? Or she did, and the only thing standing between us and mutual annihilation is this unrelenting eye contact? Both seem plausible. I wet my lips.

"I think so. What about you? Do you like it?"

She smiles. "What's with your hair?"

Oh—I scoot my eyes away from hers, toward the mirror. I thought it looked mussed. "It must be from taking my sweater off. The static." Sadie nods approvingly. I want to smile, only I'm confused, because these clothes are so good—they're *working*—but all her reaction has me thinking of is swim practice. The contortions I'd put myself through sharing a locker room with Lindsay. Desperate to see her body but also hoping, begging, *See me. See me.* My gaze drifts helplessly back to the mirror, this shimmer on my lips where I licked them.

And then I remember something.

"What's her mouth a slice of?"

Sadie blinks. Hard, like I clapped my hands in her face. "What?"

"That's what I'm asking. The lyric in your notebook." Suddenly, I don't care if she realizes I was snooping. It's more important that she understands she can tell me anything, not just whatever flashes through her mind, but—the genuine secrets. I didn't need to feel close to her; it was the exact thing I told myself just an hour ago. Turns out that was a lie.

Her nervous laugh makes my confession worth it. The way she takes my face in both hands and smooshes my cheeks together.

"Black velvet."

"Black—"

"Don't get it? Here. *Your mouth is a slice of*"—humming, she taps her thumbs on my cheeks, alternating syllables—"then *black*, okay, all good, until, *vel-vet*? Boom! Catastrophe. Doesn't work, or so Em says. You ask me, it's viable. But I'd never let anybody sing it."

"Why not?"

"Because I—stop looking at me like that." She squeezes harder, harder, until my lips pucker. Fish face. "Stop with the doe eyes. Next you know, I'll be writing about them, too, and then what? Nothing playable to show for my efforts? Another day down the tubes?"

"Writing about . . . ?" My brow furrows. Then—

The realization soars through me.

My face still cradled in Sadie's hands. That same nervous laugh. "It's no fucking riddle, kiddo. Everything I write's about Mack, and now it's just . . ." She falters, brushing a palm against my cheek. "Got a little of you."

Sadie's palms are different than Mom's, coarse and dry. The

second I stoop to pick my old jeans off the carpet, I miss her touch. "I actually brought lipstick," I say. "It's blue, though. Which is not redhead-compatible by any stretch of the imagination, but I think Lindsay would like it anyway. Like *me* in it," I correct, remembering Sadie's phrase from the other day. Still, it feels strange bringing Lindsay up just now, an extra shove when I'm already so dizzy. Sadie writes about me . . . she writes about me . . . "It's been in my pocket all day," I add quickly, afraid I'm reeling so hard that she'll see. "I meant to try it at school, except I chickened out." When I finally find the tube, Sadie plucks it from my hand.

"What's it called, *gangrene*? No—*Blues to You*. Because that makes sense." She hooks a finger in one of my buttonholes, and I get the hint somehow, bend toward her. "So what's the deal with this chick? She like you back?"

"Uh." Blood rushes to my face. "No. Well. Maybe? She dated Peter up until recently, since the fall of junior year, but sometimes I think she only put up with him because he got her into bars and concerts and stuff. He's way older. Like, twenty. But she never really talked about boys before him. Ever. And liking one guy doesn't mean you're not queer, right? She's always showing me pictures of girls she follows on Insta and telling me how pretty she thinks they are. I mean *always*. Oh—and she likes me in lipstick. After she saw my feature shots, she told me that was like, a new side of me. You had to kind of be there, to hear the way she said it, but I thought . . . it's promising?" I'm fully aware of how pathetic this sounds.

That wanting something so badly, rationalizing it into being true, won't change reality. But if it could . . .

Sadie uncaps the lipstick. My head thrums. What time is it? Lindsay could be calling any minute, but there's no room for something as ordinary as minutes, or seconds or hours, to exist in this tiny dressing room. Sadie's got my cheek cupped in her hand, forehead scrunched in supreme concentration. The lipstick tugs across my mouth. "First time we played together, up on a big stage, Mack wore lipstick. Worse than this, though. Black. That's how I got the idea for the lyric."

"I *wanted* black!"

Sadie jumps—the lipstick jags creamily up my cheek. I apologize. Profusely. Grinning, she moves to my bottom lip. "Black would be perfect on you."

Perfect? Nobody has used that word to describe me. Ever. I scramble, desperate not to show it. "I mean"—does she have wipes? A Kleenex?—"during my photo shoot, I did think it was a little much, but I totally get it now. I would've grabbed black today if my mom had it." I flick my eyes down, to see if that pleases her, but her expression is illegible as ever, and my nipples are hard. Dampness prickles beneath my arms. "What I said about Lindsay liking it feeling promising," I venture, "do you believe that? Do you believe"—I can feel her guiding the lipstick, getting it all over my face, but I laugh because I don't care, I'm Sadie's canvas—"you seriously believe Lindsay might like me back? I'm not making the hugest mistake of my life here?"

"Anything's possible."

But that's no answer at all. I press harder. "What about my father? What would he think?"

She pauses. "I don't know."

"What do you mean? Why not? You said he . . . he was this big believer in going for it, right? So obviously, he would've encouraged me to tell Lindsay how I feel. He wouldn't have wanted me hiding my true feelings from anybody—especially if I'm in love. Especially if he thought I'd have a chance. That's not what he would've done. Right?"

Sadie's face clouds. Because I'm rambling. Because she takes coloring outside the lines very seriously, and it's going to take a whole box of wipes and possibly rubbing alcohol before this blue comes off me. *Please*, I almost beg. *Tell me that's how he would be.* I've only got an hour or so until Lindsay calls. An hour to make sure. But I push those thoughts away. Focus on Sadie's freckles. The storm brewing behind them.

"Where'd you get this idea of him being so honest, huh?" she whispers. A scratchy finger smears blue down my chin. "He hid plenty from me."

CHAPTER 17

LINDSAY HATES FLYING. AND AIRPORTS.

And people in airports.

But yeah, she laughs. "I'll come."

I sit up. "Seriously?"

"Well . . . I have to ask my dad first, obviously—"

"Which one?" Lindsay has two. There's Saulo, her birth father, and Trevor, his husband who adopted Lindsay when she was five. He's up in Canada a lot, traveling for work, but when he is home, they spend hours together—planetarium trips, flea markets. Dad stuff. I push farther up in the backseat, my view blurred by rain, smears of sidewalk and neon like all of Astoria's rushing past me, even though we're standing still. Driver doesn't comment when I roll the window down, let the drops splash onto my cheeks. "Linds?"

"Oh," she sighs, "Papá." Her name for Saulo. "Trevor's in freaking Vancouver again. But we actually have winter break coming up, second week in February? So I'm pretty sure Papá will let me. And if he doesn't, I'll tell my aunt and she'll convince him by force. She'll lose her shit if I go to New York, trust me. And my cousins . . ." She seems to think about it. "I'll be getting texts for days, no lie. You don't know how obsessed they are with New York."

Frankly, I can't comprehend why anybody's obsessed with New York. But . . . winter break. Does my school do that? I'll have to check. Mist laps my cheeks, cold and prickly. "Awesome," I say.

She laughs again. "So awesome."

And then silence. Not the uncomfortable kind, but swollen with possibility. It starts raining harder, so I pull back, only to realize as I open my eyes that we've only made it a block past the thrift store, where Driver picked me up. Sadie was gone by then. Not that she said goodbye or anything. Just pressed my hand.

Now I push a button on the armrest, and the window zips up, sealing rainy Queens behind it. My reflection in the glass gleams a faint anaphylactic blue, compliments of Sadie.

Where'd you get this idea of him being so honest?

From the world, I should've said. His interviews. From *you.*

But behind that musty dressing room curtain, I couldn't say any of that, couldn't bear the thought of breaking the spell her magic had woven between us. So I'm slouched against the car window, phone to my ear, listening to Lindsay breathe. I know her visit will be spectacular. I know this simply because there's no way it can't be. Because that's the only way to turn eighteen with my head above water.

If *he* wasn't honest, then how could I be?

"Wait," Lindsay says. "What about Mariah? Did she say yes?"

"No, but"—I hesitate—"I'm almost positive she will."

"Well, ask her soon, okay? As in, this minute? Literally right now? You know my dad. He'll be way easier to convince once I prove your mom's on board."

I laugh. This is why she'll make an excellent politician. "Okay."

"Promise?"

"I—"

"Koda, you have to promise!"

"I was going to! You didn't let me finish my sentence! I'll ask her as soon as I get home in, I don't know, twenty minutes. *Promise*," I add, and then I quirk my finger against my thigh, pinkie swear, like in middle school. She can't see, but it's exactly that sort of promise. Exactly those vibes.

"Home? Isn't it practically eight o'clock in New York? Where were you?"

My backpack lies at my feet, the THANK YOU FOR YOUR BUSINESS thrift store bag bundled on top. I straighten my pinkie until it's just touching the plastic. "With a friend."

"Ooooohh. What kind of friend? A *girl*friend?"

"Oh my God." My face flares. "Shut up! It's not like that. At all. She's . . . she's actually . . . just trust me."

"Trust you? I don't think so. I think I'll have to meet this chick for myself, really assess the situation, before I take your word for it. I mean, come on, Koda." Her giggle fades. "You're so bad at knowing when people like you."

Rain knocks against the car, against the sludge in my head. What does she mean, exactly? Who's *ever* liked me? When did I close my eyes? I'm too nervous to ask Lindsay to clarify. To tell her, *Well, I don't care about people if people aren't you.* I only squeeze my eyes shut tighter, until the whole world is black velvet. No light poking through.

CHAPTER 18

CONVINCING MOM PROVES SURPRISINGLY easy. I type some remarks up in the car about why Lindsay should be permitted to visit—Mom, above all, treasures preparedness—but I've barely gotten to the first parenthetical before she's on her phone, scrolling through the school calendar. Turns out, we don't get a whole week off in February, only a random Monday that, hallelujah, coincides with Lindsay's break. A long weekend will have to do. The matter settled, Mom lifts the phone to her ear, the line already ringing. *Saulo,* she mouths. *To finalize plans.* I nod—this really is happening—and she motions me closer, presses a quick kiss to my head. "I'm so proud of you," she whispers, not a trace of sadness in her voice. The cold shoulder I gave her last night brushed lovingly aside.

Mom will forgive practically anything, provided you show initiative. One quick, reflexive smile, and I'm off, retreating to my room before she can start dispensing advice. I can just guess what that would be.

A PowerPoint, probably. Subject: Why Lindsay Should Date Me. Minimum ten slides.

With sorting details left in the hands of our ruthlessly capable parents, there's really nothing to do in the four weeks leading up to Lindsay's visit but . . . worry. And wait. I find myself zoning out harder than ever in school, gnawing pen after pen until one finally bursts, spattering black across my lip and the known world. My classmates scream. The kid beside me asks if a squid jizzed on my face.

I switch to pencils. If Mom was around to see me slogging through my homework each night, she'd notice the teeth marks sunk into the wood, ask what's wrong, but the terror roiling inside me goes deeper than teeth marks. Before I know it, a week has passed. Then another. Homework becomes impossible. Texting Lindsay, just coping with the fact of her name on my phone screen, becomes impossible. A thousand and one breathless questions about what she should bring, where we should go, our seventy-two hours of togetherness narrowed to pop-up stores in Brooklyn, the flashiest Broadway shows. Can't we just do what we used to? Cuddle up in our comfiest pajamas and watch *Blue Planet*, contemplate confessing my love while sharks devour whale carcasses on the screen? A pathetically Koda move. Not Mack at all.

I need a distraction.

For that, Sadie was supposed to have me covered.

These past couple days, instead of bringing me to Astoria after school, Driver drops me off downtown, at the East Village recording studio where Sadie and Em are frantically rewriting their quarterly batch of songs. *Studio* makes the place sound fancy, but my excitement dips once I step off the rickety elevator to discover . . . a hallway of doors. Most of the time—I quickly discover—talking, even *whispering*, in the hall is forbidden, because behind those doors recordings are in progress. Squirty pop melodies that get stuck in your head for days, that I hum despite myself, and the faces Sadie and Em make at me as we huddle at the table in their overheated writers' room. Together, they swap lyrics for hours, singing each other's suggestions back and forth until the words lose all flavor, like overchewed food. You can tell Sadie likes having Em around to argue and share ideas with. A fact made all the more annoying when you consider how little she and Sadie have in common. Em's older, for one thing. Milky blond, with rose-gold metal glasses and a big, booming voice that easily overtakes Sadie's during their more competitive bouts of harmonizing. The second she shakes my hand, her eyebrow twitching like—*Mack's kid? Really?*—I hate her.

During the rare times when Sadie and I are alone, she's too plugged into writing mode for me to ask for more guidance. She's at the studio before me. Leaves after me. Not a press on the hand for goodbye, or even a "See you later, kiddo," but a vague flutter of her fingers, the same way she turns pages in her notebook. Once or twice, I ask if she's feeling okay, then immediately regret how childish it makes me sound, how uninformed. Sadie's an *artist.* Of course work would exert a gravity on her that I've never seen, let alone experienced, for myself. She's allowed to get a little sweaty.

So. The week leading up to Lindsay's arrival is spent not *with* Sadie, but wishing for her. Curled up with my forehead against the back of the duct-taped couch, the guitar—my father's guitar—in my lap. Teaching myself to tug the strings so gently, the sound that warbles out barely counts as sound at all. Just knowing that eventually, Sadie will hear anyway. And then she'll look up from her scribblings and smile, like she's slipping me a note.

Some days, that's enough. Other days, it's not, and the memory of her calling my father dishonest makes me want to sever every string on the guitar's neck one by one. So he cheated on her. So what? I mean, cheating is wrong, irrefutably shitty, but they got back together in the end. Didn't they? Didn't they write all those songs for their final album about how in love they were, and everybody else could kindly fuck off? I don't want to hear her say another word about my father if it's going to be untrue. That might give me a reason to dislike her—and I couldn't handle that. Not now, when Lindsay will be here tomorrow. At school, I make a desperate resolution. Get Sadie talking about him again—the *real* him. The father who will help me say what I need to.

I brave the treacherous studio elevator only to find Em

alone, grimacing over the heap of papers she and Sadie call their abortions. Failed songs. "Where's Sadie?" I ask. My backpack plunges from my shoulders, onto the damp-smelling carpet. There's another beat or two before Em looks up.

"Figured she was with you."

"Nope." I don't bother squeezing the irritation from my voice.

Em stretches. She has a cat tattoo—multiple cat tattoos—on her bicep. "Hm," she says. "The plot thickens." Like she's talking to a fourth grader.

"Not really. Her stuff's right there." Guitar propped against the armrest, jacket flung across the couch.

"Well, don't let *that* fool you, Koda Rose—Sadie does what Sadie wants. Say she's gone and vanished for real. You prepared to fill in?" She points to the little brown piano in the corner, and an image wells up without me asking it to—Sadie sitting hilariously tall and proper on the hard wooden bench, her real playing interspersed with pointed key banging whenever Em gets distracted.

I swallow, realizing that her finger is now aimed at me. "I can't play piano. My dad couldn't either." The significance obviously escapes her. She throws her hands up, like, *Guess I'm fucked.* I try to defend Sadie. "It's not that big of a deal. She could be in the bathroom."

"For an hour?"

"Maybe? She always takes a long time."

Her eyes widen with what seems like alarm, but she rolls

them quickly, muttering, "If she's powdering her nose."

I pull my coat off and get comfy on the sofa arm, the guitar propped gingerly on my knee. Still muttering, Em goes over to the piano and flips the cover up. Witchy cat eyes leer from her bicep.

"Shows what you know," I say under my breath. Sadie never wears makeup.

It's snowing when we leave the studio. I can't yank my hood up quickly enough and get trapped for an extra cycle of the revolving door. By the time I'm free, Sadie and Em are lingering beneath the streetlight, smoking into each other's faces. Once Sadie finally did show up—no explanation, no apology, slinking into her place at the piano—their rental of the room had nearly expired. Em freaked out. Forty-five minutes later, she's still pissed, gesturing wildly. "Don't be stupid," she's saying. "I refuse to believe you're that naive. I refuse to believe you're incapable of change. Meaningful change, Sades. You're—you're jeopardizing your *career.* Your *life.* And what about me? Do you know what it does to me to see you doing this to yourself again, the thoughts it puts into my head? Or do you not care about me anymore, either?"

Sadie exhales, and I hang back, wanting to interrupt but not knowing what to say. Whatever they're arguing about, it clearly has nothing to do with me. So I jam my hands in my coat pockets and wait. Embarrassed. Jealous. Like I really am in fourth grade.

Clouds coil above Sadie's head. I can't make her breath out from the smoke as she says, "Here's another idea. You worry about you, and I worry about me. What do you think?" And then Em accuses Sadie of being reckless, of *not* worrying about herself, going on and on until Sadie seizes Em's face in her hands and kisses her. Once on each cheek. "Bye," Sadie chirps.

Snow swirls. I'm molten, but I wait for Em to get out of earshot, for the crowds and snow to all but erase her, before I ask, "What was that about?"

"Oh." Sadie hefts up the guitar case. "Em's like that. Thinks she knows best and all."

"Like Teddy." I slosh after her across the street.

I'm proud of myself for bringing Teddy up—proud Sadie's shown me so many pieces of herself that I can make connections, but Sadie doesn't acknowledge this at all, just shoves her hand deeper into the pocket of her coat. There are more questions I want to ask. *Change how? Doing what to yourself?* Only, I kind of don't need to. I understand what it's like, everybody demanding something different from your existence, pushing and pulling until the pressure practically atomizes you. I couldn't subject Sadie to that. Not when she's the only person who hasn't done it to me.

Besides, Em's yelling isn't a tenth as important as what came after. That question, when I finally ask it, comes out casually. "How come you kissed her goodbye this time?"

The sidewalk narrows and Sadie slips ahead of me, the case's clasps rattling. "Italian manners." The back of her leather jacket is streaked with melting snow. I count drops and don't remind her that Lindsay will be here in a matter of hours—that I still can't imagine kissing her, kissing any girl, that confidently. I don't point out that Sadie's never kissed me.

It's dark as hell for seven p.m., the air black ice. The sidewalk widens, breathing room again, and I move next to Sadie, trusting her to lead me through the East Village's twisty streets. There's a stark difference between here and where I live, dozens of blocks up—the buildings almost as low as they are in Queens, smothered with graffiti. Nearly everybody we pass resembles Sadie. Some kind of artist, draped in as many kooky accessories as they must have ideas. Not that I'm intimidated or anything. I'm with Sadie Pasquale, and even if she doesn't seem to feel like talking right now, our breath clouds are mixing, guitar case bumping against my calf. I'm worthy at last to walk among them.

At some point, we must pass the corner where Driver usually picks me up, but neither of us mentions it. When the glowing green orbs of the subway come into view, I recognize the station instantly. The same one I ambushed her at back in December. Except the Christmas carols have been shut off, the sushi restaurant closed. The metal grate makes stripes on Sadie's face as she twists her cigarette out. If she smokes another, we'll get an extra five minutes together. At least.

When she takes out her MetroCard, my heart sinks. She can't leave yet. "Can I ride with you?" I ask before I fully grasp what I'm saying.

To my surprise, she doesn't agree right away. Just glances toward the narrow, dripping steps, like this is not the best idea I have ever had. "I don't know if that's . . ." She stops herself. "We live in opposite directions."

"So? You could ride with me to my stop and then turn around. Or—or I could ride to Queens with you and have my driver pick me up. I know it's risky," I add, trying to guess what's making her so reluctant, "but we still need to make it official, right? My New Yorker status? Please." Sadie keeps her eyes trained carefully away from mine, tapping the MetroCard against her mouth.

Actually, she explains, leading me underground, public transit's not as risky as you'd think—each car anonymity heaven. "More likely to get accosted in my own neighborhood, wouldn't you say?" The grin she flashes over her shoulder seems strained. I decide not to worry about it.

The station reeks of old pee, the floor smeared with mud and half-melted snow. Sadie swipes her card for me, and then I linger awkwardly, obstructing the flow of passengers no matter where I stand, until a gaggle of French tourists distracts the booth attendant long enough for her to hop the turnstile.

"Only illegal if you get caught," she says, seeing my face.

Her knuckles are chapped, frozen stiff, and she blows on them while we wait on the platform, one foot resting on the wall behind her. A movie poster. Something about superheroes, this epic battle between good and evil, that I'll eventually have to pretend I've seen. I don't mention this to Sadie, or pull my hands from my coat pockets. In fact, I'm glad she's acting standoffish. How would I invite her to tuck a hand in with mine anyway? My newfound bravery only goes so far.

When the 6 train lumbers in, my stomach curdles. There's more people crammed in the car than seems physically possible, let alone safe. Sadie fends them off with the guitar case, hauling me aboard by my wrist. The doors shut on my coat, stagger open. I press forward, absorbing multiple death stares.

The first couple of stops are unbearable, the whole length of my impossibly long body crushed against the doors, but after Union Square, things loosen up enough for Sadie to snag me a seat. I end up smashed between some kid in an NYU cap blasting trance music without headphones, and a lady sniffing her own hair. With every lurch, the guitar case bumps against my knees. Sadie can't look at me without laughing. I laugh back, so relieved to see her out of the funk Em put her in that I don't mind how sweaty I'm getting in my sticky plastic seat. I just try to relish it. Like her—a true subterranean.

Once the NYU kid gets off, Sadie squeezes next to me. "Seat's still warm." She props the case between her knees, arms around its neck. "What a gentleman." I giggle, rolling my eyes so she'll comprehend how gross that really is. Other than that, we stay quiet. Not because there is nothing to say—there are so many things—but because our eyes speak what we're thinking anyway. Doors open. Bodies filter off. My phone hums—Lindsay wondering how cold it is and if she should pack a coat.

"What's wrong?" Sadie asks, hugging the case.

"Nothing. It's—it's just Lindsay." Then, seizing my chance: "I haven't showed you a picture yet." Except we're several feet below sea level by now, and Instagram refuses to load until we're clanking into the next station. Twenty-Eighth Street? Where is that? I realize, swiping through pics, that I don't actually know which stop is mine.

At last, I find a picture where we both look decent. I have my one-piece on. Lindsay's hair hangs in double braids.

"Blondie," Sadie jokes, passing back my phone. Her smile dips. "Must be weird having all those pictures on you. Don't think I could quite handle that, having Mack, all those memories at my fingertips."

"Oh." I scan passengers for signs of eavesdropping, but Sadie's so whispery. And everybody seems super committed to denying anything is happening around them at all, blank-faced and head-phoned. "You do have some pictures of him, though, right?" The one facedown on the nightstand, maybe. But it's hard to imagine her disrespecting him like that. "Where do you keep them? I haven't seen any."

"Ready? Close your eyes—I want you to picture this. A book, *an actual book*, with pockets for storing your most cherished memories." Sadie's still joking. Smiling huge, even as she presses the back of her hand to her mouth, stifling a yawn. "You wouldn't have seen them. I keep those photo albums . . . not a hiding place, understand. Somewhere I can get them. But they can't get me." She falls silent, rewinding back to some private memory. I nudge her out of it.

"So can I see them? Not if you don't want me to," I add quickly as her gaze slides from mine. "If it'd hurt you too much." She wraps her arms tighter around the guitar case, then shrugs and yawns again.

"Whatever you want, kiddo. Remind me."

Before Lindsay gets here would be preferable. But the stops keep coming, so many I forget to worry and relax into the motion of the train. Eyes shut, letting it lull me. Sadie will say when my stop's up. So many people are packed onto our bench that we're practically in each other's laps, shoulders jammed together, her leg jittering against mine. But as the doors shuffle open, and more and more people get off, we stay close, practicing our apathetic New Yorker faces until we catch each other's eyes and bust up laughing. It's not until we clank into another station, and the garbled voice over the intercom announces One-Twenty-Fifth Street, that I bolt upright. "We missed it, didn't we? We missed my stop?"

Sadie does not share my panic. A smirk works at her mouth. "Well, damn. Guess we're going to the Bronx."

The Bronx. I settle back against the seat, tossing her a glare in case she thinks I don't realize she tricked me, so she won't notice I'm actually too thrilled to care. This is an adventure. As we pull out of the station, I spot an ad for the New York Aquarium and wonder what it'd be like to bring Sadie there myself someday, letting her glimpse who I was before she blew my world up with her magic. Truth is, being a fish isn't that different from being in a band. You travel together, wear the same stuff, except instead of ripped-up velvet, fish have scales, and stripes for camouflage. So I tell Sadie . . . I find myself telling her about how Lindsay and I used to go to the Santa Monica Aquarium, specifically the tide pool exhibit, even as it became increasingly obvious that we were the oldest kids there. Rocks and crabs, those she'd touch no problem, but not my favorites—the silent, gliding rays. One day I grabbed her hand and held it underwater until a ray slipped past, billowing jelly across our fingers. Lindsay screamed. Me too, even though I wasn't grossed out.

Sadie smiles. "That's sweet."

I shrug. "All that story really makes me think about is . . . telling Lindsay I love her, and then . . . I . . . I'm just afraid of—"

"Showing her your jelly."

"Well, their fins are made of cartilage. But yeah. Basically. Like, this thing that's so integral to my existence won't matter to her. I don't know if that makes any sense." Now is the part where Sadie assures me it makes perfect sense. Where she tucks a lock of hair behind my ear and reminds me how she met my father, in a dusty music room while their classmates were at lunch. She didn't laugh when she heard his terrible playing. She moved his finger higher up on the frets. She whispered, *Like this.* But Sadie doesn't remind me of any of that now. I'm not even sure where I first read that story—which online article, or archived blog post.

Sadie says, "Guess I won't be seeing you for a while, then."

"No," I say, only just realizing it myself. "Well—she's coming early tomorrow, and leaving Monday afternoon."

Only three days, but Sadie and I haven't been apart that long since Christmas, and I guess . . . I guess I've been so panicked over Lindsay that I haven't fully considered how much being without Sadie this weekend will suck. Does she feel that way too? Quickly, she turns her head away, staring toward the back of the car where a man sits folded up and alone, a brown paper bag wedged under one arm. I can't tell if he's passed out or not. If that's regret, or relief, tugging at Sadie's mouth.

"I'll miss you," I say. One of us has to. "Seriously. I'll be going through withdrawal."

Her head snaps around. "You know nothing about withdrawal."

That's . . . true. I splutter, not sure how I messed up. "Yeah, yeah, I know, it's just, it's an expression? People at school say it all the time—it's not meant to be taken literally." But Sadie seems to have forgiven me already, picking idly at a pot leaf sticker on the guitar case, its edges crumbling and faded. At least, she might've forgiven me. All night, her mood's been as impossible to decode as that song of hers I found, a wad of slashed-up paper. Before I realized it was about me.

"I wish . . ." I push my fingertips against my mouth, but there's no stopping what I'm about to say, no taking the words back once they're out. "Lindsay doesn't know I know you. I keep wanting to tell her, but. I don't know why I can't, I just . . . I want you for myself." It's humiliating, telling her this. Also weirdly liberating, the closest you could come to a love confession without uttering *love* itself, not that Sadie gives indication that this pleases or disgusts her, or registers at all. The longer I sit here, the clearer it becomes that she's not going to answer. The more impossible it seems that within seventy-two hours, all my agonizing, and obsessing over Lindsay, will come to an end, that the next time I see Sadie, I'll be on the other side of this feeling, this mess of fear and excitement and dread that's plagued me my whole teenage life. That's just fact, even if once I've regurgitated my entire soul onto her, all Lindsay says is, *I'm sorry, Koda. I don't like you like that.*

Maybe I've secretly always known that response is the only logical outcome. Maybe this whole trip is just one needlessly elaborate step toward moving on. What if it's not rejection that scares me?

What if it's not knowing who I'll be, if I don't feel exactly this way?

It makes me wish Lindsay won't have an answer ready, that she wasn't so good at telling me when I'm being dumb, need to step back, take a break. Her silence I could handle.

Not Sadie's.

Hers burns a hole right through me.

"God, kiddo," Sadie murmurs. She glances around the depleted car. "You crush me. You know that?"

"I'm being honest. Like you said my father wasn't."

She looks away again, but I didn't mean it like that. I meant—maybe dishonesty's not so bad after all. Maybe both have their place. I could, for example, tell Lindsay nothing. I could choose to ache.

Sadie lifts my chin. I've been gazing at my boots.

"Mack and I used to ride the subway like this all the time, the Bronx to Manhattan, Manhattan to the Bronx, just careening through the tunnels all night. We didn't really have any place else to go, you know? And the trains were so warm. He'd wrap me up in his arms, and I'd sleep. To this day, when I ride the train, it's a damn ordeal staying awake."

"It is really warm down here," I admit. Cue my ugly, bleating laugh. "Stupid warm." The greatest city in the world, and it's not even climate-controlled.

When Sadie starts dozing, my mouth thwarts me again.

"You can put your head on my shoulder. If you want."

The weight surprises me. I dimly recall learning that human heads weigh ten to eleven pounds, which I can now officially verify. I take a swim breath. Let it out nice and slow, like I have tons of practice having people fall asleep on me. Or at least wishing Lindsay would.

The train gets held up for a while at some place called Brook Avenue, and when it resumes moving, the motion jars Sadie awake. "God," she mumbles, thumbing her chin, "drooled a river on you. I'm sorry." No prob, I tell her. I genuinely don't care. She resumes picking at the pot sticker. I pick with her—coaxing a corner up until all that remains stuck is the "4" in "4/20." Sadie squeezes my hand. "Enough."

I nod and she smiles, like maybe she thinks her voice came

out too firm. But I understand completely. Disrespectful, downright sacrilegious, to destroy what he put there.

And then—because we have a while until we need to get off, and the car is practically empty and I think both of us are wishing this ride would never end—our hands just stay together. For a second, I don't move, afraid this is an accident. Afraid she doesn't notice what we're doing or worse, that she will at any moment, and take her hand away.

CHAPTER 19

LINDSAY DYED HER HAIR BACK TO ITS NATURAL black. When she dives into the backseat, I get a whole mouthful of it.

"Surprise!" she screams. "You like?"

I promise I do, and she pulls me into another hug. The car starts moving.

"My dads helped me with it before we left for LAX this morning. It was like, beyond last minute."

We're still hugging, my chin smashed against her shoulder, her hair teasing my nostrils, chemical-stiff. It smells vaguely like bathroom cleaner. Like dye streaming into her dads' precious quartz sink that time she absolutely needed to *go purple* freshman year, and we got in so much trouble. I remember reading the directions out loud as she hunted for a suitably crappy towel, praying she wouldn't notice my hands trembling as she guided them to her scalp. *Help me rinse?*

I pull back. We're jammed up with airport traffic and Lindsay laughs, shoving me. I laugh too.

"This is wild," she keeps saying, pressed up against the window. "Oh my God, I can't believe I'm actually here. I've never been to New York. You knew that, right? Nobody at school would believe me when I told them that. Like, how is it that I've been pretty much all over the country, but never to New York? My whole family's losing their minds."

Her excitement makes the eels that have been slithering inside me since last night relax slightly. I barely slept. Barely choked down breakfast. But now, despite all that, the first flashes of heartburn I've experienced in weeks, I shake my head, grinning. "I know everything about you."

"Oh." She grins back. "Right."

Traffic loosens, and we roll down the ramp toward the highway through scraps of leftover fog. It's obvious I should say something else. Something to keep the flirtation going, if flirting is what we're doing. Except my heart thuds so loud even a passing semi can't drown it out.

"So," Lindsay continues, flopping back against the seat, "what are we doing first?"

It's just that I know how talking goes. Not being able to speak until suddenly you are, words gushing, washing yourself and everybody you love away in a torrent of anxiety. It's like I haven't thought about what to do together at all. Like I didn't whisper the details to my pillow all night.

"It's a surprise," I manage.

Lindsay says skeptically, "You hate surprises."

"Not this one. And . . ." An invisible force grips my throat. "Y-you like them. You'll like this one."

Her grin widens.

The eels slink back.

If I'd decided to leave the house with my black lipstick after all. If I'd worn the new clothes, the ones Sadie found for me. Then I'd have the courage.

Slyly, Lindsay pokes my arm. Beneath her fingernail, my flesh tingles. Electric goose bumps.

Don't tell her how you feel, this voice in my head urges. My father's voice. *But you have to,* he says, answering himself. *Do it afraid, remember?* Two throaty scratched-up whispers.

Seventy-two hours to make a decision. To choose one side of this line Sadie has drawn, that he drew, between dishonesty and truth. What if that's not enough time to work out the solution, what *he* would want me to do?

"Well," Lindsay says, taking her nail away, "you'd better have some big plans to justify . . . I don't know, how ridiculously MIA you've been lately? Did you even look at the links I sent you?"

I swallow. "Yeah, yeah, totally, it's just all that touristy stuff is—"

"Wait! Did you see the one about—"

Inauthentic.

"Hold on, let me find it . . ."

A waste.

"Here! Okay." Lindsay thumbs rapidly through her phone. "It's that thing where you can basically see the whole city from Top of the Rock, I think the building's called? Is that the surprise? Tell me"—she holds her phone to my face—"seriously, because if it is, I'm going to die"—the text blurred compared to her shiny gold jacket that Peter told her was ugly, those spirals of hair fizzing all around her cheeks. I glance away, and when I look back, Lindsay's still vibrating with anticipation, my resolve in pieces. Light-headed, I lean over her to point out landmarks as we inch down the parkway. Empire State Building. Chrysler Building. One World Trade. From this angle, it's easy as looking at a postcard. The whole island laid out in diorama mode.

"Wild," she repeats. "I can't believe you can see them all at once like this. Just, chilling there across the water. Where are we now?" I explain that I don't know the name of the neighborhood, exactly. But the airport is in Queens.

"Queens. Got it." She strains against her seat belt, riveted by the view. When we cross the Triborough Bridge, she cracks a window. More hair whips from her bun. "That flight was unending, Koda, I'm not kidding. Six hours! And you know what's crazier? You could fly from New York City to London in about that time. Papá told me."

I lean away from her lashing hair, furious with myself for not having something to add to this by now. Something like, *Well, my father would've known all about travel times and airplanes too.* Of all the questions I've asked Sadie, why didn't I think of this one? They traveled all over the world together.

Automatically, my thoughts pull to her. What she's doing today, and where, with who . . . if she'd just freaking answer the texts I sent on the way to the airport, I might know. But here I am, stuck speculating. Studio again, probably. Em. Knocking seltzer cans over with their hands as they argue.

I look over to see Lindsay tipping her head back, taking deep, ecstatic breaths of pollution.

I'll introduce them by explaining, *Sadie's the reason we don't need to see New York.*

Sadie *is* New York.

"Oh man, I almost forgot." Lindsay grabs her phone. "Insta stories. I swore to my little cousins that I'd . . ."

This will go okay. I know it will. Yesterday, Sadie said, *You crush me.* She swirled her scratchy thumb on my palm.

"Koda? Ready?"

Lindsay smushes close, holding her phone up. My body thumps.

"Should we do nice?" she asks. "Or wild?"

I hesitate. Are those not allowed to be the same thing?

She whacks me. "Okay, no, you are so not starting with the overthinking. I'm declaring it now, this is an overthinking-free weekend. Therefore"—she clears her throat—"we'll each do what we want on the count of three. One, two—"

We both stick our tongues out, like Sadie and my father in all those old pictures.

• • •

Mom hugs Lindsay almost longer than I did when we stop by her office to say hello. Squeezes her arms, tells her how great her new hair looks, while I suck the end of my braid.

"I thought we could all do dinner tonight," Mom says, leaning back against her desk. Wearing those beige suede boots that go past her knees, hair arranged in a fist at her nape. "Around—let's say six? I'm getting myself out of here early. That's a promise." Lindsay says dinner sounds awesome—can we do Greek?—and I force myself to agree, even though dinner won't give us much time with Sadie.

"Fantastic." Mom claps her hands. "I'm sure we could find a great Greek place. I'll have my assistant"—she rummages around the paperwork on her desk, peeks under her laptop—"text you the address. Do you girls have any plans in the meantime? It looks beautiful out there, with the . . . with . . ." She picks the laptop back up, like the word she's searching for might be hidden beneath it. Then she sighs. "The sun."

"Not really," I reply at the same time Lindsay says, "Koda won't tell me."

Mom lowers the laptop, a question revolving in her eyes. I think quickly.

"Down in Brooklyn. The aquarium. It was supposed to be a surprise, but now . . ." I heave a shrug, acting super put out until gradually, her suspicion passes. She pats my arm.

"I'm sorry, honey, I didn't mean to spoil it. You went there recently, right?" To Lindsay, she adds, "I'm sure you'll both have a really nice time."

"Definitely. I love aquariums." Lindsay glances at me.

Back on the sidewalk, I draw her aside. "Can you keep a secret?"

The light is sharp like it only gets on winter afternoons, lemon juice in our eyes. Lindsay's wearing a scarf. She only put it on once Driver dropped us off at the office, a hilarious ordeal that involved popping her suitcase open, a whole ski trip's worth of scarves tumbling onto the crosswalk before she found the right one. Now she squints at me from behind it.

"Did you seriously just ask me that?"

Okay—stupid question. But this is an extremely sensitive situation. "We're not going to the aquarium, Linds. We're going . . . Just trust me that my mom will flip if she finds out. Okay? And I don't mean like, yell a bunch and take my phone away for the night. We're talking ground me to freaking infinity here. So you have to promise . . ." Her mouth crumples. I rush on. "You can't tell her where we're going, or that the person I'm about to introduce you to is . . . Don't tell my mom that we know each other. Basically, just—don't mention this person. At all. Ever. My mom hates her. Like, *hates* her, and if she knew about us, she'd never let me see her again. So promise. Promise you won't say anything to her."

"Hates who?" Lindsay demands. "You're not making sense."

The scarf is the same cashmere one she piles on any time temps in LA dip below 70. It's chillier than that today—30 at least, not that there's time for specifics. As I lean to whisper in Lindsay's ear, the fabric brushes my mouth.

When her eyes meet mine, they're enormous.

"For real," I confirm. Pride swells up in me. Overwhelming, practically tidal. If I'd known Lindsay would be this astonished, I wouldn't have kept Sadie secret for so long.

Lindsay looks down, gnawing her bottom lip like she did in middle school. "But how did you meet her? Did . . . why . . . I mean, if your mom doesn't want you hanging out with Sadie—"

"Shh!" I cover her mouth.

Her eyes are even wider now, so big that you can see the brown flecks that make them hazel. Warmth oozes against my fingers as she whispers, "If your mom doesn't want you hanging out with her, don't you think that's a bad sign?" She licks my palm and I squeal, flailing away. "Seriously, Koda."

I shake my head, pushing my irritation down, my disappointment. This was not the reaction I expected. "That's exactly why we should be hanging out. One of like, a million reasons."

"Parents say those things for a reason," Lindsay insists. "I mean, yeah, it's super annoying, but she's only looking out for your best interest—"

Best interest? I laugh. "My mom's too selfish."

Her eyes flash. "It's selfish of you to say that."

Please. Like I need another one of Lindsay's hypocritical lectures about family. Like she's some authority just because she's got not just *parents*, but nieces and nephews and little cousins, grandparents she actually gets to visit, even if it's only a couple weeks out of the year. She still disobeys her dads, sneaks out, smokes, gets caught, all the time. But pointing this out will only start a fight. I move off down the street, saying, "This situation with Sadie is different. You'll see when you meet her."

The sidewalk is crowded, full of people walking too slowly, with too many bags. We're on the west side, but my phone should know the fastest route across town. I swipe and swipe, hunting for a landmark that'll bring us closest to the studio, whose address I probably should've memorized by now. Lindsay shouts questions at my back. "Huh?" I turn around. Some old church—would that be nearby?

"Your friends," she enunciates slowly. "When do I get to meet them?"

Sunlight jags into my eyes. I throw a hand up to shield them. "Sadie's my friend."

Lindsay's cheeks are pink from the wind. She shoves a bit of hair behind her ear, only for it to spring back immediately. "What about that one girl?" she says quietly. "Your not-girlfriend?"

The sound that scrambles out of me is not quite a laugh, but close enough.

A woman carrying a yoga mat pushes between us. It's yellow, with a print of cats eating pizza that Lindsay stares at long after the woman has disappeared around the block.

"I was with Sadie when you said that," I explain.

Her eyes zap to me.

I add weakly, "'Assume' makes an 'ass' of 'u' and 'me.'" An

infuriating Momism, but easier than reminding Lindsay that Sadie was my *father's* girlfriend. That she's actually easier to love than you'd think.

My ears are scalding, Lindsay's a little red too. Like we share this genetic weakness against anything too embarrassing or cold. Quickly, to stop her mouth from crumpling more, I tell her all I've held on to about Sadie. Like how cool she is, and funny. I tell her about when we went thrifting together, laughing so hard—real laughter—that there's hardly any room for the story, Sadie scribbling all over me. I explain, in hi-def detail, every last glorious instance of her comparing me to my father, how we held hands on the subway yesterday, and when I finally come up for air, Lindsay has moved away from me, turtled so deep into her scarf I can't see her mouth at all.

CHAPTER 20

THE ELEVATOR GROANS. I STAB THE *UP* ARROW repeatedly, instructing Lindsay to ignore the sign.

"You mean the one that says 'out of order'?" she asks, gazing around the dusty lobby.

"Yeah"—I hit the button some more—"it still works most of the time, so. We take our chances."

"We?"

"Sadie and me." At last, a ding. The doors shuffle open. "Who else?" I say as we squeeze inside.

"I guess this is just a lot of information to take in all at once? First you tell me that you met your dad's ex, that you've been *friends*, or something, for two months, and now suddenly you're a 'we'?"

"I told you, we hang out all the time. What else would we be?"

Lindsay shrugs. Shrugs again when I motion for her to push the button for the fifth floor, which, okay—I'll press it.

Since moving to New York, operating an elevator by myself has become an unexpected luxury. A poster behind Lindsay's head explains basic first aid. I stare at it as we ascend, the elevator sighing old-dog sighs. Lindsay fiddles with a thread on her sleeve.

"Why didn't you tell me about her?"

My leg jiggles. This is taking forever? A literal eternity? We're going to the fifth floor. Not Saturn. "I don't know."

"Bullshit, Koda, of course you know. So spill. Why?"

My turn to shrug. When is it my turn to interrogate her? I've got lots of questions. Like why, in the two hours since she's arrived, it's starting to feel like that's how long we've known each other. Two hours, two *minutes*, instead of four years. I don't recognize her attitude, or the way she's twisted up her hair, the look she's giving me . . . anything. Behind her, a genderless cartoon person clutches their throat, which words along the bottom claim is the international symbol for "choking." I don't know what this poster is doing in a music studio elevator. I don't know why I can't just tell Lindsay that okay, yeah, maybe I am selfish, a coward, but this freaking inquisition alone justifies hoarding Sadie all to myself. "She values her privacy," I say pathetically.

Lindsay shoves more hair behind her ear. Jealous, obviously.

The doors ding, launching my heart even higher into my throat. Everything here reminds me of Sadie, whispers, *almost there*—the shabby carpet and beige walls that Lindsay eyes suspiciously, her lip between her teeth. Even the woody pencil smell is totally Sadie, not that I have any way of explaining that as we approach the tiny writers' room at the end of the hall. Maybe it's pervy to notice how somebody smells. Dangerous. Like I couldn't mention the pencil thing without also confessing, *You know, like how chlorine reminds me of you?*

Pressed against me in the narrow hall, Lindsay doesn't smell very chlorinated anyway. Only slightly minty from the gum she must've chomped on the plane. A sign taped to the door says DO NOT DISTURB!!!!!! in rose-gold Sharpie. I'm about to knock when Lindsay covers my hand.

"It's different," she says.

"What is?"

"Deciding not to tell your mom, whatever, that's your business, but if you can't tell *me*, your best friend, that you've met someone, shouldn't that be your biggest clue that maybe something's wrong? I don't like this, Koda. It's weird. Just like, weird vibes. Your dad wasn't even on good terms with her by the end. Everybody knows—"

Rage riptides me. "Don't talk about him," I hiss. We'll get kicked out of here if we don't keep our voices down. "Don't tell me what he was or wasn't. You don't know, okay? Nobody knows. Only Sadie—"

"But haven't you ever wondered why Sadie wants to hang out with you in the first place? Why . . ." She sees me grimacing, and her voice comes down an inch. "Why your mom doesn't like her?"

The challenge bursts out of me before I can stop it. "Do

you like her? The girl Peter cheated on you with?"

Lindsay flinches. Pop music starts pulsing somewhere down the corridor.

"That's what I thought," I mumble, turning away. Not realizing we're still holding hands until I tug mine free, and knock on the door.

Sadie's seated at the piano with her back to us, a pencil shoved behind her ear. Wearing the same lacy T-shirt, same ripped jeans, from yesterday. "Listen, Em." Her fingers wander the keys, this tiptoe of a sound. "We'll do a bump, all right? One little bump, for old times' sake? That's all I'm asking."

"Um." I hesitate. "Sadie?"

The piano bleats. She twists around.

"Sorry," I stammer, momentarily ashamed not to be the person she was expecting, fully, one hundred percent not Em, but Sadie's already scrambling off the bench, wrapping me in a giant hug. God she smells good. I bury my nose in her bandanna, just breathing, until I remember . . . "Oh." Her arms slide from my neck. "This is the friend I was telling you about . . ." It's exactly the reception I've been craving, Sadie so frenzied and flushed to see me that introducing Lindsay feels awkward by comparison, like delivering a book report without notes. What can I tell Sadie about her that I haven't already said? That's actually coherent? Sadie gnaws the zipper on her jacket, radiating that gloriously twitchy energy that reminds me of when we first met. Lindsay, still twisting that loose thread, edges in from the hall.

Sadie offers her little hand. "Thought you'd be blond. Like in the picture Koda showed me?"

A rush of embarrassment. Lindsay blinks at Sadie's outstretched hand. "I was blond for a while," she says, "but I got sick of it." As they shake, I watch Lindsay's face carefully for a reaction—some sign that she's decided Sadie's not so bad. Her glare blasts me over Sadie's head. "It wasn't the real me."

I glare back. Sadie slips between us and shuts the door. "Your timing's impeccable, kiddo. You seen Em?"

"No."

Lindsay hangs back, the thread wound around her thumb. I'd invite her to sit down, show her the guitar—where is the guitar?—but Sadie's piano-bound, dragging me by my coat sleeve.

"Well, let me show you the hot bullshit we've been working on all morning." We perch together on the narrow bench, and Sadie dumps her notebook into my lap. I laugh, struggling to prop it open as she bangs keys, which makes me laugh harder. Sadie creates music even when she's trying not to.

"Hold on." I flip through her pages. "Which ones are we—"

"Pick! They're all trash. Wait." She snatches the notebook back, then churns through more pages, landing on a spill of wriggly blue ballpoint. "This one I'm not *that* ashamed of. All right." She cracks her knuckles. "Ready?"

I nod eagerly.

"You've got to be honest."

My heart dips. From the corner of my eye, I see Lindsay has made her way to the leather sofa without me, and that she's sitting silently, coat folded across her lap. The exact way I used to sit at the parties she dragged me to, after she'd disappeared with Peter. *Miss me?* she'd joke when she came back. I'd look away. So terrified of telling her the truth that fear locked me shut. Honesty has never been my best quality.

But it wasn't my father's, either, apparently.

"Okay." My knuckles don't crack like Sadie's, but I give them a good flex anyway. "I'll try."

She runs a finger over the keys, making no sound at all this time, and I shiver remembering that day at her apartment. *Fear's always there.* Slow, delicate trace of my jawline. Good shivers. I lean closer. Her lips part.

Sadie's voice is smoke wisping from a blown-out candle, the song unlike any of hers I've heard. A story about going for a drive one upstate winter, to a place called Grafton Lake. The boy is nervous about traveling so far just to skip stones, but the girl says no problem, she says—Sadie nudges me to reach the far keys—*"I'll watch for ice"*—and then the chorus comes in—*"Oh, oh"*—I think it's the chorus—*"I watched for ice while you drove, oh, oh, but it wasn't that cold . . ."* Sadie teases the keys, her head tipped back, and even though we're stuck in this crappy studio and the song's not done, I can already feel the snow in my eyelashes, wet wool fuzzing up my tongue. It makes me want to cry a little. It makes me want to run.

With her. To a town so distant and cold our breath freezes

around us in scarves, the whole world iced over, glinting like the edge of a blade. Up there, I wouldn't have to tell Lindsay anything. Up there, it'd just be Sadie and me, her memories of my father keeping us both warm. I shut my eyes. Piano notes wink out one by one.

Sadie scoots back, mumbling how this shit will never make it on the radio.

I giggle. "Definitely not."

She pinches me. Like this is not the best, most honest compliment I could give her. And Sadie is smiling, gazing at me with those bottomless eyes. On impulse, I rest my cheek on top of her head. Heat from her skull leaps against me.

"I'd do anything to see that lake with you," I whisper. Get my license. Snowshoe. Anything.

Chuckling, Sadie pokes her fingers through my braid.

I lift my head to find Lindsay still moping on the sofa. I want to jump on it with her. I want to grab her shoulders and yell, *Sadie wrote this song for me!*

"What'd you think?" I ask hoarsely.

"We should go," she answers without looking up.

CHAPTER 21

NEITHER OF US SPEAKS ON THE TRAIN RIDE uptown. Hands buried in our pockets, sitting piano-formal on the plastic seats. More than once I try to catch Lindsay's eye, but she's avoiding me again for whatever reason, obsessed with the electronic board that lists stops overhead. Astor Place, Twenty-Third, Twenty-Eighth . . . I stare out the windows across the car, my reflection pasted against the dark tunnel. For the first time, I look how I feel. Dizzy and flushed from the current zinging between Sadie and me. Not talking about her is unbearable. When we stop at Union Square, passengers file off until the car's as good as empty. I touch Lindsay's shoulder. "So?"

"So, what?" she snarls.

My hand snaps back. "What do you mean, what? Are we just not going to talk? Tell me what you thought about Sadie." Like, *She's incredible, Koda!* We could throw a two-girl party, howl and dance like we did the day Peter asked her out. She could at least pretend to be happy for me, too.

Lindsay's quiet a moment, chewing the gloss off her lips. "I think we should tell your mom."

The train hits a bump, tossing us forward. I grab onto a pole. "I told you—"

"But she's a freak, Koda, can't you see? Too skinny. Those big eyes, her scuzzy hair . . . You didn't introduce me by name, which would've been awkward enough, but she didn't even care! She didn't ask a single question about me, or who I am, what I like—nothing. I mean," she relents, "her songs are . . . she's really good, but she doesn't sound like she used to, on all those old recordings and stuff. Her voice sounds . . . it's all used up. And . . ." She pulls away, and I can't tell where she's looking anymore, just that it's anywhere but me. The pole I'm still clutching. A set of anatomically unlikely boobs scratched into the seat between us. "The way you and Sadie cling to each other is . . ." She doesn't bother to finish.

"You're just jealous." I flop back against the seat, only to realize how bad my stomach's cramping. "Sadie and I don't 'cling' to each other."

Lindsay shakes her head, and a sprig of dark hair falls from her bun, brushes her lips. She thumbs it back. "Well, what was she talking about when we first got there anyway? A *bump*? What does that even mean? It sounds like, I don't know, code, for drugs—"

"Shut up. Sadie doesn't do drugs." Only my father. Though

I guess . . . if Sadie says he did them . . . but I would know. Of course I would know if Sadie was high. When I say so, Lindsay laughs.

"Sorry, but I used to hang out with Peter's band all the time, so I think maybe I'm the more trusted authority on what musicians do? I'm not naive about that stuff. Not like you." She burrows into her scarf, muttering, "Ironically."

I look roughly away. Farther down the car, a woman cradles a shivery dog, and I stare at his vibrating ears, the tangles of brown fur that made me mistake him for an old slipper at first. Tears sear my throat.

She's not wrong. For all the time I've spent with Sadie—two months now—the facts I've learned about my father amount to practically nothing. Scraps. I've never really thought about this before now. Never truly cataloged the bits of him that Sadie's shown me, taken an inventory. Why would I? It'd be excruciating. But I don't know how to explain this to Lindsay without breaking down. I don't know how to admit, maybe I am naive. Maybe my hunger for Sadie is a little off. But if both Lindsay's dads were dead and gone, she'd cling to nothing too.

"Wow," I say instead, cheeks boiling. "I guess I really am naive to think we could go one weekend without bringing up your ex."

Lindsay sucks her cheeks but doesn't point out the obvious: *At least I've got one.*

The train clanks on, both of us steaming, until gradually Lindsay starts toying with the phone in her lap.

"I keep your secrets," I say desperately.

Indecision wells in her eyes.

"I didn't tell your dads how you kept sneaking out even after you got caught and grounded for a month. I didn't tell them you smoke pot in your room. That's a drug too."

The strand slides from behind her ear as she looks at me, but I will not let her ruin this. I refuse to let Lindsay ruin the one person I do have, if I'll never get her.

"You could've," she says.

"But I didn't. That's the point—"

"The *point,* Koda, is that parents find out everything in the end anyway. That's what I'd be terrified of, if I were you. Maybe you don't get it because your family's white—"

"You say that about *everything.*"

"Because it's true! Look. My dad—Papá, Saulo, you know who I mean—isn't as strict as my grandparents, not by a long shot, but he always finds out about whatever shit I'm doing behind his back regardless. Always. So by not telling, you're just helping me delay the inevitable. You're just helping me bide time until he gets wind of it and comes storming into my room all, *'I told you not to . . .'* and the shame eats me alive because I knew he was right all along. So, is it annoying that he snoops around and gets into all my shit? Yeah, Koda, it is extremely fucking annoying. But at the end of the day, maybe I shouldn't have done all that stupid shit behind his back. I shouldn't smoke in my room. It stinks."

"My mom would never snoop."

"Well," she says through her teeth, "then I feel sorry for you."

I wrap my arms around myself, and she presses her eyes shut, both of us swaying with the train.

A snag in her voice as she adds, "Don't listen to me if you don't want to. Keep worshipping Sadie, but I'm going to tell you what Papá told me about Peter. I think she's bad news."

Stops roll by. Thirty-Third Street, Grand Central, Fifty-First, and Lindsay might be crying, but maybe I don't care. If we weren't already late for dinner, I'd abandon her down here, push her away like my pillow in ninth grade, after I practiced kissing her. Tears rush up all over again at the thought, scalding me. *Peter.*

Screw that asshole.

The restaurant is aggressively Mediterranean. Homemade yogurt, chickpeas and potatoes, bulgur tossed with figs and honey. Lindsay picks diligently through the appetizers, paying strained attention to Mom while also miraculously managing to angle her entire body away from me. That feels worse than shouting at each other. Worse than eating alone at school.

Mom, unable to determine what exactly has gone awry, asks nervous questions while we wait for salads. How was the aquarium? Were too many exhibits closed? If we're looking for something to do tomorrow, what about swimming? She swipes some email alerts away to show us pictures of a health club she joined when we moved here but hasn't had time to visit. Not just yet. I nod without input from Lindsay. "Sure, Mom, sounds great." The lap pool stretches from one corner of her phone to the other. Empty as it is blue.

We ride home in brittle silence. Naturally, Mom's working through the weekend, so she says her farewells as we're stepping off the elevator, kissing my forehead, hugging Lindsay, warning us not to stay up *too* late.

"We definitely won't," Lindsay says flatly. "Thanks, Mariah." The lights are off, Lindsay hidden in shadows even though she's five feet away from me. If our day had gone better, I'd offer her a tour. Show her the windows I stare out, and the breakfast bar where I grind through homework, the exact stool I was sitting on when news broke about me dishonoring my father's legacy. There's still time to point that out as I turn and lead her wordlessly to my room. Time to put my hand on her arm in the darkened hall and make her stand with me, our eyes shut until she admits, oh yeah. The building's totally swaying.

In my room, Lindsay yanks her sweater over her head.

"Oh." I flinch. "Sorry, I can leave if you want to change . . ." She ignores me. We've seen each other naked—as good as naked—millions of times. But I find somewhere else to put my eyes, pretending to admire this new, benign oatmeal color that's been slapped onto my walls. The paint smell hasn't quite subsided. "Do you . . . we could watch a movie or something."

Lindsay's bra is dusty blue, the kind that crisscrosses over your back. She bends to peel off her socks.

"Or we could—"

She strips her jeans off like they're nothing. This is nothing.

"No, Koda, I don't want to watch a movie. I don't want to do anything. I couldn't sleep all last night because I was so worried about dying a fiery death on a plane. I'm exhausted. Good night." She curls up on top of my bed with her back to me. No blankets, nothing. Just last year's swim team T-shirt tented over her bent knees. I give her a minute, waiting for her to close her eyes, steady her breathing—whatever it'll take to convince me she's asleep. In the window, her reflection's eyes stay open, staring out at the city. Does she not realize I can see?

I inch closer, wincing in the glare of the track lighting. "You don't have to stay here with me if you don't want to. There's a guest room."

She doesn't move. The glare intensifies.

"Linds? Do you want the lights off?"

A tired voice answers, "Just go away, Koda."

I turn the lights off anyway and go into my en suite. Everything I'm wearing gets chucked into the hamper. T-shirt, jeans, damp underwear. The water drumming into the Jacuzzi is the perfect temperature. Not-quite-heartburn-hot. I sink in up to my chin, and my throat pinches, but I've been holding tears back all afternoon. I refuse to lose it now. I dry off and put a robe on, approach the en suite mirror. My face is puffy. Goose bumps stud my bare knees.

Maybe I shouldn't bother. I have already fucked up so badly. But the other part, the bolder one, whispers that this is not unsalvageable. *Do it afraid.*

I dig the black lipstick out from where I hid it, a drawer

stuffed with loose hair bands and overnight pads and Q-tips. Apply carefully. Painstakingly. So when the lights come on, there will be no mistakes.

Tiptoeing to my closet, I use my flashlight app to find the shredded black jeans and sheer top I bought with Sadie. Originally I'd planned to wear a tank underneath, but I forget, and when the mesh scrapes my nipples, there's no going back. I'm already overheating. Practically panting from nerves and a too-hot bath, but that's okay. I cancel the flashlight app, then stealthily reenter my room. Panic burps bubble. I hold them down.

A dark shape huddles under the covers. Other than that, Lindsay doesn't seem to have moved since I left her.

"Hey."

No answer. I can just make out her back to me, the gentle rise of her shoulders. "Lindsay . . . ?" When I climb in next to her, she doesn't stop me.

Asleep. I can tell the moment I curl up on my side, conscious of maintaining the tiny seam of space that I have always maintained between us during sleepovers. She's even snoring a little, once the blood stops banging in my ears enough to listen. Slowly, careful not to smear my lipstick, I lower my face onto her pillow. Her hair is still in a bun, the little wisps that fell loose during the day still tickling me. My mouth opens. Legs too. So desperate to make amends that every inch of me is yielding, parting to her. "Linds," I whisper. "Lindsay, can you please wake up?" I could give her the bracelet now. I almost forgot about it, tucked in my nightstand drawer. I could tell her I've finally picked a side, and I'm going to be honest, blazingly honest, from now until we're dead. The ache's not worth it. I get that, after today. "Lindsay?"

Still nothing.

My lips feel chalky. The lipstick drying like the entire night has dried around me.

My hand creeps for hers the same way it crept toward Sadie's on the train, except unlike that night there is nothing to hold on to, even though Lindsay feels so solid and warm. Like we haven't cuddled before. At sleepovers, sharing a bed, we always end up tangling. When morning comes, that's all she'll think this is, and it's that more than anything else that makes the tears I've been fighting since we left the studio finally seep out of me.

She smells like chlorine.

CHAPTER 22

I WAKE UP TO FIND LINDSAY CROUCHED in front of her suitcase. "Morning, Koda." Painfully casual, like she's doing her best to act normal, hit reset on yesterday. A lump rises in my throat, I'm so grateful. "I was just wondering about this interesting pajama choice." She lifts my sheer top off the carpet with one finger, where it dangles like a battered wing. "Where'd this come from?"

My mouth is sticky. Every part of me hollowed, scooped out. Sometime during the night I must've flung the Sadie clothes off, scrambled into regular pj's. Flannel scrapes my leg hair as I slide out of bed. "Thrifting. I went thrifting with—" I stop myself. "In Queens."

Lindsay sets the top down and resumes picking through her suitcase, laying out a pair of jeans and a pumpkin-colored sweater that only she could get away with. "Doesn't it show your boobs, though?" she asks, almost as an afterthought.

Then, before I can answer: "Women can go topless in public in New York, just like men, as long as they don't do it for money. This toplessness equality group set up a booth at one of Pete—one of the band's shows, so I found out all about it."

Sadie? Peter? We've got to be even now.

"Maybe I'll wear it today." My voice prickles with daring.

She laughs. "Um, to the pool? I'll believe it when I see it."

Reset.

My mouth gets drier.

Reset.

I hold my hand out. "Watch me."

The pool is gorgeous. One whiff and my eyes well up, which I do my best to hide from Lindsay as we file into the locker room and pull off our clothes. Unlike the school locker room, it's heated. But my nipples still harden as Lindsay grins at me, tugging the delicate hem. "Okay, so, points, Koda. Major points. Now for the real question—does your *mom* know you own this?" I twist away giggling. Mariah? Not a proponent of mesh.

Quietly, Lindsay adds, "I haven't been training much since you left."

I nod without looking at her, filling the empty locker with my stare.

"Me neither."

She snaps her Speedo strap. The suit is an old one of mine. Maroon, with a silver stripe down the side that I don't think

I'd buy today. When she turns away to finish getting ready, I do a quick crotch check, tuck away errant pubes.

The water is also heated. We dive straight in. My strokes are tentative at first, it's been so long since I've done this, but gradually my muscles wake up, moving in ways I thought they'd forgotten. I part water, turn my head, breathe, outlasting the early-morning lappers until we have the pool practically to ourselves. My arms might fall off. Like, there's a distinct possibility of the lifeguard having to fish me from the bottom of my lane. But I persist until Lindsay gives up, and signals for me to join her by the wall.

"How're you doing?" she asks.

"Good," I pant. I mean it. The pool's sides are marble, hard to grasp beneath my bitten nails. Lindsay grins. Cheeks pink, nose dented by the goggles she's pushed up onto her cap. "You looked great too, for not practicing much. At least you've still got Coach on your butt."

Her eyes dart away. "Actually, I . . . I guess I should've told you this before . . . I mean, I've been meaning to, but . . . I . . . sort of quit the team."

What? I blink. Almost glance at the lifeguard—is he hearing this? "When?"

"A while ago." She shrugs. "I would've told you sooner, but you kept saying how busy you were, ignoring half my texts, and I just . . . it's not that big of a deal anyway."

"Of course it's a big deal." Swim team used to be all Lindsay cared about besides video games, and me. "Why did you—"

"Peter's band played on Fridays. Those shows last until two, sometimes three in the morning. Swim meets are every Saturday. You do the math." This little wave sloshes between us as she shrugs again.

But that's a huge sacrifice. Enormous. To give something she loved up . . . for him . . . "But you're not dating anymore. So you could ask Coach about letting you join again. He'd probably be open to that. You have the best butterfly—"

"I'm just over it," she says fiercely. Then, quieter, "Believe it or not, Koda, I'm allowed to change too."

A bead of water plunks off my nose.

She smiles, shadows wriggling across her face. "*Your* butterfly, though . . ."

My arms are too floppy and weak to splash her. I settle for twanging her bathing suit strap, the smack amplified by her wet skin. Then it's on. We tussle, fighting to get our arms around each other's necks until the lifeguard shrieks on his whistle—"NO DUNKING!" We roll our eyes. Lindsay discreetly twangs me back.

"Listen," she says, once our laughter falls away. "I'm sorry—"

"Me too," I rush to tell her, even though I'm a little lost about what I'm apologizing for, what went so wrong in the first place. It's not my fault Lindsay can't handle me making a new friend. Especially somebody as amazing as—gasping, I jerk my hands up. "My calluses!" Lindsay ducks from the splash. "I have to keep my fingers as dry as possible to help the calluses form. Did I tell you Sadie's teaching me guitar?"

Water licks the side of the pool.

Lindsay looks away. "Okay, Koda," she says, "real talk . . . I know we sort of had it out on the train yesterday, and I don't want to do that again, but . . . I also still don't really understand why you're spending all your time with her? More importantly . . ."—her eyes dip toward me, back down—"why she wants to hang out with you? I mean, it's kind of weird, right? She's so . . . old. No offense. Doesn't she have any other friends? People her own age?"

"Um, yeah?" I don't mean to sound so defensive. The pool is just too warm suddenly, my face too hot. "Of course she does. There's Em, her songwriting partner, who you definitely could've met yesterday if we didn't have to run off to dinner. Not to mention Quixote's bassist, Teddy. *And*"—I muscle on, sensing another objection—"Sadie's only thirty-eight. That's two years younger than my mom. Do you think my mom's old?"

"Okay—"

"Because you should tell her that when she comes home later. You should go right up to her and give her one of your hugs and say, 'Mariah, you are fucking ancient.' I'm sure she'll really appreciate it."

"You're missing the point!"

Am not. You can't miss a point that's not there. I kick off from the wall, meaning to swim away, but Lindsay grabs my ankle.

"Let me tell you what I think is happening."

"I don't care." I struggle. "Let go!"

Lindsay doesn't let go. She paddles closer, forcing my back against the pool wall, one leg folded, pinned between our chests. My knee tingles, exposed to the air. Her heart thumps against it. "You're all she has left of your dad, Koda. Did that ever occur to you? She doesn't care about you. The real you, that *I* know. She cares about your face."

I wrench away so violently she yelps. "Bullshit," I tell her over the churning water. "That's bullshit, and you know it. I don't even resemble my dad."

She stares. "Yeah you do."

"No I . . ." I grind my palms into my eyes. How is she not understanding? "Maybe there are parts of me that are sort of like his, but they're all wrong. Scrambled, or something. That's all I am, okay? Scrambled. I'm a platypus, and you know it. Everybody knows it." The ladder's nearby. I heave myself from the water, dripping fury. "Also"—I whip around, almost eating it on the slippery marble—"what's so wrong with that, huh? Who cares if she sees him in me? Nobody else ever has. My own mother's never even pointed out the resemblance, has not for one second ever spoken about him like I'm an adult who can freaking handle knowing where half my genes come from. Do you know how weird that is? Because I didn't, really. Not until Sadie. She sees the potential in me. She's helping me become *myself*." I head for the lockers, unaware of Lindsay slapping after me until her toe clips my ankle.

"Hey." She darts in front of me.

"Go away."

"Well, I'm kind of stuck here until Monday, so." She sighs. "Just look at me."

It takes a couple of tries. My eyes burn and I'd rather die than let her see it.

"Koda." Her lips are white and taut from the chlorine. She presses them together, then says, "I've always thought you looked like your dad. Always. Even when we were younger and you first came to school and everybody was trying to figure out who you were, I knew right away. But that's not why I wanted to be your best friend. Okay? I wanted to be your best friend because you were awkward and kind of quiet like me, and I could tell that you were thinking incredible things, even if you didn't always know how to come out and say them. What I'm getting at"—she squeezes my arm, and my flesh resists like cold putty beneath her fingers—"is I like you, for your own sake. I hope someday, you'll understand there's a difference."

The catch in her throat makes mine sting. For a second, one blind, aching second, the truth feels within reach.

I pull away, ducking into the locker room.

Only an idiot wouldn't know which *like* she means.

Lindsay and Peter are getting back together. She waits until Monday morning to tell me, on our way to the airport. Like I didn't see this coming.

And they're having sex. Penis-in-vagina sex—she feels the need to specify. "It didn't hurt at all," she whispers. We're stuck on Grand Central Parkway, gray clouds clamped like a lid over the city, altogether the crappiest possible inverse of how our weekend began. I nod, listening. Because I am a good friend who listens. "They say it's supposed to hurt the first time, but it seriously didn't. It felt so good. I wanted to tell you sooner, but I . . ." Her gaze slides away. "I couldn't find the right time."

I crack my window. We're gridlocked, and in one of the nearby cars somebody is smoking. Ash and cold air slice across my cheeks.

My silence is starting to feel conspicuous, even to me. "That's awesome," I manage. "I'm . . . I'm really happy for you, Linds."

It's not until we're in the dropoff line, hugging goodbye, that I remember the box tucked in my coat pocket. At the last second, I shove it into her hand. "For Christmas," I say as she looks up in surprise. "I forgot to mail it to you."

She squeezes out one of the smiles we've been giving each other since yesterday. The same smile memorialized on her lock screen—a selfie taken yesterday, at the Top of the Rock Observation Deck.

I don't have any left in me.

CHAPTER 23

MOM IS IN OUR BUILDING'S LOBBY WHEN Driver drops me home, picking leaves off a ficus.

"That plant is alive," I inform her.

"Sorry." She looks at the leaf still in her hand. It's nice. A glossy green fingernail. "I'm late for a meeting."

She needs the car? I swing around, but Driver's already pulled away.

"It's fine, Koda. I ordered a cab fifteen minutes ago." She arranges a tight smile. "Was it hard saying goodbye to Lindsay?"

The sky has this gray constipated look that may or may not mean rain. I turn back to Mom, wanting to sprint right past her, onto the elevator, to bed. But I don't have the energy. I drop next to her on the lobby loveseat. "No." It's not exactly a lie.

Lindsay and Peter are getting back together. She still doesn't know how I feel, which has to be the very definition of failure. Both your greatest fears coming true.

Mom's frown deepens, and I turn away from her to stare at the loveseat armrest, ridiculous with its ivory silk and tassels. My chest tightens. A sob pushing up.

If she asked why.

If she tried comforting me with one of her stupid platitudes—*Oh honey, you'll find somebody better, a girl who deserves you*—I might actually believe it. Might let myself be that desperate. Just this once.

Another restless second or two between us, and Mom signals to the guy at the front desk. "This building is lovely," she calls. "The decor, these sofas—beautiful." I make a little ficus leaf memorial on the marble by our feet.

When the cab arrives, Mom reels me into a hug. "Make sure you finish your homework, okay? And go to bed at a reasonable time? I'll text when I'm getting ready to leave, but I don't think it'll be any sooner than nine, ten o'clock. There's dinner involved." She hesitates, hugs a little tighter. "Miss you." As we part, she presses my face in her hands, and I really do almost lose it. That soft, freshly powdered smell.

Back in my room, I pull my hair into a bun, put on my black jeans, my eyes looking more bruised than that day at the photographer's studio, irrepressibly blue. Grady blue, that shade should be called. Like all the want in the world.

Sadie seems startled, almost dismayed, to see me, the zigzag blanket flung over her shoulders as she peeks through her apartment door. "Hi," I say. She gives me this confused smile.

I rush to explain. "My mom's going to be busy all day, and I was wondering if . . . you didn't answer your texts, but . . . can I stay?" All my excitement on my way over here, I never realized this might be a bad surprise. That she wouldn't want me.

She nibbles a thumbnail, deliberating. "Afraid I'm not too interesting today. Just working."

"That's fine." I should've brought homework, some books or something. God knows Sadie doesn't have TV. Or Wi-Fi. "When you're finished," I add boldly, "maybe we could go to dinner? Order in? You choose. I don't care." It earns me a crackling laugh. Sadie leans her temple against the doorframe, watching me.

"Where's your friend?"

The question unbalances me. I swore on the ride over I'd stop thinking about Lindsay. "Home. Or . . . not home yet. On her flight."

Sadie's already stepping back from the door. "Too bad," she says, in the tone of somebody who doesn't think something is bad at all.

I spend the afternoon sitting quietly while she scribbles into her notebook, and fields calls from Em, who's stuck home with bronchitis but still making Sadie miserable, basically haunting her from her bed. Two hours have passed before she smacks her songbook onto the coffee table, pushing her glasses up to rub her eyes. They're the opposite of mine. Pink and swollen.

"Fuck," she says.

"Done?" I'm cross-legged on the couch, beneath the zigzag blanket.

"Well, kiddo, 'done' is a debatable concept. A real relative term. 'Done' for now, sure, but that's exactly the problem, these fucking contracts . . . Soon as you meet one deadline, you're staring down the barrel of another, X many songs within X number of months, which I guess is all right if you're a normal, organized person, but being neither of these things, I've been taking the demands very personally lately. Usually I don't. I'm good at faking normal. You know? Been a faker my whole life, but now I just . . . this winter has been . . ." She rubs her eyes again, and this little wrinkle that's wormed between them. "Damn Em."

Sadie wipes her nose. She hasn't asked at all about how Lindsay's visit went, but that's my fault for not bringing it up. Sadie has impeccable instincts. She must have sensed what a shit show the whole thing was, and didn't want to make me feel any worse. But . . . I drop my head, poking fingers through the blanket's weave.

When I finish explaining about Lindsay getting back with Peter, I'm not crying exactly. "I don't care," I sniffle, wiping roughly at my eyes. "It's a good thing, because there's no way Lindsay likes me. *Likes* me, likes me." *I like you for you,* she says, but I push that away. It doesn't matter. Not when Sadie's halfway across the room, frowning, concerned. "I would've just humiliated myself, ruined our friendship on top of it. Not that we're really friends anymore anyway. Or maybe we are. It's hard to—she hasn't texted me at all since she got to the airport, and honestly, this whole weekend has been awful, I'm . . ." My voice cracks, full of static. *I'm so lonely, Sadie.* That's all I was about to say. *I'm so lonely except for when I'm with you.*

Sadie approaches swiftly, plants her hands on my knees. "Listen," she says into my face.

Our noses are inches apart. I hold my breath. Listening.

"Sure, losing somebody hurts, hurts like hell, but all that is, Koda, is growing pains. You'll be better off for them later, trust me. Leave before you get left. That's my motto."

My eyes flood. She is so wise. Even if I can't realistically afford more growing. "I wish you could've been there," I say pitifully.

She curls beside me, and I fork over some blanket, both of us huddled together as whirling, mutant flakes thunk against the windows. That's what the gray sky meant. Snow, not rain. Except snow is supposed to be silent, isn't it? Silent like a bad feeling. Like the stomachache nobody knows you have.

There's no way Lindsay's right. No way Sadie is using me. And I can prove it. I can make her do something painful. Something she would only do for me.

"The photo albums," I say, once I trust my voice not to shake. "Show me now?"

Sadie slips her thumb ring off and on, off and on, studying it in the grayish light. Then she helps me up and brings me to her bedroom.

She slides the closet open with her foot, but the clothes

that were hung so neatly the last time I looked are torn from their hangers, spilling onto the floor like the closet's been ransacked, practically disemboweled. "What happened?" I ask, but Sadie doesn't answer. She jerks her chin at a couple of gray milk crates, shoved toward the back. I stoop to examine them. "Whoa." Records. Motionless, Sadie watches me flip through them. She doesn't have her own work—or anything from this century—but some stuff I recognize. *Let's Dance*, Pink Floyd, Fleetwood Mac . . . Knowing her, they're organized by frequency and length of guitar solos. Sadie logic. Classic. She crouches beside me. "Peter"—I glance at her freckly cheek, the industrial—"he never let us play music on our phones or anything when we hung out. He insisted you couldn't experience a song in its full glory until you heard it on vinyl. I thought that was so annoying."

"Annoying"—she tugs my ear—"but correct." I laugh and swat her away, already feeling better.

After a bit, Sadie pushes the crates out of the way to explore darker recesses of the closet, muttering and rooting around. "For fuck's sake. I thought I . . ." Whatever weird mood she was in when I arrived seems to have lifted. It makes me feel special. Like I helped. I sit patiently, trying not to fidget as the closet coughs up dust bunnies. At last, Sadie sits back, clutching a thick book with a pebbly gray cover, no title or writing on it whatsoever. My chest leaps. "Want you to understand," she says, "I haven't looked at these in years. But . . ." She thrusts the photo album at me abruptly. "No saying no to you."

I flip through it on the bed while Sadie fiddles with her guitar, smoking and letting me take my time. It's funny, but in all the hours we've spent together, I've never heard her play before. Not in real life. Her fingers drip honey while I turn the slippery pages. Slowly. Out of respect. But also so I won't miss anything. The photos—Polaroids, so retro—cover the band's early days together. Bassist Teddy passed out on a hideous orange couch. Sadie with her curls in a scrunchie, hugging a giant black dog. *SAMBUCA,* that one says. *FIRST ROADIE!!!! It's* Sadie's handwriting, every letter a lightning bolt. Of all the hundreds of photos, my father is only in a handful.

"God forbid he didn't get to play photographer," Sadie says. She's sitting against the bed, a curl of smoke and her bandanna just visible over the mattress.

"Got it." I mean—it makes so much sense I can't believe it had to be pointed out to me. Of course my father, with his wisdom and genius, would document everything. There are photos of him kissing the same black dog. Slumping on the orange couch with Sadie in his lap, a skinny cigarette pinched between his fingers that it takes me an embarrassingly long time to realize is pot. I turn the page quickly.

The final photos are more conceptual. Page after plasticky page of abandoned buildings. Too much sky. The last in this sequence catches my eye. There's a sidewalk, grass pushing through the cracks in fists, and my father—that really is my father—approaching the camera. White T-shirt, mouth snagged mid-laugh, arms outstretched like he's walking a tightrope. Along the bottom it's scribbled, *to sadie—when i die, pack my summer clothes.*

I stare at the letters until they stop being letters. Until I'm confident we write the same *i*'s. Then I clear my throat—"Sades"—and hold the album out so she can see from the floor. Still, it takes her a while to realize where I'm pointing. Her cheeks splotch bright red.

"What does that mean?" I ask. "Are they lyrics or something? A song you never released?"

"Not lyrics." Sadie stands, clutching the guitar by its neck. She sets it gently aside, then hoists herself up onto the bed with me, Doc Martens and all. "A game we played. 'When I die, don't call my parents.' 'When I die, serve me to the cats *a la mode.*' It was hilarious. We'd crack each other up for hours."

That doesn't sound like a very fun game, but what do I know? This photograph, his handwriting—the most personal parts I've discovered of him yet, somehow only make him more indecipherable. I try to smile. "Can I take it out? The picture?" Her eyes flick a warning. *Be careful.* I pinch a corner of the Polaroid and tug. Maybe if I see his face . . .

The bed creaks. Sadie's gotten up. I hear her cross to the closet.

But the photo does not reveal some new, previously unreleased side of him. He just looks like my father. Actually—my father before he was my father. A scraggly kid. I shove hair behind my ears, conscious of Sadie lingering by the closet, awaiting my appraisal. "He was beautiful," I say at last. What everybody talks about when they talk about him.

She smirks. "You're telling me."

I have to dig deeper. "What'd you like best about him? I mean physically."

"Ha! I'll tell you when you're older." Now Sadie's voice is muffled. I look up to see her on hands and knees again, flicking through the milk crates. "Frankly, he drove me wild. Don't think I could pick any one thing."

"But if you had to."

"Well, if I *had* to," she teases. "He did have these dimples . . ." She seizes a record, but then, maybe deciding it's not the one, lets it thump back into the crate. "Big ones," she adds quietly. "Like they got dug out by a spoon. They were the first thing I noticed about him, once I got past how much his strumming fucking sucked. Of course, I eventually told him his dimples were pretty. Huge mistake. One flash and he knew I'd be powerless." Sadie glances up, our gazes catch—and then she concentrates extra hard on flicking through records. "He could really reel me in. Anyway."

I look back down at the photograph, into my father's pale face. My fingers creep over my lips. "I don't have dimples."

"I noticed," she says.

I push the photo back into its sleeve.

Sadie hops up. She must've found the record she was looking for. "You like the Beatles?"

"Um." I shut the photo album and place it on the nightstand, on top of the facedown picture frame. My thoughts can't get any traction. "Maybe?" She crosses herself. I've never seen a record player in real life before, let alone the one on her dresser. I'd mistaken it for a jewelry box, but now she clears necklaces and scarves off the top to unearth ancient machinery. Musty yellow. A true relic.

When she pops the record on, it crackles the way old movies crackle, like they're clearing their throats. Noises that come after, I can't place. Snickers. Bass? "We had a cat on our tour bus"—she puts her hands out, and a nervous heat flashes through me, but I grasp them anyway, let her pull me off the bed—"JohnPaulRingoandGeorge. Mack's idea. We couldn't agree on what to call him."

"Who's the one who sings like he's got a bad cold?"

Sadie yanks me to her. "You trying to kill Mack all over again?"

I laugh even though I don't feel like laughing, my face tight and dimple-less. As the record spins, her eyes move over me. She seems a lot smaller suddenly, but that's not possible. She's always come up to my chest. "I like this song," I say, to make amends. "I've heard it before."

Her hand slides to the small of my back, which I didn't realize had gotten so sweaty. "A goddamn toddler could recognize this song. It's 'Come Together.' Now come on."

We dance. All six of us together, the Fab Four playing on a scratchy record as Sadie leads me across her scuffed-up bedroom floor. We bump into things. Upended crates and piles of clothes, holding each other so tight it's hard to tell who's laughing harder as one song blurs into the next. This one is slower, more subdued. Sadie giggles into my chest. "How late can you stay?"

"All night," I offer, and she giggles harder, like it's a joke.

When I die—I shrink myself, preparing to spin—when I die, Sadie, tell me how I reel you in.

CHAPTER 24

SADIE TUGS A MESS OF BLANKETS AND pillows down from the closet, apologizing for not having fresh sheets. “Laundry isn’t exactly my top priority.” I assure her it’s not mine, either, and then, even though she doesn’t ask for help, I spread the new blankets across the bed, heap on pillows while she disappears into the bathroom. By the time she’s back, I’ve bundled her comforter into the corner, and the records back in their crates, coaxed the sticky closet door shut. I turn to see her in the bedroom doorway. Arms folded, all shadow.

“Hi,” I say stupidly.

It’s dark, has been for hours. The streetlights cast a yellowish glow on Sadie as she crosses to the window. She doesn’t move when I come up behind her.

“You seriously don’t mind if I sleep over?” She did ask how long I could stay, but . . .

Paint flakes off the sill. Sadie picks at it. "Snowing like hell anyway."

Mom said as much once I finally answered her texts. Apparently, Driver had called her a while back, saying that it was really coming down thick and soon it'd be too dangerous to drive me home from my friend's. It could've been disastrous. My cover, completely blown. Yet somehow, Mom miraculously assumed that the friend was "Sarah." When I explained we were only doing hw, and her parents didn't mind if I slept over, she responded with a single emoji. Thumbs-up.

"Not that this is anything special," Sadie goes on. "Not like upstate."

"You should bring me sometime. Like in that song you wrote." I wait for this to register, but she turns, wiping paint dust off her fingers.

She reminds me about the bathroom—like I'll get lost traveling exactly two feet—and that I can help myself to whatever I want in the kitchen. That is, if I can find anything. Her tone has dulled, so changed from when we danced together that I almost don't realize I'm being put to bed. "Aren't you staying up?" I say, perched by the nightstand. "I can too." Sadie hesitates, then reaches to gather something off the floor. Pajamas in ratty red flannel. "You told me you never sleep the first time I visited. Remember? You said, 'Lucky for you, I don't sleep.'"

"Hyperbole, kiddo. I can hardly make it past eleven anymore."

Impossible. "But you and my father used to party like crazy, didn't you? Stay up for days and days? So you could probably still find it in you. Please? Just for tonight?"

When they meet mine, her eyes do seem tired.

"We can . . . we can talk more?" I falter. "All night. Like on the subway. I mean, like when you and my father used to ride the subway. I know we got to my stop eventually." But this is different. She *asked* how late I could stay, and I answered honestly. So what's with the mood swings? What happened between us dancing and now to make her all aloof again? "Please? I always have the hardest time falling asleep in new places."

My pleading gets me nowhere. "Keep looking through those pictures," she says lightly. "That'll put you to sleep." One by one, she clinks her rings onto the nightstand. I snatch up the closest, knowing more than probably anybody the infinite ways adults can signal, *conversation over.*

The ring is plain silver, with a tiny teardrop stone. "This is so pretty."

What's wrong with me?

Why can't I let her go?

"Did my father get you this?"

She glances away as I try to stuff the ring on my pinkie. "No. Somebody else."

"Who, though?" I think of cruising the jewelry counters at Christmastime, the topaz ring I could have—should have—gotten her. And Lindsay . . . the silver box . . . She had to have opened it by—no. I grind the thought out. Sadie looks at me.

Making her own plea with every line in her face. "You've dated other guys is what you're saying. Other boyfriends?"

Sadie reaches out and takes the ring from me, sets it so carefully on the nightstand that it doesn't clink at all. "If that's what you want to call them."

"Who?"

Her chuckle crackles in her throat.

"I'm serious!"

Mom keeps secrets from me, but not her. Not Sadie. I sit by, helpless, as she gathers some things from the closet, a couple of records, and her record player. "Sadie."

How did my father draw her back? What did he say? "Sades—"

"How's this," she interrupts. "You go to bed, and we'll talk tomorrow. Deal?"

I chew my lip, letting her think I'm mulling it over, when I'm really just counting to five in my head. "Deal."

Sadie nods.

That kind of secret, then.

She clicks the lights off and shuts the door. I peel back the covers and insert myself between them, lying very still and quiet as the faucet runs and toilet flushes, water gurgles through the pipes. Soon she'll take off her clothes. I listen harder, like naked is a sound. *Worship* was the word Lindsay used to describe Sadie and me. *Keep worshipping her, but I think she's bad news.* Before, it devastated me to think of Lindsay getting back with Peter, but now that Sadie's pulled my head together, I only feel sorry for her. Sorry that Lindsay is so ordinary. She'll never know what *worship* means.

I curl up and try to sleep, but every time my eyes close, Sadie and I start dancing again. Magically, I'm better at it, and her smile opens like it did the few times I've managed to truly surprise her. I twitch awake. Bury my face in the pillow that smells like ashes. Like her.

I'm not sure if I slept three hours or three minutes. My phone is . . . somewhere. But my hunch is Sadie's awake too. There's this restlessness in the air, stirred up by my wildly jumping thoughts and something even realer. Sharper. I bite down on the pillow for as long as I can stand it. Longer, I bet, than the band's longest song.

Slowly, I tiptoe to the door. My shirt clings to my chest. I bang my hand against the doorknob trying to find it in the dark, then edge out into the even darker hall. You don't have to go any farther to see straight into the living room. Immediately, my heart sinks. Sadie is asleep? Balled against the armrest with the blanket over her shoulders. Then—stepping toward her—I pick out little details in the lamplight, things my disappointment hid from me. Like the blanket pressed to her face. Her shoulders rocking.

"Sadie?"

Her head jerks up.

I don't ask if she's crying. It's too obvious, her face shiny and creased. I creep closer as she fumbles with the blanket. How to comfort a crying person? I need—not a whole textbook, but a chart. Diagrams that show what to do with your hands. Hesitantly, I touch her knee. I'm not sure why, since she's so tiny—but the knobbiness startles me. "Sadie? What's wrong?"

"Can't." She pushes her palms against her eyes. "Can't anymore . . ." I kneel. Snot glistens on her lip. "Teddy was right."

My vision wavers. "What do you mean? Can't what? What did Teddy say?" But I know. Of course I do, because I overheard them talking and he doesn't want us hanging out. "Sadie . . ." I am so averse to tears. Certifiably allergic. My throat narrows as they ooze through Sadie's fingers. I place my other hand on her other knee, but she flinches away and cries harder. Deep, bellowing sobs like howling at the moon.

"God," she moans. "Oh God, I can't. Every second you're here, I just—but even when you're not, I—I close my eyes and you're there. You're always there. You've got to go!"

Our faces are close, and I hear myself saying, "Don't say that." Begging her, "Don't, Sadie, please . . . I know I don't have my father's dimples, okay? I know I'll never be brilliant, or half as creative, but . . ." But if Lindsay is right and this platypus face is the only reason Sadie wants me around, well, that's okay, it's officially fine with me, because I'll take anything. I'll take Sadie wanting me around for this most messed-up of reasons, as long as it means not being alone, not being the pathetic, worthless girl I was before. "Sadie"—she shoves me away from her, but not very hard—"please!" Her forehead knocks against mine. Our mouths graze.

The sound it makes isn't the sound you think of a kiss

making, a big, dramatic smack like in the movies. In fact, there's no sound at all. Sadie pulls back, eyes huge. Bewildered.

"I'm sorry." I cover my mouth.

We stare at each other, trembling.

"I-I'm sorry. I'm—" a freak. And now I really do have to go. I wrench myself up, babbling, "Thank you so much for your time, I promise I'll never—"

She grabs my wrist.

CHAPTER 25

THE DREAM I HAVE ABOUT LINDSAY IS THE same dream I always have about her. A dream that knows exactly what it is, and doesn't pretend to be anything different. We're at the pool. Not the high school pool, but mine, in California. Cue birds. And the sting of chlorine, water skidding off our noses as I tell her what I always do. This time, though, she doesn't push me away. Doesn't say, *I don't think of you like that.* Our mouths connect. Lips. Tongue. Everything. I touch her belly. The diamond points of her nipples, stiff against her bikini top.

When I lurch awake, slippery with sweat, it takes me a moment to recognize where I am. The apartment looks so different in the morning. Chilly, filled with a thin gray light. My limbs ache from being smashed up on the couch. I stretch, wincing. Sadie's cuddled too close to my armpit. Mouth slack and drooling. I push my fingertips against my lips, gnaw awhile, to calm myself.

This is weird. I know that. A million kinds of bad, and weird, and wrong. But last night, as soon as she pulled me toward her, she busted up sobbing again, melted against me. *Hush,* I said. *Sadie, hush.* And she fell asleep. My arms promptly followed. Now I try to drift off again, but can't ignore the worries fritzing through my brain. When she wakes up, she'll kick me out for sure. Anybody with a shred of self-respect would sneak out before that happens. I wriggle out from under her and splash my face with cold water, brush my teeth the best I can with a fingertip and her chalky toothpaste, chanting to myself, *just go, just go.* But as I drip out into the hall, closing the bathroom door softly behind me, I remember our mouths touching. The shivers—good shivers—that tore through me.

The most awkward part of a sleepover is waiting for the other person to wake up. Sadie does so gradually, in a total daze, like she forgets the kiss or even passing out on me in the first place. Her confusion is . . . confusing. I curled back next to her after my face dried, but now I sit up too, wiping my hair back. "Um," I begin, but she shakes her head, fingers gnashing her temples. I wait for what feels like an appropriate number of seconds. "Do you still want me to leave? Because I can," I lie as she lowers her hand. "I can no problem."

Sadie smooths the hair off my forehead, the gesture so tender that I don't realize right away that she's shaking, doing a bad job of hiding it. "I"—she shuts her eyes—"stop it, Koda Rose. For fuck's sake."

I can't remember the last time she invoked my full name.

So—I am in trouble? This *is* messed up? Sadie swings her legs over the side of the couch. Her cheeks are wet again.

"What's wrong?"

Her laugh is more of a croak. Tears spilling, she goes unsteadily to the window and jiggles it open, letting a gust of metallic breath into the room. Snow. I forgot. I approach warily, glad I'm tall enough to peer straight over her, past the metal cage of the fire escape to the sidewalk below. Except the sidewalk—her whole neighborhood—is gone. Buried.

"Jeez," I say.

She rubs her sore-looking eyes.

"This all happened overnight?" Flurries are one thing, but snow in bulk?

Incredible. Some piles have fluffed onto the windowsill, and while I wait for Sadie to tell me what's wrong, I sear my fingertips in it, shivering.

Sadie moves a hand to her nose, sniffling. Then she lurches for the bathroom and doesn't come out. Not even after ten, fifteen minutes.

"Sades?" I call.

The guitar is in her bedroom. While I listen for movement, I pick it up, try a quick chord. It doesn't sting. "Hello?" I try again. She disappears in there all the time, but now—I don't know. Something's off. I put the guitar down and knock on the door. *"Sadie."* My mind starts to race. "Sadie, what's wrong? I'm coming in if you don't answer." I try the knob, expecting it to be locked. But the door creaks open, revealing

Sadie scrunched on the toilet seat, clutching her nose.

"Shut the door," she barks.

Her fingers glisten crimson.

"I'm fine."

I book for the kitchen. Her fridge doesn't have an ice cube maker, or trays for doing it the old-fashioned way, but when I wrench the tap on, the water is already pretty cold. I fly back down the hall to find the door still open, Sadie where I left her. It takes some prodding—I have to physically pry her hands from her nose and stuff the dripping paper-towel wad at her—but she seems to get the idea. "Put this on your nose. It'll constrict the capillaries. Blood vessels," I clarify as she blinks, uncomprehending. "That's what causes nosebleeds."

The paper towels don't help, wilting red in no time. I slide down the wall so Sadie won't see my legs quaking, but being this close to the blood makes me feel worse. Throw-up worse. "I used to get nosebleeds when I was little," I say, needing to hear a voice. "The doctor said they were from the air in LA being too dry. Maybe that's your problem? Your apartment's always so hot." Even now, I'm sweating. Sadie maneuvers around me to hawk blood into the sink.

"It's the hole in my nose."

I look up.

She slurps from the tap, rinses, spits. "Used to be I wasn't doing as much coke as when I was younger. Few lines here and there, with Em, but then she went and got all fucking sober, and you came waltzing into the picture, with your puppy dog eyes and guilt trips, and I remembered, oh right, I'm an addict. This is how I cope." She gulps more water. "Well, according to Teddy."

The tiles are ice. I draw my knees up, and Sadie softens with something like pity. "You didn't know," she says. "I knew you didn't know, which was why it was so easy to hide it from you. From the beginning I told Teddy, 'I've got this.' I was all, 'How could some kid hurt me more than I've already hurt myself?' Guess I've finally got my answer."

My fingertips ache, numb from the snow and cold water. I curl them inside my sweatshirt cuffs, mindful of my budding calluses. The baby nubs. "I—"

"When Mack died, I went back upstate to my parents'. Climbed into bed and didn't get up for a month. Anytime I considered it, I'd hear paparazzi rustling around outside, shutters clicking, and there was all this stuff Mack had given me while we were in school, photos and notes and drawings tacked all over the walls. I'd wake up sometimes and think he was still there with me. Like we were kids again and he'd snuck in through my window, fallen asleep." She paws her nose. "That's what it's like having you with me. One look at you, and I'm plunged back into a dream I haven't had in years." She squats in front of me, eyes huge behind her glasses, like fish in a bowl. "I've hated you your whole life. Bet you didn't know that, either, did you?"

I try to say what I'd meant to before, but it comes out halfway, this strangled *I'm sorry*. Sadie dismisses it. So quickly I realize, yet again, that I have said the wrong thing.

"Even *before* you were born, I fucking hated you. Who hates a baby? But now"—she grasps my face in her hands, eyes brimming, but because I remember her saying a little cry might be good for her, I don't move, even as more blood drools from her nostril—"you fill me up. Like I fill you, right? We leave no room for anything else." She pats me. I almost whisper, *Take that, Lindsay.*

A sensation, wet, warm, blooms on my knee. We look down.

"Don't," Sadie whimpers.

Blood soaks my jeans.

"Don't go." She folds against me, sobbing. "Please, baby, don't go."

CHAPTER 26

THE HOSPITAL IS FRANTIC.

"What's your relationship to the patient?"

I'm frantic.

"She's my aunt."

Doctor blinks.

"Adoptive. Adoptive aunt. Please, can I see her? Is she okay?"

I don't know if Doctor is old enough to be a real doctor, but he's wearing the right stuff, papery spearmint scrubs like you see on TV. He leads me back to where people are waiting—where I've been waiting, for way too long—and then there's pressure, his hand on my shoulder, that makes my butt hit the pleather seat. "What happened? Has your aunt had problems like this before?" His questions ding off me. Answers fall out. She was bleeding. I say this over and over. "She started bleeding and I tried to stop it, but I couldn't. It wouldn't stop!"

Doctor vanishes, leaving me alone again. I put my head between my knees and let the sobs loop. When the paramedics arrived, they wouldn't let me near Sadie. She was linoleum-clammy by then. Oatmeal-colored. They patted her cheeks and shone lights into her pupils, shouted commands she couldn't follow. They strapped her onto that thing sick people get strapped onto and brought her to a hospital. This hospital. Right down the street. I ran the entire way and a nice lady in the lobby directed me up here, but the nurses said I had to wait and I must've looked awful, because when I sat down, somebody's grandma sat next to me and rubbed my back. She said she was waiting for her grandson, who broke his arm sledding. She told me she was scared too.

Gradually, I regain composure. Return to the upright and locked position. The grandma's moved away from me by now. Or she left—her grandson is better? He's going home? Somewhere in this cavernous, beeping hospital, Sadie is bleeding. I still don't know what to do.

Blood smears my sweatshirt and jeans, mud-colored now as it mixes with oxygen. *Hemoglobin*. A science word. Others include: *aorta*, *globin*, *atheroma*. I'd take my sweatshirt off but can't remember if it's snowing. I'll need it if it's snowing.

"Koda!"

A woman strides toward me. Flapping Burberry trench. Red hair.

"Mom!" I heave myself up. "Mommy!" She catches me in her arms, and the world goes kaleidoscope. Fluorescent lights, confused flutter, and then there are hands on my shoulders again, her hands, walking me backward. She shrieks at the blood on me.

"Koda! Oh my God! Are you hurt?" Her face isn't the sewn-up professional one she reserves for meetings but open, splitting with fear. No. I shake my head. Not hurt. She yanks my sweatshirt in front of everybody to be sure. I don't have the strength to tug it down. "Your voicemail said—but our driver wasn't—what are you doing in Queens? You hung up—"

"When the paramedics got there." I remember. There was blood by then, more blood, dribbling from Sadie's mouth.

Mom draws me against her, and we collapse together onto the seats. She smooths my hair with her smooth hands, oblivious to—or deliberately ignoring—the gawkers who have gathered around us, Doctor explaining the situation in his patient doctor's voice. I jolt. Tickled by a new fear. Do these strangers . . . recognize me now? Phones are out. Doctor's expression betrays nothing. But I know enough to hold my breath as Sadie's name leaves his mouth and detonates on the linoleum.

Ka-boom.

"I'm sorry," Mom interrupts. "Who?"

My breath splinters out.

Doctor's eyes twitch from me to Mom, who, gawkers will appreciate, has exquisite posture. In their pictures, her back will be straight enough to snap.

"The patient," Doctor says. "Sarah Pascal."

A hand seizes my wrist.

"Pasquale," I scream over my shoulder. I'm caught. Being dragged away by the Mariah riptide. *"Pasquale!"*

A sign says: IN CASE OF EMERGENCY, TAKE STAIRS. Mom goes down them too fast, her nails stabbing into me. I yell at her to slow down. I'm not graceful like her. I don't know what floor we're on, or where Sadie is. *We fill each other up.* I can't leave without knowing where she is.

A minor cosmic event outside the hospital. Bursts of light so stupefying I duck automatically under Mom's Burberry wing.

"Mariah! Mariah! What happened! Is Koda Rose okay! Girls, over here! How's it going over at the magazine! Ladies, have you ever been to Queens!"

Beneath the trenchcoat Mom has her silk robe on, and her hair smells like jasmine—musky jasmine, because she's sweating. She clutches me close, feeding pazzos terse, even lines through her teeth. "Get away from my daughter. Get away. One more step and I'll have your balls."

Silver car glides up. Hands on my hips and then she's practically on top of me, scrambling to slam the door. I huddle against her. Close as I can get, close as we used to be, squashing her pretty bedhead waves. We pant. Soft thuds engulf the car as it nudges forward. Who called the pazzos? Who could've tipped them off? Somebody at the hospital . . . ? Driver's eyes skitter frantically in the rearview mirror, but I avoid them.

Mom tips her head back against the seat.

"Mom."

She really is sweating like hell.

"Mom, I—"

The hand comes out of nowhere. So fast I hear the smack before it cracks me, and everything else, wide open.

Mom puts it all together by dinnertime. "The East Village." Sarah. Queens. Driver gets axed, and that proves a whole new kind of terror, having to estimate how many times I've visited Sadie behind her back. Mom bawls some more, then sends me to my room. Until she figures out our next move.

Around midnight, when I still haven't been summoned, I summon myself. Slipping through the connector door, I find Mom slumped in bed, scrolling through her phone.

"Mom." My outstretched hand trembles. "Give it. Please." It's the same model as mine. I tap the browser open and swipe away articles without reading them, words like *MAYHEM* and *ER SCARE* jagging across the screen. "Can't you listen to those chants your last therapist prescribed? That podcast with that guy whose really boring voice helps you fall asleep?"

"You're supposed to be in your room," Mom answers. But I'm already retrieving the face goop from her vanity, which means I have to stay, at least for a few minutes. She sighs when I return with the jar. "I don't see how you can blame me for wanting to know what's being said about us, about *you*, now that this is all out in the open."

My throat is sticky, raw from hours of crying. Probably my stomach hurts too, but I can't sort that ache out from the others. Mom rakes her hair back, piling it high on top of her head before letting it fall again. I need to say something to console her. Something positive, but my mind has been scraped empty, the hospital a fluorescent blur. Mom covers her face. "You've known each other since that night at the restaurant, haven't you?" she says through her fingers. "Or before that. Weeks before."

"Only two months."

Her eyes widen in shock.

That's almost as long as we've been in New York. What does she expect me to admit—that Sadie's all New York is to me? Stepping closer to Mom, I nearly feel clammy bathroom tiles again, smell the coppery blood pouring from Sadie that I couldn't stop with paper towels, my sweatshirt, my hands.

Pain must be twisting across my face—Mom softens and busies herself with the belt on her robe, muttering, "For God's sake." Which is when I remember the jar in my hands. I can't quite look at her as I unscrew the cap. The goop smells nice. I never realized. And it's white, a good white. Not Sadie-pale at all.

Mom takes the left side of her face, I take the right. The key is to spread evenly and not gob any in her eyelashes. "Put your tongue in," I say after a few minutes. I'm icing myself a big Mariah cake. It's like swimming. My hands, my body, know what to do, move without me. I put the finishing touches on her jaw, rubbing so the heat of my fingers will activate the goop's anti-aging properties. Then she sits with her eyes closed. Breathing.

"I don't know." She nibbles a cuticle. "I don't know what I want to say to you. I've always thought—you make me so proud, Koda. That's the problem. I prided myself so much on your thoughtfulness, the maturity with which you handled the photo shoot, those leaks, that I guess I took you for granted. And now I can't really begin to articulate how disappointed I am in you, the terrible judgment you've shown. I would've found a way to connect you with Sadie, discreetly, if that was what you really wanted. It would've hurt me, but . . . all you had to do was ask." My throat pinches. She's lying. She said, *Sadie's unreliable. A mess.*

She wasn't wrong.

Tears rise up, but I choke them down.

Mom continues. "But now you've put us in a terrible position. The press is all over this, calling left and right, demanding comments, explanations. To have you defy me, to go off with that woman behind my back . . ." Her hand drops to the bedspread. "Did she get you high?"

"What! No! Mom, I would never—"

She grasps my face in both hands, just like Sadie, and it's stupid, but all I can think is—I have to text Lindsay.

I was the first person she called when her dad Trevor had those bad chest pains last summer. Mom drove me to the hospital, and waited in the car while I ran in and hugged her. The next day, as doctors ran more tests, we sat in the waiting room for an eternity together, playing gin rummy with her other dad's ratty cards. I felt guilty not knowing what to say.

But maybe words aren't the point. Maybe it's the distraction. Company. A best friend to reassure you that no matter what you're facing, you don't have to go through it alone. Mom's doing an okay job, even though she's lying. Even though she never would have introduced me to Sadie, and Sadie—why would Sadie speak to Mom? When we were together, Mom's existence shimmered invisibly between us. There, but unmentioned. Untouched. So, yeah. Lindsay would be preferable. I'd tell her, *I'm so sorry.* I'd tell her, *You were right.* It was drugs.

But drugs can't change what Sadie is to me.

A tear skips down my cheek. Mom thumbs it away.

"She was bleeding," I say stupidly.

"I know, honey."

My head's so full of Sadie—thoughts of whether she's okay, when she'll come home, that I forgot until literally now that all I'm wearing is a T-shirt and undies. My bloody clothes have been stripped off and flung into the wash. I don't remember when. I don't remember why I couldn't put on fresh clothes. "I was scared," I burble. "It was so scary." I know, Mom repeats. The saddest smile flits across her lips.

Sharing a bed with your mom probably isn't the sort of thing that can continue once you're eighteen. Maybe I don't care. Maybe I'm doing this strictly because being alone is impossible right now, although that only partially explains the unexpected pang of seeing Mom fluff pillows, pull the covers back. I can't sleep. Opt for drifting. Anchored by the warm, soothing weight of Mom's arm across me. Then—I'm not sure. My breathing must trick her. She rolls away, and the silence fills with cuticle gnawing. The pinch and scrape of teeth. I wriggle closer. And it's weird. The girl curling against Mom isn't the same girl who comforted Sadie and kissed her. But they're both me.

CHAPTER 27

BLOGS BLARE HEADLINES THE NEXT DAY about my and Sadie's *relationship*—publicly, Mom's lawyer insists that there is none—but offer no word on her condition. Huddled on Mom's marshmallowy office sofa, I check and recheck my phone. Sadie hasn't answered my texts. Or the whisper-voicemails, twelve in all, that I left last night.

She's in and out the whole morning, trailed by chirping, scribbling assistants who periodically offer Dasani and individually packaged servings of almonds. Somebody orders sushi for lunch, and she eats at her desk, using fingers instead of chopsticks. Nobody offers me anything. I wouldn't eat, even if they did. I'm hiding. Hair tentacled around me, curled in my Sadie-less shell. Misery, it turns out, makes prime camouflage.

Lindsay doesn't text me either, even though she must have seen the news by now.

Around seven, we take a taxi home. Mom makes tea. Chamomile, which I don't have the heart to remind her isn't heartburn-proof. We sit on my bed, not speaking. "I could make you something else," Mom offers. I shake my head. Ginger tea, peppermint, it's all crap, and even though I appreciate her attempts at what I did for Lindsay—the company thing—after crying for ten hours in her office, I want her to leave. Why aren't we discussing *her* judgment? She forced me to do the photo shoot. Forced me to move, never paused one second to consider what living in the epicenter of all things Quixote might do to me. And when I think of that, I don't feel sad anymore. Just this shattering anger.

"Mom." I wait for her to look at me. Steam drifts from our mugs. "You should know, I didn't do this to meet Sadie. I wanted to meet my father. She was the closest thing. And now she's I-don't-know-where. So . . ." Where's my quest for courage, and honesty and truth, gotten me? Nowhere. That's not an approximation, either. The honest-to-God, courageous truth. Lindsay won't speak to me. My father's still unknowable, as bottomless as the sea.

And now Sadie's gone too. The only person I had left has all but abandoned me.

My breasts feel tender. Another ache in a long day of aches. Maybe I'm getting my period. Maybe this is just what being without Sadie means, only I'm too wiped to think about even that anymore. Too wiped to do anything but take my phone out and dial Sadie's number. It'll go to voicemail, but I'd switch to speaker anyway. Let the song of her voice fill the room. *Hey. Leave a message . . .*

That's what I would do anyway, if Mom would just go. "Do you know what's going on with Sadie?" I demand. "What's happening? Where is she?" Then, answering my own questions, "Never mind. It's not like you'd tell me if you did know."

Rising, Mom turns to study me. She's going now, finally—only, her face is strangely blank, this moonlit movie screen. Her forehead creases like when she's working up to explaining something important. Likely logistics. Our lawyer's latest media defense strategy. Meanwhile, shots of me outside the hospital, cowering in Mom's armpit, will be forever slathered across the internet. S'MOTHER DEAREST, the headlines read. Now she steps forward, reaching for my hand.

"Koda." My name creaks out.

And I dissolve. It's not a voice you use to explain anything reasonable. It's the voice you use when somebody might be dead.

Astoria is gloomy this early in the morning. Filled with pigeons, and old people who look like pigeons. Everything smells wet, even though it hasn't rained.

A man in the vestibule of Sadie's building is doing something complicated with extension cords. He lets me in. No questions asked, just a curt "Morning." For all he knows, I live here. Thundering up the stairs, I call, "Forgot my keys!" over my shoulder. Really selling it.

3F looms at the end of the hall. I knock once. Twice. A few times. "Sadie?" I quaver. "Hello?" There is a peephole. I know how they work—but I try looking through it, just in case. "Sadie, it's me. Are you home?" I press closer to the door, only of course there's nothing there, just the grain of wood scratching my ear, and heat. I pull back. "My mom said . . ." She said Sadie had gone from the hospital straight to drug rehab. Which, okay, is not death. But close. Death-adjacent. Same with any other place that's away from me. I knock more on the door. Pound until my palms sting. Frustrated, sweating, I scream, "Dammit!" wrenching the doorknob.

It's open.

Open.

Thank you, thank you, beautiful paramedics.

The apartment looks the same. Flooded with sunlight, and in the two days since I've been here last, I forgot how good that feels, like pressing my face into my favorite pillow, breathing deep. There's the couch. Bookshelves. Clutter, of course. Her blanket lies crumpled on the rug. I fold it carefully. A bird, definitely a pigeon, coos on the fire escape.

She isn't here.

Mom didn't lie. I'm the untrustworthy one. Snuck out of the office the moment Mom got swallowed up by meetings, hailed a cab to another borough when I promised, *promised*, I'd focus on schoolwork. The take-home packets arrived today. I guess I just had to come here. Had to see for myself that this is real, and Sadie is gone, gone forever. For months. The thought trips some kind of wire inside me. I stumble blindly for the kitchen, her voice scraping through my head. *Can you cook an egg?*

Frankly, Sades, I don't have time for eggs. If Mom's meeting ends at ten, that leaves me just over an hour, but I do finish folding the blanket. I wet some paper towels to scrub at the blood crust in the bathroom, and then I open the medicine cabinet where the pill bottles are and fling them against the wall. I dump the pills out, an entire freaking rainbow of colors and shapes that I smash with my heel. We're talking worse than smithereens. I use the dustpan to sweep them up and flush them down the toilet. There's more. Once I start digging, I can't stop. I flush it all. Midol. My antacids. Everything but the baggie I find in the Tampax box, because there's only residue left. Grainy white powder. I flush the baggie, too.

Bloodshot eyes watch from the mirror. I press both hands to the glass, then cover my forehead. The coolness takes time to seep through.

Across the hall, her bedroom door stands ajar. The guitar must be lonely. Same as the unmade bed, which I wade onto. The pillows still smell like her, and I lie against them contemplating what it means when somebody calls you *baby*. Lindsay would never call me that. Mom, neither. It must be a name for somebody special. Somebody you kiss and bleed all over but never meant to abandon. No way Sadie would make a decision as major as attending rehab without telling me. We need each other too much.

I snuggle deeper into the pillow, my phone balanced on

my cheek. Time for another voicemail. I dial and wait.

Her nightstand buzzes.

Wait—not her nightstand. The drawer. I yank it open, and there it is. Her ancient flip phone, the battery nearly out of juice. 109 MISSED CALLS from "KR." A musical note dances on the tiny display screen. VOICEMAIL BOX FULL. The note has eyebrows. They wiggle as it tangoes back and forth.

I shut the drawer.

My head feels heavy, the pillow emitting its own gravitational force. But I can't sleep now, no matter how far away she is, or how gummy my eyes feel. I need to think. First I pop a Tums. Let it dissolve slowly.

Then—dimly—jingling. A dog? No . . . keys. I sit up. "Sadie?" I get tangled in the covers, splat to the floor. "Sadie!" I shout. She didn't go to rehab? She's back? I race for the living room to find a blond woman in a T-shirt and metallic down vest, tatted arms snug around a cardboard box. My heart hits my boots.

"Koda," Em says, perfectly nonchalant. Like of all potential disasters awaiting her in Sadie's apartment, I'm not so horrifying. She takes Sadie's jacket off its peg—the leather jacket with pins and sheepskin lining—and tosses it into the box. "I saw the news. Surprised your mom's let you out unsupervised. If you were my kid"—she drops the box onto the couch and picks up the blanket I folded, looks at the box—"I'd never let you out of my sight again. Like, ever." She rolls the blanket into a sausagey bundle.

"I'm eighteen. Or—will be, in a month and a half. Either way, my mom doesn't control me. What are you doing here?"

"What does it look like I'm doing?" She raises her free arm as she pushes past me, covering up a repulsively chunky cough. "What else could drag me off bed rest but a one-way ticket on Sadie's hot-mess express? She called me this morning. Apologies, list of demands, I know the drill. Figures she'd melt down this close to our deadline, but . . . here I am, to the rescue again. Don't tell me she gave the same orders to you. Otherwise, I'll feel redundant."

"You're lying," I say, unable to conceal my jealousy. "Sadie can't call you. Her phone's in the bedroom."

Em looks at me. "Listen, Koda, and I don't mean to blow your mind, but sometimes, phones aren't smartphones. Sometimes, they're hooked through a series of cables—"

"I know what a landline is!" My chest burns. I shouldn't have flushed the antacids. "I just don't buy that Sadie would call you first. She'd call me. You don't . . ." *Sadie doesn't care about you. The real you, that I know.* Em swings into the bathroom, but I'm right behind her. "Probably Sadie would've called me, but couldn't risk my mom finding out. I'm sure she's memorized my number." My justifications are thin, heart arrhythmic. If Lindsay's right . . .

Em ignores me, picking through the pill bottles on the floor, rolling them label up with her toes. "You trashed all these, didn't you? Damn—alprazolam too. I'm sober, been sober for ten months, so I shouldn't be talking like this, but trust me, benzos are fun. Figures Sadie would find a means of getting her hands on a prescription. Ain't that legit." Scooping up a bottle, she recites: "*Sarah V. Pasquale: Take One Orally at Onset of Symptoms*. Huh." The bottle clatters to the linoleum. "Must be for her anxiety."

I grab the bottle and set it on the sink. Anxious? Sadie? That doesn't compute. Em assesses various options for shampoo and conditioner before placing her selections in the box, saying more quietly, "Are you perplexed? The *V* stands for Vittoria."

No. Wikipedia told me months ago. But I say nothing. Dig my tongue against my teeth.

In the bedroom, Em moves—not purposefully, but with *authority*, filling the box with scrounged-up jeans and sweaters while I sit on the bed, arms wrapped around my aching stomach. You'd think she's been here before, or something. None of the clothes she collects off the floor. She discovers them in dresser drawers, closet compartments, even turning her back to me once so I won't see her with a bushel of black underwear. "She didn't mention how long she'd be away," she mutters to herself, folding up a fairy-green bathrobe that I can't fathom Sadie wearing. "Does she need another sweater? A real coat? On a scale of one to ten, ten being cutting glass—"

"Cutting glass?"

"You know, like how hard your nipples get?" Em chuckles at my blush. "You're a prude, then. Cute."

"I'm not a prude," I say hotly. "I just—Sadie's going to be

gone forever. Okay? The websites all say the typical rehab stay lasts ninety days." Her eyebrows jolt together, igniting a flash of triumph. At last, I've found my edge on her. "So if I were you, I'd get another box."

Em smirks. "Rehab? Like . . . drug rehab?"

Miserably, I nod. "My mom said this would be a wonderful opportunity for her." *Sadie is sick, Koda. She's been very sick, for a very long time.* "Do you know the name of the place?" I googled frantically last night, after Mom broke the news, but the links I tapped only led to reviews. Conflicting info about counselors, and the lack of vegetarian dining options.

"Shit, Koda." Em's laugh gives way to more coughing. "Sadie's not in rehab. She's up in Dutchess County. With Ted." She flips the box shut to show me the address scrawled on top. *T. DeRoche, 432 Broome Road, Dutchess Hills, NY.* "Not suggesting your mom's lying to you, of course. I've read practically all her old interviews—was always struck by her sincerity. In addition to, shall we say, her more salient qualities." Her eyelid does a little skip that's almost a wink. "God, wait, that's weird, right? It's weird to hit on your mom in front of you. My bad. But she's so gorgeous! In fact"—Em crouches over the box—"I remember when I was in college and that whole thing with your dad went down, her face just like, blasted all over the TV, and . . ." She shrugs. "I credit her with helping me realize some things about myself."

So Mom did lie, which inexplicably hurts worse than anything. Even the slap. Even if that's all she does now—lies and lies and lies. Only, that's not where my head's at right now. I get off the bed, looming over Em while she folds and refolds sweaters. "You're queer?" I venture.

She blinks up at me, nudging her rose-gold glasses with the back of her hand. "Bi, yeah. Was that not obvious?" Then she sighs, fake-wringing her hands at the chaos around us. "Of all my exes, Sadie might just be the most functional. I'm starting to think that says more about me than them. Pass me that shirt, please. Not the gray one. Black with the—yes." The shirt depicts a tarot card. A man sprawled facedown with ten swords stuck in his back. Em takes it, the cotton whispering against my fingers.

"You and Sadie . . ."

"Oh, did you not know?"

No. I never would've . . . but it . . . makes sense? I guess. All their murmuring and ragging on each other. The goodbye kiss. *Italian manners* my ass. "Sadie didn't tell me," I say.

"Not surprised," Em goes on as I bolt for Sadie's nightstand, the picture placed facedown there. "To be honest, I never really thought of Sadie as having a specific sexuality? Mostly, she seems to go where the feelings and drugs take her. That's from Christmas," she says as I flip the photo over. Like I'm an idiot. Like I couldn't have figured out from my father's jingle bell earrings, the pink in his and Sadie's cheeks, that this picture was taken over Christmas. Four months before I was born. "Their last, I think? Seems wildly counterintuitive that you'd go through the trouble of framing a picture only to never look at it, but what the hell do I know. Sadie's a mystery. You ask me . . ." I glance back at Em, and she clears her throat, maybe to hide the sadness creeping up with the phlegm. "Rehab might be the better choice."

I set the photo down.

At least it's not of Em.

Shirts properly swaddled, she pats the side of the box. "You didn't happen to spot any tape on your path of destruction, did you?"

When I shake my head, she wanders off to the living room.

Tingling, I pick the picture frame back up, run my thumb along its curved edge. Christmas. He had to have known he was going to be a father by then.

Leave before you get left, Sadie told me.

But he went back.

CHAPTER 28

ACTUALLY, GRAND CENTRAL IS GRANDER than the name implies. Massive. Bustling. A blue whale heart. It's just after one p.m. Tourists push past me, dragging children and wheely suitcases, stopping every five seconds to gawk and take pictures. I crash into the same family twice before realizing directions are inscribed on the marble archways. GRAND CONCOURSE. DINING CONCOURSE. OYSTER BAR. Gross.

On a hunch I head toward the Grand Concourse, checking to make sure my hood's still up and hair tucked away. Got to exercise caution in this swarm. The Grand Concourse thrums with echoes. A giant board posted in the middle lists departure times and track numbers. Inching closer to investigate, I notice a tourist point up, and my eyes follow automatically. The ceiling arched above us is covered in constellations. Green as our pool in LA was, before Mom hired that last groundskeeper.

I don't want to think about Mom now. The next train to Dutchess Hills departs in eight minutes, and she'll flip an absolute shit once she reads my texts. It's a risk I have to take. I meant what I told Em about being practically eighteen already, Mom not controlling me. I can do what I want, go where I please, and in the three days that have passed since I ransacked Sadie's apartment, Lindsay's started posting latergrams with Peter. The two of them kissing, all hearts and brain-dead lyrics.

Except Sadie, nobody wants me. Not even this stupid city. Which is why I have no choice but to go and be with her. Wherever that is.

Nearby, some guys my age are arguing about what is either a sport or a video game. One smiles my way, a perfectly benign, being-friendly-to-a-stranger smile, and I push quickly past them, guitar case aimed in front of me. "Hey!" they shout. "Watch it!" I mouth a silent thanks to Sadie, for helping me become so train-savvy.

The train drops me off just to the left of nowhere. A desolate, waterlogged field. The rain picked up as we were leaving New York City, and now it's really belting down. Luckily, Teddy's farm isn't that far from the train station, according to Google. Three miles. I head north—what my GPS eventually insists is north, after several false starts—squishing along the side of the increasingly busy road, sidestepping roadkill and headlights. A bridge appears, so I cross it, not stopping to examine the churning gray water below. Em wasn't kidding. It's chillier here than down in the city, my throat slick with snot. A ninety minute train ride shouldn't make that big of a difference. Fields unfold on either side of me, darkened to velvet by the rapidly setting sun. After what feels like hours of trudging, the fields start to come with white fences. I find a mailbox carved in the shape of an alpaca.

The driveway is steep and rutted as hell. I climb carefully, one hand thrust in my coat pocket and the other lifting the guitar case extra high to avoid the mud. Gradually, the house comes into view. Yellow. Two stories. A wraparound porch with a swing, and two upended tricycles. My fingers knit themselves around my mouth. I breathe on them fast, hard, but how can I focus on getting warm when the house is right here, and okay, maybe not the kind of house you'd expect rock stars to inhabit, its vinyl siding the color of old gum, but they're inside just the same. Lights are on, and I'm here, I'm *here*. All I'll ever need is locked inside.

The doorbell croaks. Nobody answers. I nail my finger to it, and the croaking echoes all through the house.

"Okay!" somebody yells. A man. Teddy? But I don't really know his voice. He never sang. "Okay, okay, coming!" The door flies open, revealing a man in jeans and a Beatles T-shirt with the sleeves pushed up. I start to introduce myself, only to close my mouth mid-hello. His eyebrows swoop. Recognition.

"Where's Sadie?" I ask.

Before he can answer, a little boy runs up, sees me, and dives behind Teddy's legs in terror. My excitement plummets. I forgot he had kids.

"Um," I say. Teddy's staring at me, his gaze bright but no-bullshit, exactly like in the pictures. He tells the boy to stay inside, bending to whisper instructions in his ear that I don't catch. Then he joins me on the porch, shutting the door firmly behind him.

"What are you doing here?" he demands.

"I—"

"This is private property. You're trespassing."

My stomach clenches. I didn't think he would be like this. Serious, yeah, but not . . . furious. I shove my hands in my sweatshirt pocket. It's not the same one Sadie bled all over, my JV swimming sweatshirt that I've lived in for months. This sweatshirt is charcoal gray. Artfully distressed. I thought it might complement the guitar. "I'm sorry. I know you've probably seen the news about us, and I get that Sadie's your best friend and you think you're protecting her, or whatever, but Em told me she was here, and—"

"Em?" He grimaces. "Who? Look, yes, I am very aware of what happened—" He reaches for me but stops, fingers just shy of closing around my shoulder. "I'm afraid you need to leave. Really."

"I can't—"

"Please. I'm sorry, Koda Rose, this isn't easy for me, either. . . ."

No. Fuck this. I didn't come all this way to get chucked off Teddy DeRoche's property like some crazed stalker fan. How do I tell him that? How do I explain that I might do something really stupid if he doesn't cut the crap and let me see Sadie, something like—I don't know, lie down slowly in that disgusting river? But this is exactly what I say, and in that pause that follows, I become aware of a gentle patter. Rain? Again? A drop slides off my nose and I realize, I'm the patter. Soaked and shivering.

The door creaks wider. "Ted, what the fuck's taking so long—"

Sadie freezes when she sees me. We both freeze. Her dreads are pulled back, and she looks the same, only worse, in this puffy-eyed, bare-lashes way, not one but two sticky kids barnacled to her legs. Their braids are identical. Their faces.

One waves. I hate kids. But I'm so shocked, I wave back.

"Language," Teddy sighs.

"Language," the boys mimic, pinching her. She yelps.

A white cat wanders out and writhes around my ankles. Ted and Sadie remain silent, trading fire with their eyes. Meanwhile, she's barely looked at me. *Sadie.* I try to beam her some kind of message. A reminder that she told me not to go, and I haven't. I never will. Then she spots the guitar, and something seems to loosen inside her.

"Listen up, troops." She squats to address the twins, not that she technically needs to. "Remember that pack of cards from last night? I want you to go downstairs and throw them all over the rec room. Fifty-two-card pickup. I know your daddy yelled at us before, only now"—she fishes for his eye, but he's turned away from her, pinching the bridge of his nose—"I've got a hunch he won't care." The boys run off shrieking. Sadie stands. Her jeans are too long, cuffs rolled but still piling over her bare feet. I don't recognize those jeans. Or the saggy Yeti sweater.

"Hello, Koda." This wrinkle in her voice.

"Sadie," Teddy says.

I want to touch her.

"Sadie, I swear to Christ—"

"What?" she barks. "You think I called her? How would . . ." The word catches. Our eyes connect, and I get this feeling—this fizzy, reckless feeling. Teddy steps back. Too close not to have felt it too.

"A minute," Sadie says.

I go molten. Full-body flush.

"Give us a minute, Teddy, won't you?"

"A minute," Ted says, holding up a finger. Just one.

The room Sadie pulls me into off the entryway is dark and musty-smelling, but I don't care, because I'm here. Sadie's here. And now she's shutting the door and rushing toward me, whispering my name. I don't know how I catch her, but I do.

"Sadie, oh God, I missed you. I missed you so much!" I was hoping to say something better than this. Something cool, and clever. But with her skinny legs hooked around my waist, I don't need to be either. The force of our impact smashed me into the furniture. Some kind of humungous desk that I can barely make out in the darkness.

"I know," she says quietly. "Kiddo, I know, I thought about you every goddamn minute. What are you doing here? Are you crazy?" She takes my face in her hands. "Does your mother know—"

No. Mom has no idea. Presumably. My phone's deep in my backpack, on silent—but mentioning Mom has made Sadie paler. "I thought you were dead," I say, wheezing with excitement. Relief. "I thought I'd never see you again. My mom told me you went to rehab. She's doing everything she can to keep us apart!" Sadie slides from my arms.

"Did go, but I couldn't . . ." She falters. "Rehab's a little been there, done that for me, you know? That kumbaya twelve-step garbage, it's not exactly my style."

"Oh." I guess it wouldn't be. But if she's still using drugs . . . if rehab could help . . .

"Of course, Ted'll tell you I should've stayed. So why, I ask, would he help bust me out?" A thread of hair clings to my lips. I feel it tickling, and then the brush of Sadie's fingers as she pushes it impatiently away. "You're wild," she murmurs. A compliment. It must be.

I grab her hand. "Will Teddy let me stay?"

"Minute's up," he booms through the door.

While Sadie goes to open it, I smooth my hair, right my sweatshirt. No way she would've told him that we kissed. He's just doing his overbearing concern thing. At least, that's what Sadie accuses him of as he steps into the room. Light from the hall spills in, and I realize we're in some kind of office.

Paperwork stacked in piles, a slumbering MacBook. The whole far wall is lined with trophies. Alpaca trophies. BEST FIBER ART, STUD OF THE YEAR, BEST FLEECE. I almost don't realize that Ted's staring at me.

"He would have done this," he says after a long moment. His voice is so ordinary. Not deep. Not high. Even if he could sing, I can't imagine my father letting him.

Sadie leans against the door, arms folded. "Told you." In the sallow light she looks worse than ever, her mouth swollen and bruised. I swallow, ignoring memories of her lurching from my arms that day in the bathroom, heaving up the blood that had drained into her stomach. The memory is so visceral, that I struggle to work out what they're implying.

Of course my father would've done this. That's the point. But their acknowledgment still makes me breathless. "Thanks."

Teddy tugs thoughtfully at his curls and says we might as well move into the kitchen. An impossibly green kitchen at the back of the house, with avocado-colored appliances and some other vegetable—cabbages?—dotting the wallpaper. That's also how the place smells. Old cabbage. And manure, courtesy of mucky boots stacked by the door. The table is covered in what appears to be more paperwork. Teddy jerks out a chair but then sits in another, across from it. Sadie begins puttering around the cabinets.

"I feel," Teddy says, not ungently, "that you owe us an explanation, Koda Rose. I assume that your mother doesn't know where you are, and is probably going out of her mind with worry. I also assume Sadie's told you my rule about the guitar. Not that that's more important than your mom's peace of mind, but . . ." He pulls one of Sadie's dreads as she passes by, making her cringe and smack his arm. "Let's say it is."

The guitar case is propped in a corner. Teddy must have carried it in while I was reuniting with Sadie. He must've hunted around the kitchen for a clean, uncluttered place to put it, far from the shit boots.

"You've got to do something about these locs, Sades," Ted's saying.

She flicks him off.

"This is your last warning, and I mean it. As your sole Black friend, I do not, nor will I ever, condone this." He turns back to me, eyebrows raised. "So?"

I linger by the chair he pulled out, wondering if it's for me. If it'd be too presumptuous or totally beside the point if I asked him to call me Koda. There are cabbages on the back of the chairs, too, but painted. I trace one with a fingertip. Where to begin?

"Ted's been real hot for the *I feel* statements lately," Sadie says, spooning grounds into a coffee maker. She faces the counter—I can't read the slope of her shoulders, if she's trying to cover for me, or what. Once again, Teddy grimaces, which must be a thing with him. Every line in his face seems to be waiting for it. *"Sadie,"* she mocks, in Ted's nothing voice, "*when you do X, I feel Y.* Which, you know, makes me feel like total shit, but there you have it."

Deciding the chair is for me, I sit down. A cat jumps immediately into my lap. Not the white one from before, but a ginger tabby determined to show me her butthole. I dodge her stringy tail while Teddy cradles his head in his hands.

"Okay." He straightens, rubbing his big dry paws together. "Okay, Koda Rose—"

"Koda," I rasp.

He doesn't seem to hear. "I'll explain, since Sadie refuses. This is the third—no, fourth time?—that Sadie's attempted rehab. First couple, she almost makes it through the program. Then some big anniversary rolls around, Mack's death, their first date, whatever, to make her relapse, and here I come driving all over the state to pick her up and bring her home. Third, she gets clean. Stays clean until"—he points at me, then wiggles his fingers, boom, confetti flying—"she meets you. And now her nose is bleeding again. She's got to have surgery. Okay? I'm sorry. I know you're just a kid, and this must all be very exciting for you, this grown-up person with her grown-up problems, but you've got to accept responsibility for your actions. That guitar represents . . ." He stabs a finger at it. "How the hell did you get ahold of it anyway?"

I'm too busy processing this new information—Sadie only mentioned rehab didn't work for her; I didn't realize she'd tried and struggled and been bailed out so many times—that I don't see her mouth pressed into a thin, white scar. Not until I'm saying, "What do you mean, how did I get ahold of the guitar? I didn't. Sadie showed me. In her apartment," and her whole face collapses. *What's wrong?* I try to ask with my eyes. What was my mistake?

"Seriously?" Ted says.

She turns away, wiping her cheeks with the back of her hand.

"The guitar was in storage. I got—you're supposed to be using the goddamn storage unit, Sadie!"

Storage unit? What is he talking about? "Sadie's been teaching me to play," I say with all the snottiness I can muster. "She's an amazing teacher, even though I'm pretty much hopeless. Bad just like my father."

At that, Ted tilts his head. He glances back at Sadie. "Bad?"

"Started bad, stayed bad," I quote proudly. Sadie swirls a finger on the countertop.

"I mean . . ." Ted's looking at me now. "Don't get me wrong, he wasn't a natural, not like Our Lady of Chaos over here, but he was never *bad*."

"I don't believe you."

"So don't. But that's the truth. We met at jazz band practice—he played bass too. Whooped my ass at bass, in fact."

A crash downstairs. Yelling. There might be more than cards being thrown in the basement. I want to scream at Ted that I'm not a kid, that my very presence in his kitchen, my refusal to buy into his stupid lies, proves as much. But he pushes up from the table, glancing at the clock. "I've got to take the boys to their grandparents'," he announces, then moves off into the hallway, bellowing, *"Boys!"*

Say something, Sadie. Come on. *Say something.* Tell Teddy he's wrong.

Sadie nibbles her sweater cuff.

The cat purrs into my face.

She moves away from the counter when the boys stampede into the kitchen, clutching jackets. Sadie screws herself together to help *them*, maneuvering arms and zipping zippers more expertly than expected. Either the boys aren't old enough not to stare at strangers, or Teddy hasn't gotten around to imparting this valuable lesson yet. I glare back at them, rooted to my chair.

"That's Koda," Sadie says, not quite looking at me. She points to a twin—the stickier-looking of the two. "Archie." She points to the other. "Jet."

"*I'm* Jet!" the stickier one screeches, and Sadie makes a show of acting astonished, clutching her head, which makes them howl. The fury I've been holding back crashes over me.

"Don't you realize she's humoring you?" I demand.

Sadie flinches, but I might as well be talking to the cabbages. The boys hop around her. Too stupid, and little and naive, to understand what I meant anyway. I stand. My chair shrieks against the linoleum. "Are you going to be here when we get back, Aunty Sadie?" one asks as I push into the hall. I glance back at her. One last, helpless grab of a glance—does she not care where I'm going? Sadie chuckles, pretending to bonk the boys' heads together.

"Depends on how well you behave. . . ."

Teddy's in the foyer, sorting through a heap of sneakers.

"Sadie wouldn't lie to me," I inform him.

He pauses, a different shoe in each hand. "Did I say she lied?"

"You contradicted what she told me. Same thing."

Teddy digs two more shoes from the pile, then takes something from the closet. Stiff, brown canvas, more tarp than coat. I look back toward the kitchen, and when I refocus on Teddy, he's adjusting the tarp-coat's collar, watching me closely. "You're incredibly tall," he says.

"Five ten," I reply automatically. Then, "Taller than him."

I meant this defiantly, but he laughs, the sound big and unexpected. A door slamming. "Not hard."

The boys appear. Teddy grabs his keys off an alpaca-shaped hook on the wall. "Archie, wait," he warns, but they're gone already, tumbling out into the night. The white cat slinks inside. Teddy sighs. And it's not until he steps closer to me that I understand how blue his eyes are. Not the deep, broody blue of my father's, but flickering, practically holographic in their intensity. "Your dad . . . he's been gone a long time. Eighteen years, just about. You've got to excuse us if our memories of him aren't perfect."

No. No. Memory fading is no excuse at all. Sadie and Ted lived with my father. They did drugs together, and laughed and had sex and fought about songs. They *knew* him. If I'd had the same privilege, every second I spent with him, every word he spoke, would be in my head forever. Wrapped in velvet paper.

Damp air trickles through the door, smelling like grass, and rain, and more shit. I shiver, stuffing my hands in my armpits.

"I'm heading one county over. Two hours, round-trip," Teddy tells me. He starts for the porch, then stops. "Please don't be here when I get back."

When I return to the kitchen, Sadie has the window cracked over the sink, a cigarette tucked in the corner of her mouth. As I approach, she removes it with a guilty swipe.

"Just me." The words seem weighted somehow. Like just by saying them, I'm disappointing her. She lights up, takes the hard, hungry drag she's probably been dying for since Teddy bailed her out of rehab. Now his words—*You've got to excuse us if our memories of him aren't perfect*—tumble through my brain. "Sades?" I wait for her to look at me. "How come you told me my father was . . . you never said he played bass."

Sadie studies the cigarette's red-hot tip. "You try it, ever?"

My last remaining defense—a casual shrug.

I have acid reflux and a pet frog. Every instrument is a mystery to me.

"Easiest goddamn thing to play in the world, let me tell you. Stand there and pluck it." She ashes the cigarette over the sill.

Her crumpled pack of Newports sits on the counter. I sense her watching with approval as I draw one out. A charge leaps through my fingertips, and I almost drop it. The insides of my cheeks start to sweat.

She smirks. "Make you puke."

One puff and I'm coughing. Sadie rubs my back in that

funny way of hers. Up and down instead of in circles, like Mom would.

For a few minutes we just stand here. My head spins from the nicotine, this caving sensation opening inside me that I don't know how to acknowledge without everything else caving too. Mostly, I try to copy Sadie. The cool, easy way she balances the cigarette between her fingers. Hers is a stub, mine ashy, when we crush them out in the sink.

Sadie mutters, "Ted'll kick my ass out too if he smells smoke on me."

So she heard us talking in the hall. She heard him say I had to leave, and didn't do anything to defend me. I don't know how to process this. I can't go home yet.

Sadie's lighting up again when I touch her shoulder.

"Shower," I say.

CHAPTER 29

UPSTAIRS, TEDDY'S HOUSE IS THICKLY carpeted, the mat in the little guest bathroom noodly between my toes. Water drums into the tub, Sadie silhouetted by the plastic curtain. I hear her gurgle and spit. "Tastes like shit," she complains.

My legs quiver. I try to draw them up, but the toilet is unacceptably narrow, especially with the seat down. Steam billows, blurring the medicine cabinet and tiny window. Bottles line the tub ledge. I study the labels. Pantene, and some kind of off-brand body wash that's supposed to smell like cupcakes.

Sadie says, "Big risk, coming all this way."

"I had to."

She sets something down. "Teddy—"

"I don't care what Teddy thinks. He's an idiot. Okay? Best friends, they say they want what's best for you, maybe even put up a really convincing front, but they don't know anything.

They're all idiots!" If she agrees, she doesn't show it. The body wash bottle disappears. Sadie sticks a hand out, and I reach to pull a washcloth from the shelf above the toilet, doing my best to ignore that she's naked.

She laughs. "Well, excuse me, princess."

I close my eyes. Squeeze them tight, tighter, until sparks shower across my lids. When I open them, Sadie's silhouette is squirting shower gel into the washcloth. It actually does smell like cupcakes. Sprinkles, and vanilla, and yellow dough. I push my breath out my mouth. *This grown-up person with her grown-up problems* . . . like mine don't qualify. Like no matter how old I get, how much I learn about my father, I'll never be grown-up enough to fully comprehend him.

In Sadie's version of my father, the version that I have clung to these past two months, he's this wild renegade. Reckless, only functionally talented, a quiet loner. In the other version, Teddy's version, a crucial new detail: he played bass. I don't know why that matters to me. It shouldn't. Not this much. He could have played bass, and been all of the other things Sadie claimed he was. This image I've cherished of him helping me with Lindsay and teaching me guitar, laughing at our mutual suckiness—that could still be true. Couldn't it?

My phone jolts against my thigh.

Hey. The bracelet is beautiful. thx <333

just wanted to let u know that.

It must be my disbelief, the shock at finally hearing from her, that makes me type, Ur welcome.

Also I . . .

Ugh idk how to say this but

When ur ready to talk about my visit

Just know that I am 2. Ok???

Talk? About . . . ? If the visit had gone better, I could tell her what happened with Sadie. Omg, Linds, guess where I am right now??? Obviously, she hasn't been following the blogs.

Then again, if we hadn't fought, if I'd chilled out and maybe just *listened* to her concerns about Sadie, I wouldn't be here at all.

I don't say anything more, and neither does Lindsay. While Sadie finishes up, I doodle a hole in the foggy window and look out of it, at the blank space where the moon should be.

"Got nothing but Karen's stuff for the time being," Sadie explains, rooting through a dresser in the room where she's staying. A guest room, with a pullout bed heaped in quilts that I think somebody actually sewed. The walls are yellow. Happy yellow. Sadie sits next to me on the bed, half-dressed in flannel pj pants and a wireless bra, a sweater lumped on her lap. She doesn't seem to have the strength to put it on.

"Em said she was going to the post office right away."

Sadie seems satisfied by that. The sweater stinks. Old-lady-lavender. I can't stand it. Lurching up, I seize her towel off the dresser. But where to put it? Too much carpet and wood.

Sadie gestures for me to drop it on the floor, so I do, trying not to stare at her ribs. The belly button charm I didn't know she had.

She picks at the black polish on her toes. "So, it's good to see you. You look well."

"I don't feel well." For precision: I currently feel like a lot of things. Just not that.

"I regret"—Sadie keeps picking nail polish, dreads obscuring her face—"don't have time to list them all, frankly. But I especially wish I'd been more honest with you about the drugs. I meant to, but then it seemed like . . . you were so innocent. Naive, to tell the truth. And then when you told me you'd never drank, never smoked pot, I figured . . . I guess I was terrified you might think less of me."

My weight makes the mattress fart as I sit back beside her. "I'm not mad at you about the drugs," I say quietly. "And you're not the first person to call me naive. That honor goes to Lindsay."

It's like Sadie wants to smile but doesn't have all the pieces. She doesn't look like a rock star anymore; even a retired one. Just bony, and fragile and sad in a way that makes me want to push away from her, even though I've also never wanted to hold her so bad.

"She's your Teddy, then," Sadie says.

Possibly. But also . . . more.

So much more.

I suck my cheek. The curtains are tied, and the view, despite the stuffiness of the room, is spectacular. You can see the entire valley spilling out below, including the twinkly village, the ice-choked gray river that I crossed to come here. "That's the Hudson," Sadie says as I get up for a closer look.

"How'd you know I was thinking about that?"

She chuckles. "Me and Mack saw a whale in it once, when we lived on the west side."

"What?" I look at her. "A whale? What kind?"

"Dumb one, obviously. We were walking along the Greenway. It was late, after midnight, and suddenly Mack points out at the water and—I didn't know what I was looking for at first. You know how it can be at night, and Mack sometimes . . . but then he grabs my shoulders, all, 'Look, Sades! Look!' and no shit, there's this massive goddamn whale out there in the river."

Likely a humpback. Their migration routes take them up the Atlantic, straight to Canada. "What'd you do?"

"Watched it. We both did. His arm was around my shoulders, right, and I could feel his heart slamming against me and this giant whale out there breathing and I thought, *This is it. This is the happiest I'll be in my whole life.*" She wipes her eyes. This furious brush of her knuckles. "We never told a soul. You going to ask Teddy if he remembers that?"

Well, that's precisely what I'm starting to realize. The exact trouble with justifying your existence around somebody so famous and so gone.

As beautiful as Sadie's story is, as much as it could reveal about my father, I'm not going to pull it apart this time. I'm too exhausted to go in with my Koda scalpel, dicing details to figure out exactly who my father was. I don't want to know that he saw a whale with Sadie, or put his arm around her shoulders. I don't even want to know anymore if he was talented, to tell the truth.

I must've sat back down, because I feel the quilt beneath me, and Sadie kneeling, her wet cheek pressed against my knee. Hesitantly, I touch her callused fingers to my lips.

Which was it, Dad? Guitar or bass? Six strings or four? I don't care.

None of that reveals who you would've been to me.

CHAPTER 30

I FEEL THE SILENCE BEFORE I STEP OFF THE elevator. The doors shut behind me, and there are no footsteps. No Mom in my face, demanding to know where I've been or what the hell I was thinking. Silence coats everything—kitchen and great room, silvery city views—like a layer of dust. The carpet, too thick to begin with, squishes beneath my wet shoes. I click on a lamp.

"Mom?"

Nothing.

God. Where is she?

I bend to unlace my All-Stars. A lock of hair slithers into my eyes and I swipe it back, smelling Pantene.

"Koda."

I jerk. Mom's at the hall entrance, blue robe and a chignon again. One look at her, the bones jutting in her face, and I know I'm done for.

"Didn't you get my texts?" I say. "I told you not to worry—"

She turns and goes back to her room.

When my eyes unstick, it's practically noon. I lie for a moment in the blackout curtains' manufactured darkness, uneasiness spreading through me. The smell emanating from outside my room doesn't help. This vague, familiar odor that I can't place, thick in the air and the back of my throat. My phone is somewhere under the covers. I fell asleep with it cradled against my cheek.

In the kitchen, Mom frowns over a mixing bowl, chrome appliances glinting ferociously in the late-morning sunlight. She doesn't look at me as I approach the breakfast bar, slide uneasily onto the stool across from her. "Good morning," I try.

Usually, Mom ties her hair back to cook, but today, it's brushed out over her shoulders, so red it throws sparks. I fold my hands, bracing for her to yell, slap me, like that day at the hospital. She licks her thumb and turns a page in the cookbook propped on the counter.

A funny feeling flickers through me. I push onto the balls of my feet, trying to make out the recipe. "You're cooking?"

Snow drifts lazily from the sky. Even winter is over winter.

"Mom?"

She grabs the mixing bowl and pivots, her back to me.

"Mom." The slaps of my bare feet echo as I join her, almost gouging my hip against the counter. She hasn't made anything but smoothies since we moved. "Mom? What are you doing?"

Her mouth dips. I am useless. As irrelevant as the pazzos yammering at her elbow in those old clips. "Please," I beg. "What's wrong?" Finally, she glances my way. An incidental glance as she wipes the wooden spoon on a rag.

"Nothing's wrong, Koda. I'm making brunch."

"Brunch?"

She keeps wiping the spoon.

"But . . . aren't you mad at me? Aren't you upset?" Stupid questions. She must be furious. It's just that this is a mood, a Mom, I don't recognize. "I broke a rule. I . . . I ran away—"

"You must have seen the news."

"What news?" I haven't been on my phone at all. But then Mom looks at me, *really* looks, and the flickering sharpens to a sting. I sprint to my bedroom, return to the kitchen with my phone. Mom's expression remains maddeningly neutral as I scroll through it.

Blogs got the scoop. Candids of me in Grand Central—Koda Rose Grady strolling through the grand concourse, gawking at the departure board. Bystanders argue about which stops I peered into, mock my futile disguise—*"A sweatshirt? Come on. Mack's a legend around here. We know what his kid looks like"*—even though that was an accident. Literally how I dress. The article continues: *The impulsive getaway appears to be just another in a string of incidents involving the late rock god's troubled daughter and his equally troubled ex, Sadie Pasquale. Although Miss Grady's ultimate destination could not be verified, it seems more than slightly coincidental that she would travel upstate hours after news broke of Sadie's latest rehab stint.*

My eyes fill and I shut them, savoring the tiny burn. Of course I was spotted. Of course. What's next? Ever since we moved here, the thinnest membrane's existed between me and the rest of the world, and now it's been torn open for good. "That's not fair," I say. "There's no connection between me and Sadie. Not anymore. I"—it's almost too painful to say—"I said goodbye for real this time. For good." Mom sticks a finger in the mixing bowl and licks it, my phone on the counter between us.

"Maybe you should have thought of the consequences of your actions beforehand, Koda. Time after time, I swoop to your rescue, and yet none of my efforts really seem to work in the end, do they? No matter what, you're bent on doing things your way." She pushes the bowl aside and smiles. A silk-rose smile. "Let's do that, then. Let's see how it works. You are, after all, so grown-up."

My stomach tightens.

Mom shuts her eyes. I watch her throat kick around a little before she says, "Please set the table."

CHAPTER 31

I'VE BEEN AT THE MAGAZINE'S HEAD-quarters for exactly five seconds when an assistant I don't recognize accosts me with a sandwich.

"Mother's orders," he explains.

"I know." It's multigrain. I thank him and continue to Mom's office, working the crust off beneath slippery wax paper.

"Figured you'd run off again," she says as I drop my backpack by the sofa.

"No. I decided to walk." Cold air has been feeling better and better lately, helps clear my head.

Mom looks angry. *Walking* has not been part of the arrangement—I've been taking taxis here after school—but now I thought of it, so it will be. That's part of our agreement. Her whole, *let's do things your way.* I sink onto the sofa, and the leather squeaks accommodatingly. Mom continues studying whatever fashion quandary is currently laid out on her desk.

Apologizing won't help. I've said sorry five thousand freaking times in the week that's passed since I got home. Last night was the worst. I went into her room, bawling for no reason other than that I suck, and have lost everybody, and there's nothing in the world, *nothing*, I can do to win Lindsay back. She was right about Sadie. About all of this. I should've understood that. I should've listened. . . .

Haltingly, I unwrap my sandwich. Pesto. Roasted red peppers. Mozz. Inexplicably, my vision blurs, and I take a breath. Let it out slow.

Mom doesn't talk to me while I eat, but composes herself in increments, tugging the various strings of her body until her mouth inches up and nostrils quit flaring. It creeps me out how she can do that. She flexes her fingers, and every knuckle cracks.

"Mom."

She waves at the mess I made on the coffee table. "Clean that up."

Rolling my eyes, I ball my trash up and head for the next room—a kitchen with a microwave and espresso maker, for her use only. The trash can is against the wall.

At first the flowers don't register. All I see in the trash is my wad of wax paper, and beneath that shreds of color—yellows and browns and reds. "Whoa," I say, my voice sounding strange even to me in the tight, airless room. "Who are these from?" She pitched the whole bouquet. I lift it carefully, dusting off coffee grounds. Not the greatest flowers. Pretty, because who would give flowers that aren't, but the sleeve is thick plastic, like I've seen wrapped around bouquets outside bodegas. I stroke the scraggly petals. "What are these called?" I ask, turning. At the desk, Mom remains motionless, sun on her face. "Black-eyed whatevers, right?"

A card is tucked inside. Well, more of a note. I unfold it.

KODA—
FORGIVE ME

The bouquet tumbles from my hands. I lunge after it, scrambling for a cup, a glass, but it's no use, the cabinets don't have anything tall enough. Mom approaches.

"Cut them."

Noise in my head.

"Honey, hang on. You can cut the stems."

I let her do it. We place the glass of flowers in the center of Mom's desk, and then I pull up a chair beside hers and we sit together, her knee resting periodically against mine. After a minute, I scoot the flowers closer to the sun.

"They wouldn't let her in," Mom says. "Security escorted me downstairs to the entrance. If you hadn't decided to walk, you might not have missed her."

I ignore that. "How did she look?"

"Like Sadie."

I pinch a petal between my fingers.

"She asked about you. I told her you were fine, we were both fine, and she just smiled at me, like—I don't know, like she knew I was lying. She's so hard to read."

"Sometimes." Her texts, though.

I've been deleting those all week.

"Why did you put them in the garbage? Did you not want me to see them?"

Mom gets up and shuts the cabinets. Pours a glass of water, inspects her cuticles. "I don't know what I was thinking, Koda, other than that I wish we'd never come here. This is hard for me. Letting you do your own thing, after all that's happened—and knowing you'll eventually make more mistakes. Knowing my first instinct will be to fix them, but accepting that sometimes the best I can do as a parent is step back and let the consequences fall how they may. Should I have invited Sadie to wait for you?"

"I don't know," I say quickly. "I don't know what I'd say. I didn't know she was back in the city. Ted—that's who she's been staying with, the bassist—"

A funny smile. "I know who Teddy is."

"Oh, okay. Anyway, he said she'd have to have surgery. I thought he meant right away."

"She does." Mom sets the glass down. "And after she heals, another go at rehab. We discussed that a little—honestly, I think she's more nervous about getting clean than having the doctors cut her up. But I told her about some of my friends who have been in recovery for years. Staying sober is hard, but she's tough. I'll pay, of course."

When you're in the ocean and a wave smacks you hard, hurls you forward only to rake you back again? Whatever words I'm looking for probably mean that. I go up beside Mom. She's not crying, but her face is red, chest heaving. Her fingers are splayed across her mouth.

"Why?"

She shakes her head.

"But—"

"She's so sick, Koda, but that's only part of why I didn't want you to meet her. Mostly, I was . . . I was afraid you'd blame me."

I ask what she means.

"For everything." Mom shrugs, helpless. "For her life. Eighteen years I've tried to convince myself, Sadie chose this. She chose to use drugs, but the way you talk about her—the way she talks about you—I could tell you were both helping each other through something huge." She laughs. This breathy, shimmering laugh she bottles for parties. "Bigger than I'll probably ever understand, right? But that's okay. I have to be okay with that."

I bite down on one callused fingertip, the most grounding thing I can think to do that she won't see. "You could've helped me."

Sometimes I think Mom's as mirror-averse as I am. She looks up, turning from her reflection in the window.

"You could've told me more about my dad from the beginning," I say. "You could've . . . I just wanted stories. Pieces of him that only I would get to see. I know you hate him, but—"

Her eyes widen. "I don't hate him."

"You—"

"I didn't *know* him."

My fingertip is still in my mouth. Mom pulls it away.

"We met at a party. I slept with him once, and whatever small talk we made before that, I—well, it's gone. I remember different things from that night. Like, how windy it was on the walk home. Ridiculously windy, even for LA. I didn't think about him at all. Even after I found out I was pregnant, I didn't think about him. That was other people, pushing their concerns onto me. It was a chaotic time. I learned to live with it." She shrugs. "I don't mind that we were never officially 'together,' never had this grand romance like him and Sadie. The press treated it like this massive 'screw off, Mariah' once she took him back, but that was all of their construction. Spin, to sell magazines. I never thought of it as Mack *choosing* her—there was nothing between us in the first place. I'm not embarrassed by my choices. I'm not ashamed. If you want to ask me anything . . . ask about that."

I sneak a fingertip back in my mouth. These last two months, all I've done is ask questions. And now with every day that passes, I find out they were exactly the wrong ones. But—

"You could've brought that up yourself, Mom."

She seems to think a moment. "Yes." She tugs my hand away again, more firmly. "That's probably true."

Back at her desk, I help her get organized for her next meeting. It involves combing through a portfolio of concept sketches—the work of up-and-coming designers The Magazine might bless with a feature. One designer in particular catches my eye. Their clothes are so chaotic. Major themes include slashes. Splatters. "The pattern on this dress kind of reminds me of a whale." A jumbo red swirl on the front, surrounded by speckles that could be plankton, if you squint hard enough.

Mom smiles, rolling sketches into a canister. "You would think it's a whale."

Actually, I don't think that's true. I haven't thought about whales, really thought about them, since I met Sadie. Or before Sadie. When I got mocked into taking my posters down. I regret that. Mostly, though, I regret judging Lindsay for choosing Peter over swimming. Those choices, it seems to me now, happen so easily.

The sketches are almost all packed away. Mom eyes the whale sketch, half-rolled in my hand. "Honey, could you hand me—"

"I do have one question."

She pauses. Nervousness glossed with a smile.

When we get home, I'm putting my posters back up. I'm going to ask even more questions. But I'll start with her and my dad and that night. "I was just wondering . . . what you did after you met my dad. After you walked home."

"Oh." Her cheeks are pink. So much for not being embarrassed. "It must've been around three a.m., but my roommates were still up. We made pancakes."

"Drunk pancakes?"

"Pancakes," she repeats, reaching for the whale sketch. As I hand it to her, I can almost see her on the walk home that night, red tendrils of hair whipped up by the wind. Sprinkling cinnamon into pancake batter, laughing with her roommates like I used to laugh with Lindsay.

Mom freezes when I hug her. So shocked, and quiet and still, that I put a hand to her mouth to make sure she's still breathing. She bats it gently away.

Soon an assistant will bang on her office door, reminding her that she is needed immediately. But for now, her fingers are edging through my hair. I tip my head up to let her kiss my forehead. Some things you'll never be too old for.

CHAPTER 32

I ALREADY HAVE OUR COFFEES AND A half-moon cookie, snuggled in cellophane, when Sadie shuffles into Fazes. We don't say hello, but I have to hug her. It's too weird not to, even with half the café and Register Guy watching. She smells exactly like I remember—like ash and wet mittens. My hands nest in the small of her back and she touches her head to my chest, locked in this hug that warps the world.

Until Register Guy asks if we want lids for our coffees, and we both mumble no.

Sadie grabs our cups off the counter. It's freezing, but she insists on sitting in the little courtyard out back, which in all my trips here I never realized existed. The ashtray on our spindly iron table is crescent moon–shaped, the day overcast and windy. While Sadie rips through sugar packets, I gather the empties that haven't blown away, then pull my backpack onto my lap. Partly to keep pigeons from investigating, but also because I won't be nearly as tempted to touch her again with this much bulk between us. I won't fantasize about running a foot up her leg or cupping her cheek or squeezing her fingers, since soon her calluses will be getting soft anyway.

Sadie pulls her scarf back over her mouth, and we sit together in silence, huddled in our coats.

"That scarf's longer than you," I say.

She picks a fleck of paper off her tongue. "Five feet, one inch. Didn't I tell you Ted's a comedian?" Her smile's a sliver, but a sliver's still something. I press my foot against the guitar case she stashed beneath the table.

"Thanks for meeting me." I look down into my coffee, at the cream making lace on top. "And bringing the guitar."

"Your wish is my command." She gives a twitch to her cigarette, her smile flimsy suddenly. Propped up. I've been dabbing my eyes on her scarf, but now she takes it from me, covers her face.

"I'm sorry."

"Sadie."

"I'd never lie—"

"I know. Stop apologizing." Her knee jiggles beneath the table. I keep my shoe on the guitar case, hoping New York hasn't made the treads too gross. "You really don't mind me taking her?"

She shakes her head. "She belongs with you. Besides, it's not like I'll be getting much work done anyway, where I'm headed. Just here getting my things in order. Promise you'll update me every once in a while, though. Pictures and such. I want to know what you're playing."

I smile. That's a very optimistic read on my abilities, but I figure it's time to stop thinking I'm bad and inept at everything. My father clearly wasn't.

Depending on who you ask.

"Will do," I say.

We finish our coffee in silence. Or pretend to. She doesn't mention visiting Mom at the office, and I don't bring it up. Beneath a nearby table, pigeons on crumb patrol battle over a scone. Sadie leans her chin on her fists, watching them. I ask her, "Did you know they're actually doves?"

"These things? Really?"

"Rock doves. They're like, coastal pigeons. But we built cities and took their habitats away."

"Coastal pigeons." She bends to crumble the scone, and the doves go wild. "Killer band name."

We giggle and her eyes crease, and the feeling that's always bubbling when I'm with Sadie rushes to overtake me. Love, no doubt. But something else too. Gratitude. "Maybe you could start that band once you're doing better. Coastal Pigeons. Except"—I scrabble for a joke—"no bass. Okay? No matter what, there absolutely cannot be bass."

"Got it. Only obscure percussion." The cigarette jitters to her lips.

"Sadie." I swallow. "Promise you'll send me updates too? When you can," I add, assuming there'll be restrictions around these things at first. From what I've read about rehab, it sounds pretty strict. "Even if it does take a long time for us to get back in touch, I want you to know I'll be thinking of you. No matter what. I want you to know that . . ." The crack in my voice widens. "You *can* get better."

The cigarette smolders, caught between her lips. She grinds it out quickly. "Doesn't feel that way. It feels like . . ." A dismissive laugh. "Told you I was a wreck, didn't I? Told you I wasn't brave."

She gets up, and this is the part I've been putting off. What neither of us knows how to do, a goodbye more official than me rushing from Teddy's house in my still-wet clothes. I take a finger, my chord-playing one, and trace a path from her forehead, down her jawline, to the tip of her chin. And I tell her—thank you. Because she did teach me a lot besides guitar. How to make a mess. How to be bold. She tucks a kiss into my palm.

"Hey, Sadie?" I whisper.

Those wide, wary eyes.

I slide my hand away. "Do it afraid."

Riding to a last stop is strange. The train screeches up to the platform, and instead of telling you which station is next, the conductor crackles, "This is the last stop!" Overhead the marquee flashes. LAST STOP. LAST STOP.

I wait until I'm alone in the car, and then I gather my backpack and my guitar, and the coat I don't remember shedding, and step onto the outdoor platform. It got chillier during the two-stop ride from Thirtieth Avenue, and my fellow passengers walk briskly ahead, tugging on beanies and scarves. I don't have either. Above me, the sky is gray mold.

I've never visited this side of Astoria before. The park side. But as I descend the creaky iron steps onto the street, I know exactly where I'm headed. Nine blocks west, kiddo. Straight shot. Walking is still good. It feels necessary—I'm almost disappointed when I reach the park as quickly as I do. It's deserted. Barren in that hopeless, pre-spring way, but then again, to me New York has always seemed a little bit hopeless. A little pre-spring. Yellow grass crunches beneath my shoes. I park myself on a bench and zip my coat, facing the sludgy water. The East River, not the Hudson. But I'll pretend they're just about the same thing.

The bench makes my butt cold, but I'm not finished here yet. Guitar case planted between my knees, I dig my phone out, tap open my long-neglected thread with Lindsay. My fingers know what to write. Hey Linds—I'm sorry I've been such a monster lately. I'm not trying to make excuses or defend my behavior or anything. You don't even rly have to respond to this if u don't want to. I just want you to know that I miss u. And that there is something big I've been meaning to get off my chest. Then I type, with no hesitation: FaceTime me?

Send.

My phone starts pinging almost immediately, but I can't answer. Not just yet. There's more that I need to say to her.

Words like, It sucks that you're back with Peter. Really, truly blows, but if that's what she wants, there's nothing I can do but grit my teeth and support her. Maybe someday after I've said what I need to, they'll break up and she'll give me a chance. Maybe she won't. And that's okay. I don't need her to be my girlfriend to be happy. I need her to be my friend.

So I lift my phone to my face and pick up my guitar. I toss my hair back and turn toward the river, the whales that I know are out there, singing.

ACKNOWLEDGMENTS

I've been working on this book for so long that to adequately acknowledge all the people who helped me along the way feels downright impossible. But . . . here's where I try.

First, I'm grateful to Danielle Burby, my indefatigable agent, who saw the potential in this wild story from the beginning and never let me doubt that she'd find the right home for it. Thank you for being such a champion of my work, and for providing insightful, helpful feedback and guidance every step of the way—in addition to all the reassuring cooing noises you made, repeatedly, in response to my neurotic emails. We did it! At last.

Equal thanks belong to everybody at Simon & Schuster who helped usher this book into the world, but especially Liesa Abrams, my extraordinary editor whose notes ("More daddy issues") gave me so much for me to sink my teeth into. It has been an absolute pleasure. This book is better because of you.

To my MFA cohort at Stony Brook Southampton: Wow. Thanks for just literally putting up with me. It's hard to know where to begin, but I'd be remiss if I did not thank everybody in Patricia McCormick's Young Adult Literature workshop who read scraps of this novel in its nascent tadpole stage and responded with, "Actually, I don't hate this . . . ?" to the point that an early draft of this novel ended up being my thesis! On that note, thanks to Patty herself, and Sara Jaffe, for being such insightful thesis readers. And an extra special massive thanks to Ursula Hegi, my advisor, who provided me with ceaseless encouragement, wisdom, and helpful audio notes with gentle bird and water sounds in the background. It was soothing.

Thanks to my badass friends: Faye Chao, Laura Barisonzi (who shot my fantastic author photo in such a pinch! And digitally refined my quarantine eyebrows without complaint!), Erin Reale, Darcy Rothbard, Heather Frey, Dana LePage, Eunbee Ko, Natalie Hamingson, among others, who surely must all have second-hand anxiety from me by now. Of course, extra *extra* thanks to Jenna Marie Hallock and Jason Seligson, my Write Club buddies, who likewise never tired on the encouragement front even when I'm sure I got really unbearable. You guys are amazing. Also, I'm so sorry, but I think there might be about . . . thirty cookies over there?

Thanks to my wonderful family: particularly Mom and Dad for instilling in their Virgo daughter an unfailing work ethic. Dad, I'm sorry that the father in this story is dead. This is not a commentary on our relationship, but a testament to my powers of imagination and empathy, which I only got to develop because you and Mom were such great parents. Thanks to my brother, Dan, and his wife, Grace (Finally, a sister of my own! Yay!), and my brother-in-law, Mike, and his girlfriend, Allison.

I beat *Sekiro* while finishing a NOVEL, and Dan and Mike still haven't. Lastly, on the family front, inexpressibly huge thanks to Kellie Maisenbacher, my wife and the light of my life. This book would not exist without you. No exaggeration.

And to my students, past and present, you guys rock. Thank you for acting interested when I explain how I'm a writer, and putting up with my rambling about thesis statements and characterization and the horrors of sentence fragments, even as I insert them into my own work with gleeful abandon. Do as I say, etc. Additional thanks to my SAT students for letting me hijack your summers, and for laughing (usually) at my jokes. Every single one of you will crush college and beyond. Meanwhile, I still don't understand the bat passage.

Similarly, thank you to all the teachers who encouraged my writing from elementary school onward, especially Mrs. Arner (though to me you were Miss Ufferfilge!) who gave me space in her second-grade classroom to write stories about frogs and bumblebees. And to Shealeen Meaney, favorite professor, who introduced me to the work of Edith Wharton and let me be pretentious in undergrad classes while I was still figuring myself out. Thank you to my therapist, Amy. And to my beloved dog, Koda (my other therapist), and Todd, my big-boned kitty who never withheld criticism. I miss you every day.

Finally, for those of you who have lost a loved one to suicide, be patient with yourself. Grief knows no time limit. If you or anyone you know is struggling with suicidal thoughts, substance abuse, and/or mental health concerns, know that that's okay, and that there are people who are here to listen and support you. The following national hotlines are here to help:

Suicide Prevention Lifeline—1-800-273-8255

Substance Abuse and Mental Health Services Administration Hotline—1-800-662-4357

The Trevor Project (for LGBTQ+ youth)—1-866-488-7386

ABOUT THE AUTHOR

Jennifer Nissley is an instructor of writing in a developmental college program, where she has the privilege of working with native and new English speakers from all across the globe. She received her MFA in Fiction from Stony Brook Southampton and lives with her wife in Queens, New York.